REDLINE

A JOHN TYLER ACTION THRILLER

THE JOHN TYLER THRILLERS
BOOK 8

TOM FOWLER

For Lisa and Isabel

1

When he saw the same car pass in front of the jewelry shop a third time, John Tyler knew the place was about to get robbed.

It was a black GM sedan—maybe a Chevy SS or a Pontiac G8. Something with a V8 under the hood to enable a fast getaway. The car stopped at the curb just past the main door. Tyler spotted two men inside. From what he could tell, the driver looked shorter and slighter than the two passengers. Could it be a woman?

All this because he wanted to buy his daughter Lexi a nice pair of earrings for her upcoming twentieth birthday.

He thought about leaving but felt he should at least warn someone first. Tyler came to Stanley's Jewels in Baltimore County because he remembered his late mother mentioning the place twenty-odd years ago. Two other customers browsed from the various displays and locked cases, and a pair of employees walked the floor. A thick metal door led to the back area of the store. Tyler imagined they kept the real valuables there—most likely in a safe—and not where the public could see them. The store didn't employ a security guard, but obvious cameras popped out of the walls and ceiling at many points. Tyler figured some less visible lenses also provided surveillance.

He made his way to the nearest worker, a thin man way too young to be the proprietor. "I hate to tell you this, but I'm pretty sure you're about to get robbed."

"What?"

"I've seen the same car three times now," Tyler said. Once could simply be someone driving by. Twice could be an accident. Someone drove past where they wanted to go. A closer parking spot opened. A third pass made a pattern not boding well for a store whose inventory stretched into the hundreds of thousands of dollars and probably beyond. "It can't be good."

As if on cue, one man burst through the door. He stood a shade over six feet—the measurement lines on the frame helped—and carried an average amount of weight. He also carried a Remington twelve-gauge shotgun. A dark ski mask covered his face except for the eyes, almost making a uniform when combined with blue jeans, a black T-shirt, and black leather jacket. Two more men, both carrying pistols, filed in a few seconds later. They were dressed similarly, and their masks were the identical off-white shade. "This is a robbery," the first one said, making the events obvious. "Hands up. If you cooperate and stay quiet, no one has to get hurt."

Tyler often carried a pistol. A sign on the door of Stanley's Jewels proclaimed no firearms other than by law enforcement, which aligned with a recent and restrictive Maryland law. In cases like these, he left the 9MM in the car. At the moment, he wished he abided the law a little more loosely. Unarmed, Tyler wasn't going to try and play hero, so he put his hands up like everyone else. One of the gunmen stood nearby, his gaze alternating between Tyler and the employee. The one with the shotgun walked to them and pointed the Remington at the worker. "Open the cases."

The third man tossed a couple cloth bags onto one of the

glass surfaces. "Don't skimp on the good stuff, asshole. We want diamonds."

The other employee, a middle-aged woman with her graying hair in a bun, cried. "Shut up," the bag man barked at her. She managed to turn the volume down a little but continued her sobbing.

"Everyone stay calm," the Remington wielder said, making sure to look at the customers and workers. "Keep your hands up. We don't even want your wallets. What's in these cases is worth a lot more."

The two other customers were a young black woman and an older white man with thinning hair. Both held their hands aloft, though the man grimaced a few times. Sweat appeared on his face, and his breathing quickened. When the guy wobbled on his feet, Tyler stepped close and grabbed him around the torso.

"I said keep your hands up!" one of the robbers barked, waving a pistol.

"You want to steal jewelry, go ahead," Tyler said. "If this guy dies . . . even from something like a heart attack . . . it's going to go down like you murdered him."

"You a doctor?"

"No. Just someone who's seen a truckload of people react to stress over the years." The older man continued taking shallow breaths, and his face looked ashen. Tyler felt on the guy's neck for a pulse. Rapid but weak. "We need to get him on the floor."

"Stay there," the masked man ordered.

"The hell is going on?" Remington demanded as he approached. The third gunman moved from his post near the door to badger the other employee into filling the bags faster.

"This man is probably experiencing some kind of cardiac issue," Tyler said. "I'd like to get him off the floor." He jutted his chin toward the door. "Maybe back there. We need to get him lying flat." Thanks to an abundance of displays, floor space in the small interior of Stanley's Jewels was at a premium. There was room to get the old man onto the carpet, but he'd still be in the middle of everything. Removing him from the stressful environment would help.

"This is bullshit," the pistol-wielding bandit said. "You just want to run out the back."

So there was a back door, and this crew knew about it. "Even if I did, who cares?" Tyler said. "I don't have the Hope Diamond in my pocket."

The volatile one started to say something, but the guy with the shotgun—and the cooler head—talked over him. "We don't need someone dying while we're here. Get him to the back. You're carrying him, though. Or dragging him. Whatever."

"Fine." Tyler kept the victim upright but moved behind him to wrap his arms around the man's chest. Other than an occasional groan, the guy seemed out on his feet, so Tyler needed to provide all the force. Thankfully, the poor fellow was pretty slender and not too tough to drag behind a row of display cases and toward the metal door. "Is it open?"

The weeping woman nodded. Tyler braced himself against the frame and kept his right arm around the old man's torso. He reached back with his left hand, found the knob, turned it, and opened the door. It closed behind itself once he dragged the guy through. Lights flickered to life, illuminating a hallway. A door at the end led to the outside. A break room was on the left, and an office on the right.

Tyler got the elderly gentleman into the break room and set him down on the floor. The guy still had a pulse, but his color remained poor, and Tyler didn't think he'd survive a lot longer without paramedics or an AED. He stood and headed back into the corridor.

The office was occupied.

2

———————

A MAN EVEN OLDER THAN THE CARDIAC VICTIM SAT IN A LARGE padded chair behind a desk. Dim light from two monitors glowed on his face. "Stanley?" Tyler mouthed. The owner nodded. "Alarm?"

Another nod.

"How long?" he whispered.

Stanley shrugged. "Only a few minutes now."

"I want to try and get people to safety. The door there is heavy. Bulletproof?"

"More or less."

"Let's hope for more, then," Tyler said. He padded up the hallway and opened the door a crack. All three robbers yelled at the employees. A third bag joined the mix. One was already full, and the other two were on their way. Tyler waved, got the black woman's attention, and gestured for her to join him.

She shook her head.

He beckoned her again. She frowned, got low, and hustled as best she could toward Tyler. He opened wider to let her pass before returning the door to a crack. "Break room," he whispered. "On the left." She headed there. Tyler hoped he could get one of the employees to safety, but the robber with the pistol and the short temper noticed him. Tyler studied the man. He looked older around the eyes than his fellow burglars.

"Get out here!" he ordered. Tyler raised his hands, opened the door wider, and moved through into the main part of the store. He would need to keep improvising. "What the hell were you doing?"

"Making sure no one was about to shoot."

The bandit stepped closer. "Maybe I'm about to shoot you." His finger remained outside the trigger guard, but he leveled the gun at Tyler. The fellow's green eyes took on a maniacal look. Tyler wondered if this crew had robbed other places and what the body count might have been. He slowly turned his upper body to move his left arm closer. If the gunman's finger disappeared, Tyler would need to act. He didn't relish the idea of a shootout in a public place with an innocent person in harm's way, but he also wasn't going to stand around and let this asshole fire at him point-blank.

"Fill the last bag!" the third member of the crew ordered the employees. The woman kept crying. At Remington's insistence, the pistolier backed away from Tyler. Both of them eyed other cases in the store. Even if nothing there contained a diamond, then gold, silver, and other jewels would be worth plenty on the black market. The female employee continued to cry. The man looked between Tyler and the rear door. Did he want to make a break for it?

Tyler shook his head. Making a dash now would be inviting trouble—and probably a few bullets from the unstable guy with the Glock. Bolting and leaving a woman to deal with three armed men was also the sign of a true coward. The employee looked again. Tyler gave his head another small shake. "Don't do it," he mouthed.

A few subtle movement and posture shifts told Tyler the guy was going to ignore his advice. People were unpredictable, and sometimes, this worked against everyone involved. Scenarios danced and played in Tyler's mind. The trigger-happy guy would be most likely to shoot. He was still the closest, and Tyler inched nearer. If things went south, he would need to disarm the crazy one, kill Captain Remington to eliminate the most dangerous weapon, and then take his chances against the other crook with the handgun. From his current position, there was no easy way to get to cover. The options were use Shotgun Guy as a shield or rely on experience, get low, and be as accurate as possible.

Not ideal, but Tyler had faced and survived worse in Afghanistan and closer to home.

The worker turned toward the door. A predictable sequence of events happened in rapid succession. The wild-eyed gunman opened fire, hitting the employee in the side with all three shots. Loud voices combined into a dull yell muted by the gunshots. The man who tried to make a break for it slumped to the floor, and trails of blood on the wall followed him. Tyler stepped toward the shooter, but the shotgun wielder pulled his compatriot away.

"What the hell!?"

"He was running. Son of a bitch was making a break for it."

A horn blared outside as the female employee bawled and wailed. The driver stepped out of the sedan and moved closer to the shop. She held a pistol against the outside of her leg. Blonde hair peeked out from under her ski mask. Tyler stared at her.

She stared back.

Her blue eyes remained locked on Tyler. She wore the same kinds of mask, clothes, and leather jacket the guys did. Why was she staring? Tyler didn't know anyone who both fit her description and would serve as the getaway driver for a trio of burgling assholes. The three crooks sprinted from the shop. A few unintelligible yells filled the air, and only then did the driver turn away and climb back behind the wheel. The sedan sped away on shrieking tires as sirens grew closer.

Tyler checked on the employee who tried to make a break for it. Considering the volume of blood pooling around the man, Tyler knew what the result would be, but it only took a second to confirm the lack of pulse. The female worker continued crying. A few small pieces of jewelry lay scattered around the floor. The rear door opened a crack. Stanley peeked into the main area of the shop, looked around, and walked out to console the poor woman. "I think the old guy will make it," he said. "Thanks. You made a difference today."

Tyler didn't say anything. He wished he could have done more. These situations were always fluid and unpredictable, however, and someone making a run for it at the wrong time rarely turned out well. Tyler pondered moments where he might have been able to act, but despite having a crazy man with a Glock, the crew worked the scene well. "I wish I could have done more," he said after a moment.

"You can't save everyone," Stanley said, sparing a forlorn look for the dead man. "You just have to save the people you can."

"Yeah." Tyler sat on the floor as an ambulance stopped out front.

3

The county police were keen on talking to Tyler.

For his part, he wanted to be sure the old man was all right. Paramedics got to him right away, even before the cops filled the empty spaces, and they now wheeled him out on a stretcher. The fellow's eyes were open at least, and he seemed to be alert. "I asked you a question," one of the officers said in an agitated tone.

Two cops stood in front of Tyler. Both were tall and thin but fit—built like baseball players, he thought. One was white and the other black, with the latter serving as the mouthpiece so far. Stripes on his sleeve indicated he was a sergeant. "I wanted to see if he was all right," Tyler said. "It didn't look good at first."

"You got him off the floor?"

"Yes."

"The robbery crew let you?"

"I had to make my case a little," Tyler said. "I told them holding the place up was one thing, but having someone drop dead while you did would be quite another." He shrugged. "I guess they agreed."

"How many were there?" the white one wanted to know.

His nameplate identified him as Summers, and his sergeant was Lawrence.

"Three in the shop. A driver waiting in the car outside."

Summers jotted a few notes into a small spiral book. "You get a good look at them?"

"They all wore masks. I can give you eye colors, heights, builds, and my best guess as to ages, but not much else."

"Sure," Lawrence said.

Tyler ran down each of the trio. He'd clocked their heights as they came in. One remained on the other side of the store, so the description was a little lighter there. "The driver was a woman," he added at the end.

The comment made Summers pause his writing. "Really?"

"She was dressed mostly like her friends including the mask. Blonde hair, blue eyes, and my best estimate for her height would be five-seven. At the risk of sounding sexist, I would guess she has a nice figure."

"Good driver?" Lawrence asked.

"Good enough or they wouldn't let her do it. In terms of what I saw, she peeled out of here but kept the car under control. It's a rear-drive sedan with loads of power. I know plenty of guys who think they could handle it and would have steered it straight into a parked SUV."

"Why'd you come here today?" Summers said.

"To buy my daughter some earrings. She has a birthday soon."

"How old?"

"Old enough to appreciate nice earrings," Tyler said, "and young enough to still be okay with her dad giving them to her."

"It's a simple question."

"It's also irrelevant. You want to know what happened here? I'll be happy to tell you what I can. My helpfulness is confined to those borders, however."

"You ever seen this crew before?" Lawrence said.

"No."

"You sure."

"Haven't been in a store getting robbed in quite a while," Tyler said.

The cop shrugged. "I'm just saying. You got a lot of details. Convinced them to let you get a man off the sales floor. Maybe they sent you ahead to check out the place."

"Maybe you finished last in your class at the academy."

Summers took over when Lawrence glared at Tyler. "These crews often have an insider. Sometimes, the person is a member of the crew. Others, they've either bribed an employee or promised them a percentage of the cut."

"I guess you finished second from the bottom," Tyler said. "I don't know these pricks. I didn't help them. I managed to save one guy, and the fact I couldn't save two is going to gnaw at me for a while. This place is covered in cameras. Watch the footage. See if I'm lying."

"We might have more questions," Lawrence said.

"You can direct them to my lawyer, then. Major Kevin Lowery, Judge Advocate General's office, Fort Meade."

"You Army?"

"Retired."

The pair walked away in search of the proprietor. Stanley led them behind the heavy door. About ten minutes later, they emerged again. "You can go," Lawrence said. "Thanks for your cooperation."

Tyler turned and left.

~

Lexi waited outside the office of her academic advisor.

She was midway through her fourth semester and had yet to declare a major. At least a few hundred of her fellow University of Maryland sophomores must have been in a similar boat. She'd figured taking general requirements early would be the best thing to do, and then choose courses with a focus starting in her junior year. Thanks to her dad's occasional extracurricular activities, Lexi had gained some experience with acting outside the law.

Now, she wanted to color inside the lines—for the most part at least.

After some deliberation, she'd chosen a major—criminal justice. Enough time remained to take everything required in the curriculum, and if she needed to pick up a course over the summer, that would be fine. The degree would open numerous possibilities for her, but Lexi had already figured out what she wanted to do.

Now, she just needed to work out which side of the aisle was right for her.

The goal was to work as an investigator in a lawyer's office. This offered two possibilities—look into alleged criminals for a prosecutor, or do the same thing but with an eye toward exoneration for a defense lawyer. Lexi's dad had clashed with the law a few times, and she felt he didn't always get treated fairly. She'd also experienced some of this herself thanks to a couple incidents on campus. Police often brought assumptions and accusations especially early in their cases. The more she thought about it, playing for the defense made increasing sense. She didn't want to see someone get railroaded in situations like hers.

Her thoughts drifted to what she might have to do to obtain the degree. The online course catalog detailed the classes she would need to take. Some seemed more interesting than others. The college expected internships in many disciplines, and criminal justice counted among them. Lexi wondered if she could get an early start on the process by looking for opportunities in the coming summer. She still had a couple months until exams and the end of the semester.

Lexi glanced at her watch. It was time for the appointment, but she still waited outside her advisor's closed office door. She could hear muted voices through the dark wood. At least the chair was comfortable. No one else waited, so the only other people in the space were two administrative assistants who looked to be Lexi's age peers. A moment later, her phone buzzed in her pocket, and she saw her dad was calling.

"What's up, Dad?"

"I was just at a jewelry store when it got robbed," he said.

"What?" One of the secretaries looked over at Lexi. She put up a hand and stepped out of the area. "Are you all right?"

"I'm fine. One of the employees didn't make it. He got shot sprinting for the back door. I tried to tell him not to do it."

"You can't save everyone, Dad."

"I know," he said. "I did manage to get an old man to safety. He had a heart attack or some cardiac thing."

"Are you still there?"

"No, I'm in the car. The place is full of cops. They had some questions for me. Some of them seemed rather pointed. I saw the same sedan three times, so I had a feeling the shop was going to get robbed. By the time I told one of the employees, the first gunman walked in."

"First? How many were there?"

"Three-man crew inside. All armed and masked. Their driver was a woman."

"How do you know?" Lexi asked.

"She got out of the car at the end," her dad said. "Stared me down before they all drove off."

"What the hell was that about?"

"No idea."

"I'm curious why you were in a jewelry store. You hate all that stuff. Get a new girlfriend I don't know about?"

"If I did," he said, "I don't know about her, either."

"You sure you're all right?"

"I'm fine, Lexi. I didn't pull you out of a class or anything, did I?"

"No, I was just going to meet with my academic advisor. No big deal. I can reschedule. You getting out unscathed is the most important thing."

"They were a good crew . . . even if the one guy was trigger happy. I get the feeling they've done this before."

"Dad," Lexi said, "stay out of it. Let the cops do their thing."

"I will. I'm not getting involved."

"I'd like to believe you."

"Me, too," he said, and they ended the call. Lexi put her phone back into her jeans pocket. Trouble had a way of finding her dad, and he wasn't wired to walk away from it. She returned to the interior office and changed her appointment to the afternoon when the advisor had another opening. The robbery would gnaw at her dad. She knew this. Until he let it go, it would gnaw at her, too.

4

"Three bags full!" Chains dropped the largest of the sacks onto the bare wooden table.

"Like a goddamn nursery rhyme," Connor said.

"Almost went off without a hitch." Chains plucked a bracelet from the bag. He didn't understand much about jewelry, but he knew it was gold. "Why did we leave a body?"

"He was making a break for it," Pop said. The gray hair serving as the source of his nickname shimmied as he shook his head. "Couldn't have the son of a bitch getting outside and telling someone."

Chains sighed. "We were almost finished. It wouldn't've mattered. Considering how close the sirens were, we obviously tripped some kind of alarm."

"Guys, look at this haul," Rock said. His beefy hand swept over all three bags. "I tried to keep a tally as we went. Couldn't see some of the prices, so I had to guess here and there. My best estimate is about two hundred large in terms of retail value."

"Nice," Chains said with a nod. "Make sure this goes to our usual fence. He should be able to get us close to a hundred."

"You got it."

The group met in a large industrial area. It had been a machining shop back in its heyday, but years of dwindling economic growth drove businesses away. The structure was still solid, however, and with a little care, most of the remaining equipment worked. Adding some more turned the space into a functional garage. The group needed it to make sure the vehicles they used were up to the task of getting away from law enforcement.

In the past—even recently—the group employed a mechanic to handle these duties. After falling out with the last one, however, they let their driver handle working on the cars, too. "How about a hand for Felicity?" Chains said. "Two cop cars came after us, and you showed some nifty driving skills. Those drifts were good enough to play in Tokyo." He chuckled. "Goddamn pigs are down a pair of cars now."

"Thanks," she said. Felicity offered a small smile. She never seemed overly social, but it could have been an effect of being the lone woman in a group of men. Chains knew Connor and Rock tried to pick her up and got shot down, the former complaining she must have been a lesbian. If she was, it would be a shame. Felicity was a pretty blue-eyed blonde, with the kind of car skills to quicken the pulse and the kind of body to draw your attention. Finding pretty women who could drive and work on cars was rare, and as much as Chains wanted to get her in bed, she had value to the group. Pushing her away would be a bad move.

"Where'd you learn to drive like a demon?" Pops asked.

Felicity shrugged. "My daddy taught me."

"Props to him, then. He teach you to work on cars, too?"

"More or less. I picked up stuff by watching sometimes, too."

Chains knew the group would function better with a mechanic. He'd need to bring one in. It meant each person—except for their founder and leader—taking a smaller share of each haul, but it would be worth it. Felicity could only do so much. This was a problem for a different day, however. For now, they needed to torch the getaway car and get three bags of hot goods to the fence.

~

Hope Raines frowned at herself in the mirror.

She loved her red hair, and it took time to start getting used to seeing herself with blonde locks. A fresh bottle of hair color every ten days or so kept her looking consistent. Her blue contacts were out. She preferred her normal green hue. "Almost four months," she muttered to the empty room in her apartment. The FBI owned it, and when her boss gave her the assignment, he also provided her a place to live the gang couldn't trace to her or the Bureau.

She knew it was a shit job when she took it, and so did her supervisor. The death count was up to four, however, and the gang continued operating across multiple states in the Mid-Atlantic area. Charlie—who went by the moniker Chains—was her point of contact, but she knew the group had a leader who never appeared in person. Her mission was twofold: take down the robbery ring, and unmask the mysterious leader.

So far, she was oh-for-two.

On her drive from the garage, Hope dictated a series of notes on the events of the day, including Pop killing the jewelry store employee. Once she got dressed, she sat at her desk. The dictation app synced with her PC, and it would take her voice memo and transcribe the words. Hope reviewed the output, made a couple minor corrections, and sent the results to a few people in the Bureau. She connected via a non-attributable virtual private network, so even if Chains and company tried to spy on her and sniff her traffic, they wouldn't get past the VPN.

She left one detail out of her report—the man inside the jewelry store she locked eyes with before driving away. From her perch in the front seat, she couldn't see everything happening in the store. However, it looked like the guy helped an older man experiencing some kind of medical issue. Hope also spotted the changes in his movements and posture as the situation unfolded. Probably ex-military, maybe even some kind of special forces. Whoever this guy was, he stood ready to disarm Chains and start shooting if necessary.

This was the kind of help she needed.

The FBI wasn't going to send another agent. Her boss made that clear on more than one occasion. "Who are you?" she wondered aloud, staring at her screen. She'd seen the man's face before during a routine case review. It wasn't remarkable except for his dark, pitiless eyes. He'd been tangentially involved in some investigation the FBI did into a militia. Where had it been? "West Virginia?" It went back at least six months if not more.

Hope knew what she needed to do first—find out this man's identity and reach out to him for help. The boys in the gang saw him, yes, but they could get past that problem. Hope looked like a different person in her guise as Felicity Snow. The same people who helped her could do similar work for this fellow. Considering one employee died, she didn't think she'd need to do a lot of convincing.

First, however, she had to overcome the challenge of his identity.

5

———————

Lexi walked into her advisor's office.

"Thank you for coming, Alexis," Ms. McGinn said. She was a tall, slender woman about the same age as Lexi's dad. Today, she wore a long blue dress with white stripes, and her brown hair was up in a bun. A pair of glasses rested on her forehead, and something in the woman's mannerisms made Lexi think she would wonder where they were at some point. "This is the first time we're meeting in person, I think."

"Yes," Lexi said, settling onto a guest chair near the desk.

"Well, I'm sorry to disappoint you. The Library of Alexandria was just a Zoom background. My office is much less cool."

The real office was rectangular—pretty deep but also narrow. Bookshelves took up a fair bit of the floor space. A small table held a single-cup coffee maker and a folded University of Maryland sweater. The office was neat and tidy save for the desk. If someone detonated a bomb on it, Lexi imaged the effect would have been the same. She'd never be considered the world's neatest or most organized person, but looking at the mess of papers and office supplies almost made her shudder. "But much closer than Alexandria," Lexi said.

"Yes," Ms. McGinn agreed. "You mentioned you're ready to declare a major, but your email kept me in suspense as to what it is. Are you going to be a writer?"

Lexi chuckled. "No. I want to do criminal justice."

Her counselor smiled and nodded. "I think it'll be a good program for you." She reached into the giant mess on her desk and somehow pulled out Lexi's file. "Looks like you've made good progress on your GERs." For four semesters now, Lexi had packed her schedule with general education requirements. Her advanced placement classes in high school got her out of a few, but her goal was to be done with them by the end of her sophomore year. "I presume you've looked over the courses you'll need to take for this major?"

"I have," Lexi said. "Once you get past the intro, there's criminal law, criminology, corrections, law enforcement, juvenile justice, research methods, and a few more."

Ms. McGinn nodded. "I shouldn't be impressed because I know you, but I am. Have you thought about what your electives would focus on?"

Lexi had reviewed the choices. One obvious one stood out. "Cybercrime." She shrugged. "I like computers." Her dad had leaned on her several times to help out in this area during some of his off-the-books work. He could turn a computer on and send an email, but anything more strained the limits of his knowledge and comfort. Lexi filled in the gaps by doing research—some of it illicit—and even figuring out how to bypass an alarm system or two.

"I'm sure you'll do very well in it." Ms. McGill wrote a few notes onto the printout. Entering them directly in the electronic version would have been more efficient, but Lexi got the feeling this was the woman's process. However weird it might have been—and regardless of the mess it produced—it worked for her. "There's one other factor to consider . . . an internship."

"I've thought about it." Lexi sighed. "I know I'm coming to this kind of late. Do you think there's still time?"

"I hope so. You'll need to spend some time your next three summers working. Employers like to see those sorts of things. You never mentioned what you wanted to do with your criminal justice degree."

"Work as an investigator for a lawyer or firm."

"Defense, then?"

"Yes," Lexi said.

"I think you'll do well there," Ms. McGinn said with a smile. "You might want to consider an internship in a prosecutor's office, too. It would let you see how the other half lives, so to speak."

"Know your enemy."

The advisor put her hands up. "I wouldn't say it like that, but I understand. You'd better start looking into places. Some of your classmates come from connected families, and they've probably already locked down the top-tier spots."

"I'll manage," Lexi said.

They wrapped up a few minutes later, and Lexi left the building. She wondered where she could find an internship, especially considering she hadn't taken a single criminal justice class yet. The big firms would be out. They'd want to see 4.0 averages in the relevant curriculum and probably some sort of independent side project. Lexi would need to target smaller firms. Maybe even private investigator's offices. Some attorneys hired PIs to handle the dirty work especially if they were one-person operations.

She would have her work cut out for her.

∽

TYLER SAT behind his desk with a weary sigh.

He could see out into the service bays at his shop, Special Operations Classic Car Repair. Tom "Smitty" Smith, an experienced mechanic about ten years older than Tyler, worked on a vintage Mustang. David Ortiz, Tyler's most recent hire, finished a job on a Chevy pickup. When it looked like both men were at a pause point, Tyler rapped on the window and waved a hand for them to join him.

Both washed their hands, entered the main building, and sat in Tyler's guest chairs. Smitty often made cracks about Tyler being late. Today, the man's mouth opened, but he must have seen Tyler's expression because he remained silent. "What's going on, boss?" Ortiz asked.

"Obviously, I'm late today," Tyler said. "I didn't plan on it. If all went well, I should have been in at eleven."

"What happened?"

"I went to a jewelry store to buy Lexi some earrings. Her birthday is coming up soon, and I saw the place was running a sale. Turns out a robbery crew wanted an even bigger discount."

"You all right?" Smitty said.

Tyler waved a hand. "I'm fine. I saw the car drive by three times, so I knew something was going down. I tried to let one of the employees know, but it was too late. Three guys came in and stole a bunch of stuff."

"You didn't try to . . . get involved?" Smitty wanted to know.

"I did," Tyler said. "An old guy looked like he was having a heart attack. I caught him before he fell, and I persuaded one of the crooks to let me take him into the back room."

"You trigger an alarm back there?" Ortiz asked.

"No. The owner was in the office. He said it already went off. I went back out. I'd be lying if I said I didn't look for an opportunity to disarm one of them. Almost got a chance, but then one of the employees tried to make a break for it." Tyler paused and shook his head. "I don't think he made it three steps before someone cut him down."

"Jesus," Smitty said in a voice barely above a whisper. "You're probably lucky you made it."

"We heard sirens. The crew grabbed their haul and left." Tyler frowned and studied the top of his desk. "No one needed to die."

"The old man all right?" Ortiz said.

"He was alive going into the ambulance," Tyler said.

"Then you saved the person you could."

"Ortiz is right," Smitty added. "You did what you could. Unarmed against three guys with a few civilians in the area. Preventing a bloodbath was the best you could have done."

"We're going to disagree there," Tyler said.

"Maybe . . . but it's not like you know who this crew is. They probably beat it in a stolen car. You're not gonna find 'em."

"I know. I just hate not doing anything."

Echoing their sentiment once more, the elder member of the pair said, "You did what you could." When Tyler didn't respond with anything, Smitty added, "Quit moping. These cars won't fix themselves."

Tyler grinned. "You're right. It's why I pay the two of you. Go ahead. I'll get some coffee and get to work, too."

Smitty and Ortiz returned to the service bays. A black Trans Am waited in the third. Every time Tyler saw one, he thought of *Knight Rider*, one of his favorite shows as a kid. Even though he was a teenager by the end of the show's run, he'd still enjoyed it. Between KITT and the General Lee, Tyler figured he'd wanted to be a mechanic most of his life. He poured some coffee and walked to the third bay, trying to push his brooding thoughts of the robbery down.

6

———————

At home in the evening, Tyler ate a couple slices of the pizza he picked up. He'd managed to get the work he needed to do finished, but the events of the morning still gnawed at him. Could he have acted sooner? Should he? Even if he did, would the scenario have played out differently? Tyler trusted his experience and training to get him out of the situation unscathed, but the employee still might have caught a bullet.

Playing what-if never did any good.

Tyler pulled up a local news site and searched for stories about the events of the day. It didn't take him long.

Brazen Robbery at Stanley's Jewels in Carney: One Dead, Another Hospitalized

Carney, Baltimore County — A seemingly routine Monday morning turned tragic at Stanley's Jewels when an audacious daylight robbery left one employee dead and another bystander hospitalized. The incident, which occurred shortly after 10 AM, has shocked the community and left authorities scrambling for leads.

According to witnesses, the heist began quietly but ended with a sudden burst of violence. Three masked individuals, dressed in dark clothing, stormed into the popular jewelry store located on Harford Road. Armed with pistols and a shotgun, the robbers wasted no time in asserting their dominance, shouting threats and brandishing their weapons to intimidate both customers and staff.

One of the most harrowing moments of the robbery came when an elderly man, identified as Harold Whitman, 72, collapsed from an apparent heart attack amid the chaos. Paramedics later confirmed that Whitman is in stable condition at a nearby hospital, thanks to the swift response of first responders. A witness said an unknown customer got the stricken man into the back of the store to keep him safe.

The robbers' aggression escalated when one of the store's employees, later identified as 28-year-old Jake Miller, attempted to leave the sales floor. In a chilling display of brutality, one of the assailants shot Miller three times at point-blank range. Despite efforts to save him, Miller was pronounced dead at the scene.

"They didn't have to kill him," said a shaken witness, who asked to remain anonymous. "He was just trying to do his job."

The robbers, having incapacitated the only immediate threat to their plan, proceeded to fill three large duffel bags with an assortment of high-value jewelry, including diamonds and gold watches. The entire robbery lasted less than ten minutes, during which the assailants maintained a tight control over the scene, preventing anyone from making calls or escaping.

Sergeant Sarah Collins, a media relations officer with the Baltimore County Police Department, addressed the media later in the day. "This was a well-coordinated and ruthless crime," she stated. "We are pursuing all leads and ask anyone with information to come forward."

As the community grapples with the aftermath of this violent episode, a makeshift memorial has appeared outside Stanley's Jewels, with flowers and notes left in memory of Jake Miller. The store, a local fixture for over 30 years, remains closed as the investigation continues.

The police have released details of the suspects based on witness accounts and security footage. They are described as three Caucasian males with ages ranging from thirties to mid-fifties, all of medium build, wearing dark clothes, leather jackets, lightly-colored ski masks, and gloves. They fled the scene in a Chevy sedan likely to be a stolen car. Authorities are urging anyone who might have seen something suspicious in the area around the time of the robbery to contact the Baltimore County Police Department immediately.

Sergeant Collins did not offer a comment when asked if this robbery was connected to others in neighboring states.

The last sentence caught Tyler's attention. Was this some kind of interstate crew? Until the FBI got involved, local police departments were stuck in low gear or idled in neutral. Many didn't share information willingly or well. A group operating in the right part of Maryland would enjoy easy access to several states and the District.

It made Tyler wish he'd grabbed one of the robber's guns even more.

~

HOPE MADE sure no one followed her before she parked at the FBI facility.

It wasn't one they publicized. Anyone could use Google Maps to find the location of a field office. This one was off the books, meant for agents in the field to use when they couldn't make the drive to a proper office—or, in Hope's case—didn't want to risk being followed to a known location. She drove her personal car, a late model Dodge Challenger with the larger Hemi V8 and a six-speed manual. The only modification was a concealed compartment in the center console to hide the burner phone her boss gave her when she took the assignment.

Hope smirked at the thought. "Took" did some heavy lifting there. She and her supervisor both knew the options were accept it or get ready for a pink slip. Now that she was invested in the mission, she still thought it was a bad assignment but wanted to bring it home . . . both for her own career and in the interests of justice.

The alarm on her car chirped as she walked away from it. This office sat in a nondescript building that could have been a small local drug store. Maybe it was before it folded and the Bureau bought it. Hope checked again for followers, found none, and headed to the back. Her smart card unlocked the door, and she deactivated the security system.

Inside, desks were arranged in rows. A single office took up the corner on the left. Rows of lights turned on as Hope moved away from the door. She picked a desk near the wall and logged in. The militia incidents had been at least six months ago. Hope remembered a few discrete events culminating in a shootout at a compound in rural West Virginia. In total, two related militia groups saw their numbers dwindle to zero.

Hope entered some parameters for her search, pressed Enter, and waited. She wouldn't need to wait long. The query returned several results. This made sense as the Bureau opened multiple cases to track different aspects of the events. In short order, she found the information she sought. While the man who brought the groups down managed to stay out of any news coverage, the FBI questioned John Tyler at the scene before releasing him.

A couple more searches told Hope Tyler was a decorated Green Beret who retired from active duty about a decade ago with a slew of medals and an Army file with a lot of black on the pages. Following a spell in private security, he worked as a mechanic before opening his own business. While the FBI didn't keep tabs on him, other agents' notes indicated some other extrajudicial actions which he likely took part in but couldn't be directly attributed.

Hope scanned his personnel file. It was unclassified and redacted in numerous spots, but the highlights proved good enough. Four combat tours, successful operations against the

Taliban and their supporters, and a trophy case's worth of awards and commendations.

John Tyler was exactly the kind of help she needed to take down the robbery ring.

Now, Hope only needed to convince him of it.

7

─────────

THE NEXT MORNING, HOPE MET THE GANG AT THEIR USUAL spot.

It proved to be an excellent place to work on cars. Chains and the crew spared no expense when it came to equipment and tools. They'd certainly earned enough from their illicit activities, including the time before Hope joined. Plenty of empty space remained for gatherings like this. Chains, Rock, Connor, and Pop were already there. Chains' iPhone—it was easy to spot because of its large and gaudy case—sat in the center of a round table. Hope pulled up a metal folding chair and joined the others.

"Nice of you to roll in," Rock said.

"I'm on time," Hope said. "Bite me."

Chains chuckled. "You guys should know better than to rag on Felicity by now." He picked up the phone, dialed a number, put the call on speaker, and set the device back down again.

"Hello," a gruff voice answered a few seconds later. It sounded a little unnatural as if under some mild electronic distortion.

"We're all here," Chains said.

"Good." The group's mysterious leader spoke from an unknown location. Hope had never met the man, and she'd yet to learn anything significant or actionable about him. Chains was the robbery ring's number two, though he served as the de facto leader most of the time. "I heard we had a casualty. Almost two."

"Some old guy nearly croaked while we were there," Chains said.

"And the one who actually did?"

"He was making a break for it," Pop said before Chains could answer.

"Did you have the situation in hand?" the leader demanded.

"Yeah."

"You were close to wrapping things up, correct?"

"Yeah," Pop said with a sigh.

"Then, let the man go," the boss said. "What was he going to do? Considering how soon emergency services got there afterward, someone already activated the alarm. There's no way the guy was going to come back with an Uzi."

"I thought—"

"Don't think," the leader broke in, cutting off Pop. "I only pay Chains to think, and even then, I'd rather do it myself most of the time. Robbery is bad, and stealing high-end stuff gets attention. You know what gets even more attention? Killing a goddamn store employee. No matter how much shit we steal, larceny is a crime against property. These places are insured, so I doubt there's much of a financial loss for most of them. Murder, however, gets you much more serious sentences, and the statute of limitations never runs out. It can even get you the chair in some states. Personally, I don't want to keep looking over my shoulder, and you shouldn't, either."

Pop remained silent. Probably a wise choice. Hope always thought he was the weakest link once they were operational.

For being the eldest member, he shouldn't have been such a hothead. "We don't want anyone to die," Chains said.

"Good. Let's talk about the take. I presume the fence has everything?"

"He does. No estimate on the value yet, but it should be a nice haul."

"All right. Good job . . . most of you." Pop scowled but again held his tongue. "Let's start thinking of another target. We just worked in Maryland, so we'll go somewhere else next time. I have a couple ideas percolating. I think getting another car should happen quickly."

"We need a new mechanic," Chains said. "Felicity's been filling in, but she's the driver. We're asking her to take on a lot. She's doing fine, but I'd rather she focus on one thing."

"Me, too," the leader confirmed. "Do we have a line on a replacement?"

Hope decided to shoot her shot. "I might know someone."

"You trust him?"

"I do."

"You're pretty new, too," Rock said.

Hope waved a hand at him. "So were you at some point."

"I mean maybe we ain't supposed to trust you yet."

"You trust me to get you away from the cops, don't you?"

"Enough," the main man said over the phone's speaker. "Felicity, reach out to the person you know. We'll see if he's a good fit. I don't want to hear about someone else getting pulled apart for being suspicious."

Hope shuddered. The last mechanic did a subpar job, and after a couple close calls with the cops, accusations swirled he'd talked about the group's secretive business. As punishment, Chains, Rock, Connor, and Pop each tied one of his limbs to their rear bumpers. When all four of them stomped on their accelerators, the poor man became a quadruple amputee in the worst way possible. At least he bled out quickly and didn't suffer long. Could Hope really ask John

Tyler to step into such an environment? He could always tell her no—she figured he probably would—but she clung to the chance he would agree to join her shit assignment.

"He's not going to dime us out," Hope said.

"All right," Chains said. "If it's good with the boss, it's good with me. See if he's interested . . . but don't tell him too much."

"I know how this works."

"Be sure you do," Rock said.

Hope did, and she would make sure John Tyler did as well before he made a decision.

LEXI SKIPPED her two morning classes.

When it was clear she wasn't leaving the apartment, her roommates got curious. "You inviting a boy over as soon as we leave?" Kim asked with a sly wink.

"I have something else I need to do," Lexi said.

"Or some*one*," Emily said, and she and Kim enjoyed a good laugh.

"You two would know if I had a boyfriend," Lexi protested. Emily and Kim were two of her longest-lasting friends. They'd met ages ago, went to the same high school, and their plan to attend Maryland worked out. This marked their second semester living together in an off-campus apartment. Emily elbowed Lexi in the shoulder and winked at her as she passed. Lexi smiled. She and Emily looked a lot alike, with the two inches of height advantage Lexi enjoyed being the main difference. Kim was a pretty half-Asian girl with coal black hair and a strong sense of style.

"I can't be the only one," Kim said. "You two need to step it up." Lexi couldn't recall Kim's boyfriend's name. She'd only met him a couple times. Raymond? Something like that.

"I've picked a major," Lexi said.

Emily grinned. "Took you long enough. What'd you go with?"

"Criminal justice."

They both nodded. "I figured you'd get there eventually," Kim said.

"Really?"

"Sure. All the things that have happened over the last couple years? How could you not?"

It made sense. Between needing to shoot two men involved in a trafficking operation, a gunman on campus targeting Lexi and her friends, and the Israeli assassin who went after her dad a few months ago, Kim reached a reasonable conclusion. "I guess I didn't realize you all were doing the same math I was."

"Are you trying to say I'm good at math because I'm Asian?" Kim feigned offense and put her hand over her chest. "*Such* a microaggression."

Lexi laughed. "Get out of here and go to class. I'll see you later." They both filed out the apartment door. Lexi had turned her assignments in last night, and neither of her morning professors were sticklers for attendance. She preferred it that way. By and large, college students were adults, and the idea of making check marks in a book based on someone coming to class or not struck her as absurd.

Once Emily and Kim left, Lexi got on with her research. She'd been looking up law firms in Baltimore, Columbia, and similar areas she could drive to easily from her apartment or her dad's house. In the process, she eliminated the big ones. Summer internships there would go to people in pre-law programs or relatives and friends of the partners.

A few mid-sized firms looked interesting. Lexi hoped she didn't decide on a major and start this process too late. She could always do an internship next summer, but she really wanted to get started on building experience. Rejection was still the most likely outcome, but at least Lexi gave herself good odds. She picked the top place on the list and called.

"Grimes, Mortimer, and Howe," a perky-sounding receptionist said. "How may I direct your call."

"I'd like to speak to someone about summer internships," Lexi said.

"I think most of those spots have been filled. Hold, please." Elevator music filled the line before Lexi could even answer. She sighed and waited. A minute later, the woman came back on. "Are you in law school, miss?"

"No, I was hoping to get experience as an invest—"

"I'm sorry, but we only accept interns who have already started law school." She hung up.

"Thanks a hell of a lot," Lexi grumbled to the empty line.

She tried the next firm on the list and inquired about internships. This time, the receptionist connected her to someone speaking with authority. "We're evaluating candidates already," the man said in a nasal tone. "If you applied now, you'd just get in under the wire."

"I'm okay with that."

"What kind of law were you looking to study?"

"I actually want to work as an investigator," Lexi said.

"We don't offer any internships there," the man said. "Good luck on your search, but I honestly think you'll run into a similar answer elsewhere. Have a nice day."

At least he made an effort to be pleasant before ending the call. Going oh-for-two didn't represent an auspicious start, but Lexi wanted to keep at it. She skipped her morning classes for this. Might as well give it a good effort. The third firm also connected her to someone else. The woman who came on the line didn't give her name but said she was the intern coordinator. "I'm afraid we're pretty far down the road of making our choices. What school do you go to?"

"Maryland," Lexi said.

"And you're a law student?"

"Criminal justice. My goal is to work as an investigator for a law firm."

The lady's sigh hissed in Lexi's ear. "I can't think of any firms who take interns there. Some hire out that operation completely. I think you'll have better luck calling PIs."

"Maybe it's something you could add for next summer," Lexi suggested. "Criminal justice is a popular major."

"We'll think about it," the woman replied, and Lexi took her comment to mean no consideration would be forthcoming.

After getting the hat trick, Lexi set her phone down. She'd expected an uphill climb, but she also thought firms would accept summer hires working with their in-house detectives. Apparently not. She still had two and a half hours until her next class. Lexi changed into athletic attire, grabbed her keys, and headed to the local kickboxing gym. She could take her frustrations out on a heavy bag.

8

____

HOPE MADE SURE TO POP HER COLORED CONTACTS IN BEFORE walking out the door.

She'd gotten into the habit of wearing them almost all the time. Someone like Chains could drop by unannounced, and she didn't want to give him a reason to be suspicious. Hope fired up the Challenger and headed toward Baltimore. It would take over an hour in traffic. She drove east on I-70 and picked up the Baltimore Beltway where traffic slowed almost as soon as she merged. The pace ebbed and flowed, and she rarely got above the suggested speed of 55.

Even the off-ramp onto Harford Road proved slow going. She turned into the lot at Special Operations Classic Car Repair just after six. Before leaving, she called to make sure they'd be open, and whoever answered the phone said they would. The place looked like it might have been a gas station in a previous life. It was a rectangular building with a waiting area, long counter, and three service bays. Yellow bollards kept cars from driving into the structure at certain points, and a few set away from the main building still framed what had likely been a separate car wash.

Inside, three men worked. Tyler was easy enough to spot.

The older man must have been Tom Smith. Tyler worked for him for a while before Smitty and Son burned to the ground, and now their roles were reversed. The third man was a Latino, and Hope didn't know who he was. She couldn't guess how long the other two would remain, so might as well get the sales pitch over with. Hope got out of her car and walked inside. The Latino approached the counter from the service bays. Something in his gait made Hope think he had a prosthetic leg. Probably ex-military like Tyler. "Can I help you, ma'am?"

"I'm looking for the owner."

"I'll get him for you."

"Thanks."

Hope turned and took in the inside of the shop. Two desks stood on the other side of the lengthy counter along with an office. Out here, a few chairs, a table, a flatscreen TV, and a coffee machine formed the extent of the furnishings. The TV was off, and the coffee pot was empty. Footsteps approached. Hope turned and stared at Tyler like she did toward the end of the robbery.

He looked confused at first, and then a glower came over his features. She met his gaze, but she understood how a lot of people might avert their eyes. Tyler had what her father called a thousand-yard stare, and he clearly used it to good effect. Hope pulled her windbreaker back just enough to reveal the badge on her hip. "I want to talk," she whispered.

Tyler didn't say anything at first. His dark eyes flicked to the badge and then to a clock on the wall. "Come back in an hour. Bring food."

Before she could answer, he turned and walked away.

∼

After the woman left, Tyler told Smitty and Ortiz they could pack it in.

Each toiled away for another twenty minutes or so before leaving. "You hitting the road, too, boss?" Ortiz asked as he shrugged into a light jacket.

"Not yet," Tyler said. "I'm going to try and get ahead on some paperwork."

"The curse of being in charge." Ortiz clapped Tyler on the shoulder as he walked toward the exit.

"Heavy is the head that wears the crown."

Ortiz's truck rumbled to life and pulled out of the lot a moment later. Tyler looked at the clock again. The woman would be back in a half-hour or so if she wanted to talk. Seeing her again threw him for a loop. He'd wondered how she managed to track him down, and he briefly regretted leaving his pistols in other areas of the shop. The blue-on-gold badge answered all his questions. The resources of the FBI allowed her to identify him. Tyler wondered what the woman did to get embedded with a robbery crew. It couldn't be a prestigious assignment.

A pair of round headlights pulled into the lot shortly after seven. A throaty engine soon followed. At least this woman drove a good car. She walked inside carrying a brown paper bag with a couple grease spots. "You got a place we can eat?" she said.

"My office." Tyler led her to the rear of the shop. She set the bag down and dropped into one of his guest chairs.

"I didn't know what you wanted, so I got burgers and fries."

"Can't go wrong there." Tyler set out some paper towels and ripped the bag open. Two foil-wrapped burgers and two cardboard trays of crinkly fries were inside. The contents soon spilled out. Tyler grabbed a pair of paper plates and set one in front of his guest.

"Thanks for talking to me," she said. Up close, Tyler could see she was very pretty. He wondered how often she needed to fend off the testosterone-fueled jerks she worked with—

and not only in the robbery gang. "My name is Hope. Special Agent Hope Raines."

"I'm gonna presume I don't need to introduce myself."

"I know who you are, Mister Tyler."

"Tyler is fine." He glared at her as he checked out the food. "And don't presume you know me because you read what I'm guessing is a redacted version of my file." The burger lacked cheese, which was fine, but lettuce, tomato, and chopped onions threatened to spill out. Tyler opened a mustard packet and added it to the top bun.

Hope put up her hands. "Fair enough."

"Why'd you stare at me?" Tyler wanted to know.

"I thought I recognized you. I know we've never met before now, but your face looked familiar. Turns out I'd seen it during some routine case review work. The militia in West Virginia." Tyler grunted. "You definitely landed on the Bureau's radar with that one."

"Don't remind me."

Hope arched an eyebrow. "Bad experience?"

"With three of your colleagues, yes. It took a supervisor to get things sorted. Roland Johnson."

"I know him." Hope nodded, and her wavy blonde hair shimmied. "I even talked to him about you."

Tyler chuckled around a bite of burger. "Good things he had to say would be like a green Army driver told to find the keys to the Humvee in its glove box."

"I get it." She smiled. "Neither one exists . . . but in your case, you might be surprised."

"I rarely am," Tyler said.

"All right." Hope spread her hands. "I'm an open book here. What do you want to know?"

"Three things. What are you doing with the robbers, what's the endgame, and why did you come and see me?"

"I'm under cover with them," she said. "You probably noticed I was the driver. It's my job. The endgame is taking them all down. I've been on this assignment for a few months and only managed one arrest . . . the first guy they used to fence all the shit they stole. It was a bad posting from the jump, but I'm not exactly making a name for myself. As for why I came to see you . . ." Hope trailed off in a sigh. "I want your help."

"Don't you have a few thousand people you can call on?" Tyler asked. "Go and arrest them. It's not hard."

Hope shook her head. "It's more complicated than that. The group has a leader I've never met. I'm not sure anyone has. We talk to him on speaker. Never on video. I've never even seen his face. I don't know where he is. Before you ask, yes, I told the Bureau the dates and times of some of the calls. Nothing. We can't figure it out. This group has been on the radar for a while. They operate across multiple states, steal a ton of stuff, and have left a few dead people in their wake."

"I noticed."

"It's one guy, mostly. The crew really tries to leave no casualties."

"You sound a little bit like you're defending them."

"I'm not." She paused to take a bite of her neglected burger. Tyler did the same. Wherever Hope went, she came back with good food. He also munched a few fries during the brief break in the conversation. "Like I said, I came here because I want your help. The group used to have a mechanic. They thought he was a rat, and they killed him. I've been doing double duty since then, but they want me to focus on driving. There's an opening."

It was Tyler's turn for a head shake. "They've seen me. All of them. I didn't exactly sit on the floor with my head down during the jewelry store heist."

"I know," Hope said, "and we can work around that. I'm a natural redhead with green eyes. I dye my hair and wear blue contacts. We'd come up with something for you."

"Why me?" Tyler said.

"I'm a fed. I'm with the group, but there are some things I can't do. I have redlines. You don't."

"If you're bringing me in, wouldn't my actions reflect on you?"

"Let me worry about that," Hope said. "I told the gang I know someone who might be a good fit for the grease monkey spot. You can work with a person at the Bureau on your appearance." She chuckled. "I hope you don't mind dyeing your hair. It's normally a requirement. Basically, you'd get a legend. A fake identity."

"I know what a legend is," Tyler said. "Is there a time-frame on this?"

"My superiors want the gang taken down sooner rather than later. It's been a while already."

"So I would need to come in, earn their trust quickly, and still take them down . . . all within a couple weeks?"

"Pretty much," Hope said.

"You're optimistic." Tyler finished his burger and wiped his hands on a paper towel. Hope remained silent. She seemed sincere—in over her head on this case, most likely, but sincere. "All right. I'm in. Those guys are bastards. Someone needs to take them out."

Hope's smile was dazzling. "Thank you. I really think this is going to work out. I—"

She stopped when Tyler put up a hand. "I don't need a song and dance. You're not going to make me a fan of the Bureau overnight. What are the next steps?"

"I'll work with someone on getting a legend set up for you, and you'll meet with an agent about changing your appearance enough to fool the guys."

"I'm taking a pretty big risk here," Tyler said.

"I've been doing it for months."

"At least you won't be toiling away by yourself anymore." Hope flashed another bright smile. It was hard for Tyler not to follow suit. "Answer a question for me."

"Sure," she said.

"What got you into cars?"

"What do you mean?"

"At the risk of sounding like a sexist middle-aged codger," Tyler said, "most women can't drive like you do and work as a mechanic. The ones who *can* don't tend to look like you." Color came to Hope's cheeks. "I'm wondering how you got into all this."

"My dad," she said. "He loved driving fast and working on his muscle car. I picked it all up from him."

"He ever see you drive like you're making a getaway?"

"No. He's dead."

"Oh. I'm sorry."

"Well . . . my mother had him declared dead when he abandoned us." Hope raised a hand before Tyler could apologize again. "It's fine. Long time ago." She finished her fries. "I'm going to head out. Thanks, Tyler. I'll be in touch soon."

Hope cleared all the trash, threw it away, and walked out. Tyler watched the way her jeans hugged her hips as she approached her Challenger. After she left, Tyler wondered what he might be getting himself into. Someone needed to stop the gang, however, and he and Hope seemed like the best bets.

9

———

"WE NEED PROGRESS, HOPE."

It was late, and Hope called her FBI boss when she left Tyler's shop. Supervisory Special Agent Jason Hess took over the case when the gang's targets kept crossing state lines. He worked from the Baltimore field office, a place Hope had visited a few times over her career. She'd expected him to be more excited about getting some help in taking down the robbery crew.

"I'm going to get you some progress, Jason."

"With an outsider," he said. "A civilian."

"A 'civilian' with twenty-four years in the Army and four combat deployments with special operations. Come on. I'm not plucking some mousy mechanic from Jiffy Lube, for Christ's sake."

"I know this has been a challenging assignment. We all wanted the fence to give us more." Hess chuckled dryly. "I guess he made enough money to afford a really good lawyer. You sure you don't want to just roll a Tac team up to the next meeting? One of these assholes might crack."

"I doubt they would," Hope said. "No. I want the leader. If no one talks, he just gets a few more guys and starts again."

"And you think this John Tyler is going to make the difference?"

"I do. He's willing to put his neck on the line."

"Seems out of the blue."

Hope sighed. "Turns out he was in the jewelry store when it got hit. He got the old man with the heart attack to safety and watched the employee get killed."

Hess fell silent for a couple seconds, and when he spoke, Hope heard an edge in his voice. "I'm going to guess you didn't just learn of this earlier tonight."

"No, sir."

"You left it out of your report." Not a question.

"I did," she admitted, "but his identity wasn't relevant. He was a customer in the shop. I got out of the car at some point, and we locked eyes. I thought I recognized his face from somewhere. When I learned who he was, I wanted to bring him in."

"This is very irregular, Hope," Hess said.

"The whole goddamn case is irregular."

"It is." Hess sighed. "I know you think it's a shit job. Maybe it is. This is the kind of stuff we do, though. Don't get discouraged."

"We're way past that point."

"All right. Try to have a positive outlook with your new helper in tow."

"I'm working on it," Hope said.

"You're on the clock, you know. We can't devote infinite time and resources here. The sooner you can wrap this up, the better for everyone."

Especially me, Hope thought. "How much time do I have?"

"I'd have to see something really significant to give you more than two weeks."

Hope took a deep breath. With Tyler's help and a more aggressive approach to solving the problem, she could make this work. "Fine. I'll keep you updated through the usual covert channels."

"Make sure you do . . . and please be careful."

"I will," Hope said, and she ended the call. It had been a long day. Tomorrow, the Bureau would set John Tyler up with a legend, and she could try to get him into the group. Getting them to accept him was something of an unknown, but she tried to stay positive. It needed to work. Her career was on the line, and if things went off the rails, her life would be, too.

❧

THE NEXT MORNING, Tyler made coffee at the shop and waited for Smitty and Ortiz to roll in.

As the magic liquid brewed, he thought about the events of last evening. The woman he locked eyes with during the robbery turned out to be the crew's driver and an undercover FBI agent. Based on his own reactions to the incident, he'd agreed to try and help her take down the group by posing as their mechanic. Tyler chuckled at the thought of Lexi seeing him with his hair dyed blond or some color other than his usual salt and pepper. Or pepper and salt as he liked to call it —the black still took up more real estate than the gray.

Ortiz's truck hit the lot right after the coffee finished, and Smitty made the turn from Harford Road a few minutes later. Once all three poured themselves a mug, Tyler gathered them in his office. "You both know I was in a jewelry store when it got robbed recently."

Smitty nodded. "Let me guess. You've already found and shot the offenders."

Tyler grinned. "No. Not yet, anyway. I'll be working on it. The FBI is looking into the group responsible, so I'll be working with one of their agents."

Ortiz sipped his coffee. "She the one who came by last night?"

"Yes," Tyler said.

He bobbed his head. "Pretty."

"It didn't matter."

"It always matters," Smitty said.

Tyler shrugged. "All right, her looks didn't hurt her cause." He remembered Hope's high-wattage smiles. "I want to get those bastards, though. There was no need to kill the guy who worked there. They could have taken their haul and left."

"Not your problem to solve," Smitty said.

"I guess it is now. Mine and the FBI's anyway."

"I guess you'll be taking some time away?" Ortiz wanted to know.

"Yeah," Tyler said. "It'll start soon. I don't know exactly when or for how long, but I get the impression we don't have a ton of time."

Smitty set his mug down and crossed his slender arms. "You know there are a bunch of ways this could go pear-shaped on you, right?"

"I do. I've probably thought about most of them. It's a risk. The group might not even accept me as their new mechanic. If they do, there's no guarantee they're going to keep me around."

"Haven't they already seen you, boss?" Ortiz asked.

"Yes, and we'll work on it. Hope . . . she's the FBI agent . . . says they can alter my appearance enough to where the gang won't recognize me."

Smitty snorted. "I want to see pictures of this shit."

"Get in line. I'm sure Lexi will be first."

"Does she know?"

"Not yet. I'll tell her." He probably should have talked to her up front, but Lexi had a college course load and the life of a soon-to-be twenty-year-old woman to lead. She had friends who lived with her and counted on her. Her father's problems shouldn't always be a burden.

"We'll manage," Smitty said. "I can probably pull Jake in for some extra shifts." Smitty's son—who was almost as good a mechanic as his old man—worked once a week or so at the shop.

"Thanks." Smitty and Ortiz left the office for the service bays. Tyler's cell phone buzzed with a number he didn't recognize. *It's Hope. Do you have a name you want to use?*

He thought about it and tapped out a reply.

Floyd Tyler Rayford.

What the hell??

Floyd Rayford played for the Orioles in the 80s. Kind of obscure. If my middle name is Tyler, I can go by it and don't have to get used to answering to something else. I'm too old and stubborn to start now.

Fine. I'll tell the team . . . Floyd. ;-)

It's Mister Rayford to you.

Uh-huh.

Tyler smiled and slipped his phone back in his pocket. He wondered anew what he'd signed himself up for . . . this time with Hope Raines.

10

HOPE WAITED IN THE OFFICE WEDNESDAY AFTERNOON.

The legend for John Tyler was supposed to be ready today. She glanced at her watch. It was just after six. The ticking clock on this case and her career made her nervous. Tyler seemed like someone she could trust, but the group's acceptance of him was far from certain. The whole situation was a powder keg, and Hope's plan represented either a way to defuse it or a match to light it.

The computer she used dinged with a new email. It contained some ideas for altering Tyler's appearance—hair color, glasses with clear lenses, lifts of an inch or two in his shoes—and a new identity. Hope knew the Bureau kept a stock of them ready to go in case situations like these arose. A little modification here and there, and an asset could have a whole new life story in a day or two.

Floyd Tyler Rayford—Hope chuckled and shook her head at the moniker—spent a decade in the Air Force as a mechanic, bounced around from job to job across several states, and lived in an apartment that must have been owned by the FBI. He'd recently turned fifty, had never married, and had no children. The rest of the file contained information on his made-up family.

She'd nearly finished reading the file when her phone rang. Agent Hess called. "Everything look good?" he asked.

"I think so. Yes, sir."

"Good. We put a lot into this one. He's even getting a Bureau apartment."

"Based on the address, I don't think it's a great place."

"It's not, but it's the kind of apartment someone like Floyd would rent."

"He's still going to go by Tyler," Hope said. "Something about being too stubborn to change now."

"Do you think he can do this?"

"Of course. Nothing in his record suggests he would fail."

"He's a wild card, Hope," Hess said. "This investigation has gone on longer than we thought. If he helps you bring it home, great. Just remember you don't have infinite time, and this is the end of the resources we're dedicating to it."

"So I'm sunk if I don't deliver," Hope said.

"Not what I told you."

"I'm reading between the lines. Our agency values critical thinking, right?" Hess didn't answer. "Thought so. This'll work. We'll bring it home, and you'll get to tell everyone at the Hoover Building how you oversaw the arrest of a major interstate crime ring."

"Hope, this isn't about—"

"I'll talk to you when this is over," Hope said. "When I've succeeded. Maybe I can even catch a ride into DC with you." She ended the call before Hess could reply. Poking the bear wasn't a great idea, but her career already teetered on the edge of a cliff. Hope printed the email and attachment, slipped everything into a manila folder, and left the office.

She needed to get this legend to John Tyler tonight if possible or tomorrow morning at the latest.

~

Tyler had run about a mile when his phone vibrated.

He wore it in a special sleeve strapped to his arm. It always felt a little silly, but the device would bounce and move too much in his pants or shorts pockets. He stopped and looked at the caller ID. It was a number he didn't recognize, but he answered it on the odds it was Hope Raines. He turned out to be right.

"I have your legend," she said. "We need to meet."

"I'm out on a run. Can you come to my house?"

"We're out west, Tyler. Frederick, Hagerstown . . . places like that. You'll be staying out here, so it's easier if you come to me."

"All right. I take it you've worked out the housing?"

"The Bureau isn't even going to charge you rent for your apartment."

"Where am I staying?"

"We have you in Hagerstown."

It made sense. The gang would use those places for easy access to the highway. Interstates 70, 68, and 81 would take them anywhere they wanted to go, and enough cars and trucks drove those roads at all hours to allow any vehicle to blend in. "I want a car, then."

"What?"

"I'm not risking mine."

"I don't have a car for you," Hope said.

"Do you use your personal ride?"

"No, but—"

"Mine is older and cooler," Tyler said. "A 'seventy-two Oldsmobile Four-Four-Two. I'm not running the risk of some asshole shooting it up if things go south. I don't need anything fancy. Get something your people were going to send to the excess lot."

Hope sighed. "Fine. I'll get you a car. How soon can you meet me out here?"

"I need a shower. Send me the address and give me about ninety minutes."

"I have hair color for you. Might as well wait on the shower. See you soon." She ended the call.

Tyler headed home. He'd already packed a bag with a week's worth of clothes and supplies. Before he threw it in the trunk, he texted Lexi. Last night, he told her he'd be doing some work for the FBI. She seemed surprised at first considering his history with the Bureau—and maybe their shared experiences with law enforcement in general. Now, he told her he was headed out to Hagerstown. Despite the early hour, she replied quickly.

I want a pic of you with blond hair, lol.

Tyler laughed, fired up the 442, and headed out. He used his phone to navigate to the coordinates Hope sent him. It was an apartment complex called The Bradford in what looked to be the eastern end of Hagerstown. With a few spots of heavy traffic, the trip took most of the ninety minutes Tyler allocated. He pulled into the lot. Hope, dressed in a T-shirt and a pleasingly tight pair of jean capris, stepped out of a Dodge Charger. "Don't expect anything so fancy," she said when Tyler approached.

"What are we going to do with my car?"

"You can leave the keys with me. Someone will drive it home for you."

He frowned but nodded. "I'll get my stuff out of the trunk." He opened it, collected his duffel, and locked the car. Hope snatched the keys out of the air when Tyler tossed them. "I'm billing you for any scratches and dents."

"Fine." She smiled and extended a hand toward the buildings. "Your palace awaits." The place looked like a lot of other apartment and condo complexes Tyler had seen over the years. Brick exterior. Three stories. Basic wooden balconies with small gardens on the ground floor. He could probably predict the floor plans. Hope led the way toward the structure on the far right. She entered 4673 on the alphanumeric keypad next to the door. Tyler noticed the numbers spelled HOPE. The green metal door's lock disengaged with a *thunk*.

Stairs led down to the ground floor and up to the top two levels. Hope took one flight up and stopped at the second door on the left. It was tan and blended in well with the color of the interior walls. "I'll leave the key with you," she said as she opened up and walked inside. Tyler followed. A small foyer and coat closet led to a living room. To the right, a small dining area opened into a galley kitchen. The lone bedroom lay down the hall on the left. "You have two bathrooms," Hope said. "Try not to have too many wild parties."

"No promises," Tyler said, setting his bag down near the dresser.

"You'll find the hair color, glasses, and shoe inserts on the sink." She inclined her head toward the connected bathroom. "You'll be a blond with glasses and about an inch taller. Considering the guys see a lot of people and aren't exactly rocket scientists, I think we'll be all right. If you think you've been made, though, we can pull the plug."

"I'll be fine," Tyler said. He realized the group heard him talk. Maybe he would need to alter his voice a little. This volunteer gig got more complicated all the time. "I thought I was supposed to meet with an agent about changing my appearance."

Hope spread her hands and smiled. She had a good one. "You get me."

"Budget cuts, I guess."

"You'll meet the boys this afternoon, so be ready," Hope said. "My guess is they'll want you to prove yourself by fixing an engine or something."

"Should I have brought tools?"

She shook her head. "They have everything there. It's a nice setup, actually. I'll text you the address." She looked at his hair and smirked. "Go make yourself a blond."

"It'll take some getting used to."

She ran a hand through her own hair. "I understand." Hope paused, and her face grew serious. "Thanks for doing this. I know you're putting your neck on the line at my request, and you barely know me."

"These guys made me a witness to murder," Tyler said. "We need to take them down . . . along with their leader."

"Yes, we do." Hope clapped him on the shoulder. "See you this afternoon."

"Oh, I almost forgot. What do they call you?"

"I'm Felicity Snow."

Tyler chuckled. "A little on the nose, isn't it?"

"It keeps them off my real trail," Hope said. "It's good enough."

When she left, Tyler read the directions on the hair color package and took his time applying it. A fifteen-minute set-in period and one shower later, he stared at his own short golden locks in the bathroom mirror. It would definitely take some getting used to, but the color looked even and natural. With the horn-rimmed glasses and an extra inch on his height, he just might pull this off.

Tyler got dressed, sent Lexi the picture she wanted, and opened the fridge. Someone stocked the kitchen, so Tyler made bacon, eggs, and toast. His daughter sent a string of laughing emojis as her reply and then followed it up with a reminder to be careful. Pretty much what he expected. Tyler ate breakfast and pondered how the afternoon meeting would go. If it went off the rails, he thought about the best way to take out the members of the group.

11

———————

Lexi lost track of what strike she was up to.

She'd swung and missed at several law firms. Since then, she set her sights lower. Private investigative firms made sense, but none of them seemed interested. "Do you have any experience?" one woman asked.

"No, I would be trying to get it," Lexi told her. "It's why I'm willing to come in as an intern."

"We've taken interns, but you need to have some hours already. We're a regulated business. It's not amateur hour."

Another couple places gave her the same song and dance. "So let me get this straight," Lexi said in frustration when a man turned her down for being a rookie. "You tell me I need experience, but no one will take me on so I can earn some. How do we solve this paradox?"

"I wish I could help you," he said.

"Maybe I should have looked into cookie thefts when I was in the goddamn Girl Scouts." He didn't have a reply, so she hung up.

Lexi deleted another entry from the note she'd made on her phone. Not many options remained. She fortified herself with another cup of coffee and pondered whether she should continue. Maybe a year's worth of classes with some lab time would count as experience for the picky gatekeepers who worked the phones at these agencies. It couldn't hurt to exhaust her list in the meantime. The next entry was a small firm called Ferguson Investigations. Her research showed they made the news for being a tiny outfit who closed tough cases pretty often.

The woman who answered the phone sounded young and introduced herself as T.J. "I'm looking for an internship this summer," Lexi said, beginning her spiel. "I'm a criminal justice major in college, and I want to gain some meaningful experience. Paid or unpaid is all right."

"We've never had an intern. It's just me and my boss."

This wasn't an encouraging answer, but it stopped well shy of the outright rejections Lexi had been hearing all morning. "How long have you been there?"

"Almost two years now."

"Do you think you might need an intern for the summer?"

"I really don't know," T.J. said. "Winter tends to be our slow season."

Lexi sighed. "Look, I'll be honest with you. You're the first person who hasn't dismissed me in the first twenty seconds. I'm going into my junior year of college, and I just picked my major. The problem is most students who chose it from day one already have summer internships or jobs in the discipline, and I want to keep pace even though I got a late start. You wouldn't even need to pay me. I'll live with my dad over the summer anyway. I just want to get a couple months' worth of experience under my belt." She paused. "You sound young like me. Did you take criminal justice?"

T.J. didn't answer for a couple seconds. "I guess I'll be honest with you, too. I haven't been to college."

If the boss hired an assistant without a degree, this gave

Lexi hope when it came to landing an internship. "There are days I would tell you you're not missing much."

"Maybe I'll get around to it."

"What do you think my chances are?"

"I'd have to talk to the boss," T.J. said. "He's out right now. He trusts me as his executive assistant, but this is a decision he should make."

"I understand."

"Maybe I could screen you for him. Want to get a late lunch?"

"Sure, but I'm in College Park," Lexi said.

"How about someplace sort of in the middle, then? Columbia?"

"All right." Lexi couldn't help but smile. This was the only promising call of the day, and while she didn't get an affirmative answer, this represented a big step in the right direction. "Where?"

"You pick the place." T.J. rattled off her phone number. "Text me where you want to go. How about two-thirty? Should let you go north ahead of traffic."

"Sounds good," Lexi said.

After breakfast, Tyler spent some time going over Hope's invented backstory for him.

He'd brought a notebook and colored pencils in lieu of his easel and watercolors at home. The apartment had a few pens in a kitchen junk drawer, so Tyler jotted down important details more than once. This had always been the way he learned best. Floyd Tyler Rayford lived a simpler life than the real John Tyler. No time in private security. No extracurricular activities to put him on the radars of law enforcement at multiple levels. An inconsistent job history.

No living family.

It would be a much more boring and lonely life, but Tyler needed to inhabit it for the next couple weeks or so. However long it took to put these assholes out of business. He didn't know what Hope would tell her fake friends about the mechanic she knew, so he made sure to be familiar with everything in his alias's life. If the gang were cautious—and they seemed to be—members would have questions. Tyler reviewed the file and pondered where he might be able to expand something or provide a little extra detail. The military service portion was pretty barren, and he could draw on his own time in the Army to fill in the gaps in Floyd's Air Force ledger.

Hope texted him a short while later with the address and some other info. *Your car is en route back to Baltimore. There's another waiting for you in the lot. Driver's door is unlocked. Key is in a hidden compartment under the seat. See you at 2:30. Don't be late.*

Tyler checked out the address. It was in an industrial park on the outskirts of Frederick. The street view showed some rundown facilities and a lack of cars parked anywhere, leading him to think the complex fell into disuse. The bones were still good, however, and it made a great place for the gang to gather and soup up a car for their next heist and getaway.

How many he would be involved in remained a large unknown. Tyler unpacked a few days' worth of clothes, hanging up shirts and pants and putting everything else into a drawer. The bedroom furniture matched, but it looked like it came from a discount store a decade or more ago. No matter. It was functional for the people the G-men needed to stash here, and Tyler had lived with older and worse furniture over the years.

Before he left, Tyler reviewed the notes from what Hope liked calling his legend a couple more times. He walked outside and spotted a Ford Crown Victoria in the parking lot.

Ford hadn't made the vehicle in over a decade. This specimen looked like a second-generation model with its larger headlights and grill. Tyler opened the door. The newer gauge cluster contained both a speedometer and a tachometer and confirmed his suspicions. A sunroof overhead let in the weak light making it past the clouds. This had been a good car in its day. The V8 would be underpowered by modern standards, and the ride aimed more for plush than sporty, but Tyler had driven a hell of a lot worse in his day.

He felt under the seat, and his fingers brushed against a small gap in the plastic. He pulled a hidden tray out, reached in, and found the key. It shared its ring with a fob allowing keyless entry. The interior was dated, but the agency motor pool maintained the car well. Tyler started the car, and the 4.6-liter V8 rumbled to life. It sounded less throaty and more muted than his 442, but so did a lot of cars with stock exhausts. He made sure his phone displayed the fastest route and got underway.

Tyler turned onto the road leading to the industrial park six minutes before the appointed hour. The asphalt bore cracks everywhere, and most of the structures at this end were in bad need of paint and general maintenance. Conditions improved a little as he drove along. Tyler scanned for other ways out. The one street was the main source of entry and egress, but if he needed to, he could drive across the grass and hop a curb. The Ford might protest, but they'd always been pretty tough vehicles.

Faded numbers marked the address Hope gave him. A few muscle cars and some ugly European model sat outside. Tyler parked the Crown Vic, took a deep breath, and walked inside the yawning door. It was a large open space, the right half of which had been repurposed as a repair bay. A nice lift took up much of the area, and tool racks surrounded it. It reminded Tyler of the setup he got familiar with at Smitty's old shop and tried to duplicate at his own.

Four men stood with Hope, and none of them looked friendly. "This is the guy I was telling you about," she said. "His name's Floyd, but he goes by his middle name, Tyler."

One of the men snorted. "If I were Floyd, I'd go by something else, too."

Tyler spotted the oldest member of the group. His graying hair gave him away. He'd been the shooter at the jewelry store. The others looked to be in their late twenties to mid thirties. All were taller than Tyler and kept themselves in at least decent shape. "I'm Chains," the one who mocked Tyler's assumed name said. He wore a large chain from his wallet around a belt loop. "The old guy there is Pop. This is Rock and Connor." The latter two were of similar height and build, differing only in hair color. Rock's was coal black while Connor's was more of a Scottish red-brown.

They stood near an older silver Audi TT. Tyler figured this would be his test. Considering the reputation the model carried in its earlier years, he could be tasked with fixing any one of a litany of things. Chains gestured to the car. "Connor wants to give this to his girlfriend." For his part, Connor's expression didn't change from unfriendly glower. "It needs a new turbo, though. You know how to work with one?"

Tyler nodded. He tried to think of what Floyd might say about this. "It's not a helicopter or anything, but I can fix it. Not a big fan of turbochargers, but I get 'em."

"Good. You have all the parts you should need to install it. The current one is still in there. Connor wants his girl to have a bigger turbo so the car will be faster." Chains looked at his watch. "For an experienced mechanic, this shouldn't be hard." He pulled a phone out of the front pocket of his jeans and a pistol from his waistband at the back. "You have two hours. Either the car works properly at the end, or you're dead."

12

———

Lexi ordered at the BGR in Columbia and snagged an available table.

She'd never been to one of the burger chain's locations before. Classic album posters—most of which she knew through her parents—hung from the walls, and even the tabletops reflected pop culture. Lexi's forearms rested on a large Superman logo. Meat sizzled behind the counter, and the smell of cooking beef filled the air. A minute later, a young blonde woman exited a Mustang out front and walked into the restaurant.

She looked pretty tall—at least Lexi's five-eight and maybe an inch or two more. She wore her blonde hair pulled back in a ponytail. Jeans and a sweater framed an athletic body. She saw Lexi and waved. "Hi! I'm T.J."

"Thanks for coming," Lexi said.

T.J. waited behind one other customer, ordered her meal, and joined Lexi a moment later. She couldn't have been more than twenty-one or twenty-two. This boded well for landing an internship. T.J. was pretty, but Lexi noticed she didn't wear too much makeup. "I've never been here before," she said. "Don't get to Columbia very often."

"Me, either. Do you live in Baltimore?"

"Yeah. I have an apartment there."

"Two friends and I share a place in College Park," Lexi said. "It's an easy drive to campus. We even walk on nice days."

"You're taking criminal justice classes?" T.J. asked.

"I just picked a major. It's my fourth semester, and it was time. I wasn't really sure what I wanted to do before, though I guess I always felt something of a pull in this direction thanks to my dad."

"Is he a cop?"

"No," Lexi said. "He's a mechanic, technically. Retired Army. He has a complete inability to walk away from trouble, even if it's someone else's, and even when he should." She snorted. "Right now, he's helping some FBI agent track down a robbery ring because he happened to be in a store when it got hit."

"What's his name?"

"John. John Tyler. I guess all his time in the Army made him used to going by his last name. No one calls him John."

T.J. nodded. "I've met him. He helped my boss with something about a year ago."

"Really?" Lexi smiled. "You think it'll help my cause?"

"I'm . . . not sure. I got the impression C.T. didn't like the way he handled something."

Lexi felt there was more to the story, but T.J. stopped talking. The guy at the counter called her order number. Lexi collected her cheeseburger and fries, filling a small plastic container with ketchup on the way back to her table. "I hope your boss will judge me on my own merits," she said. "I'm not my father."

"I'm sure he will."

"Have you told him about this?"

"Not yet," T.J. said. The fellow yelled out another order number, and T.J. got up to collect her food. Her burger looked and smelled much like Lexi's, though T.J. didn't get tomato.

After a few bites of a good sandwich, Lexi asked, "What can you tell me about your agency?"

"It's pretty small," T.J. said after munching a fry. "Just my boss and me. We could take more cases if he contracted out some of the investigating, but he hasn't wanted to yet."

"You think he might change his mind?"

"Hard to say." T.J. shrugged. "I thought he was leaning that direction. We worked a serial killer case a few months ago. The whole thing got a shitload of press throughout, and it made for some good publicity at the end. We got a ton more calls than normal. It's been a busy period, but C.T. hasn't brought anyone else in."

"Why not?"

"I think he's very . . . particular."

"He a by-the-book sort of guy?" Lexi said.

T.J. laughed. "No. Not at all, really. He definitely colors outside the lines." She lowered her voice as someone sat at the table behind them. "His background is in computers . . . if you catch my drift."

"I think I do." Lexi nodded. "I have a little experience there, too."

"Really?"

"Yeah. My dad worked private security for a while after he retired. They gave him a nice laptop. Preloaded with quite a few interesting tools. He barely knows how to use it, of course." She chuckled. "Old people and computers."

"I know, right?"

"Anyway, he's gotten into the habit of asking me all the tech stuff," Lexi said. "I knew a little going in, but I've taught myself plenty in addition. It's definitely helped on some of his more interesting extracurricular jaunts."

"I think C.T. will value that experience," T.J. said.

Both women ate more of their meals. Burgers and fries

disappeared quickly. "Broad experience is something I don't have much of yet," Lexi said. "I haven't even enrolled in the intro class yet. Your boss would need to see something in me, I guess."

"He just might." T.J. smiled. "He took a chance on me when he didn't have to. I came to him with almost no relevant experience . . . only a recommendation. It's worked out really well." She didn't elaborate, but Lexi got the impression there was more to the story. Maybe T.J. would trust her enough to give her the full version one day.

"Good to know." Lexi drank the last of her soda. She realized her knee bobbed under the table, and she stopped it. "Do you think you could put a word in for me?"

"I can." T.J. grinned. "I don't know if he plans to take on an intern, but if he's willing, I'll recommend you. It's like paying a good thing forward."

"Thank you." Lexi beamed. "I know I'm getting a late start major-wise, but something like this will really help me."

"What do you actually want to do with a criminal justice degree?"

"Not one of the big two things," Lexi said. "No interests in going into law enforcement or being a lawyer. Ideally, I'd want to work as an investigator for a defense lawyer. No firms seem willing to take me on, though, and some even said they hire out that aspect of the job."

"Not many of them seem to come our way." T.J. shrugged and glanced at her phone. "I should be getting back."

"Thanks for coming today. It was really good to meet you."

"You too!" T.J. and Lexi both stood, and the two shared a quick hug. T.J. bussed her tray, walked outside, and climbed back into her Mustang. Lexi had gotten better at spotting makes and models thanks to her dad, so she noticed the car was a recent vintage but not a GT. She took care of her trash and walked out of BGR with a little spring in her step.

～

Tyler sweated, and not just from the stale air in the makeshift garage.

He knew how turbochargers worked, what they did, and the basics of connecting everything. Logically, it made sense. The TT's engine bay, however, must have been designed for technicians with long, slender arms and tiny hands. A few small cuts dotted Tyler's skin as he worked. By his own estimation, he had about forty minutes remaining and should finish ahead of the deadline.

He remembered the TT when it came out. The design was revolutionary for its day. Tyler felt the car didn't age well, however, and preferred the more streamlined looks of the third-generation version. The new turbo the gang gave him was a little larger than the stock version. The piping all connected, but a few extra millimeters on the turbine would cause more boost and thus more performance.

Twenty-five minutes later, he stood up, wiped his hands, and said, "There. It's done."

"We'll need to test it," Chains said. He tossed the keys to Connor. "Take her for a spin." Connor got behind the wheel, started the engine, and pulled out. The group's de facto leader leaned closer to Tyler. "You'd better hope he thinks it's an upgrade."

"Those weren't the requirements."

Pop, who took over pointing the gun a short while ago, made sure Tyler knew a weapon still pointed at him. "Maybe we changed them."

"Maybe you can keep looking for a mechanic, then." Hope frowned but didn't say anything. She crept closer to Pop.

Connor returned a minute later. He got out, shut the door, and pocketed the keys. "Seems good." He nodded. "Lag is better than before. I'll need to dyno it to see how the power and torque shake out, but it feels and sounds fine to me."

"All right," Chains said. "Looks like you passed the test . . . Tyler, isn't it?"

"Yes."

"Maybe we should call him Floyd," Pop said. He still kept the gun trained on Tyler despite Connor approving the repair test.

"Maybe you should put the goddamn gun away," Tyler said.

Pop stepped closer and made the mistake of putting the muzzle within Tyler's reach. "What's the matter? You don't like . . . ow!"

Tyler hit his wrist, pushed the muzzle up and out, and disarmed the man in one fluid motion. Rather than escalate the situation any more, he ejected the magazine, popped the round out of the chamber, and tossed all three components to different corners of the area. "As a matter of fact," he said, "I'm not a fan of people pointing guns at me . . . especially for no reason."

"That was my pistol, you son of a bitch." To their credit, the other three men seemed content to stand by and watch this play out. Chains smirked like he expected something to go down. Maybe they all knew Pop was volatile, and dealing with his crap was a part of the test.

"Still is. You just need to put it back together. You do know how, right?"

"You prick." Pop drew back his fist and threw a punch at Tyler, who saw it coming and stepped out of the way. He did the same thing a second time. Undeterred, Pop went for a third. This time, Tyler blocked the strike and gave the other man a hard two-handed shove to the chest. It made him stumble backwards and nearly topple over.

At this point, Chains and Connor stepped between the

two. "All right," the man in charge said. "We don't need to throw down. I think we're all on the same team here."

"You're letting him join?" Pop demanded. "I don't like him."

"You don't like most people." Chains jabbed a finger at the older fellow. "It's your problem. Not mine and not anyone else's. This guy did a fine job. We need a new mechanic, and in case you ain't noticed, there ain't exactly a line outside the door."

"Does it need to be him?"

"I'm not going to be threatened," Tyler said. "If you can't control your people, I'm out."

"I got him," Chains said, a little testiness creeping into his voice. "So long as you do good work, get it done when we need to, and keep your mouth shut, there's no reason we can't make some money together."

"You learn to fight in the Air Force?" Pop asked.

"Yeah," Tyler said.

"You seem to move pretty well for someone who wasn't in too long."

"I'm a good mechanic because I remember what I've learned."

"So?"

"So apply it to other areas."

Pop grunted and turned away. Maybe he couldn't make the connection. Tyler made a mental note about the crew knowing he'd been in the Air Force but didn't make a career of it. Certainly no Green Beret training. Tyler wouldn't allow anyone to intimidate or bully him, but he'd need to get by on the basics if push came to shove. Hope offered a small nod.

"We'll be in touch," Chains said.

13

———————

Tyler left right after the group accepted him.

A few minutes later, Hope called. He looked into the rearview mirror and saw her car. "Miss me already?" he quipped.

She snorted. "Good job back there. I know they can be unpredictable."

"I don't work on many turbocharged engines. Maybe Floyd is better at it than I am." It felt weird thinking of his FBI-created identity as a different persona. Then again, it felt weird working under a cover story in the first place. He eased off the gas, and Hope's Charger pulled closer. "You got the nicer ride."

"Well, I *am* an active agent. All things considered, I don't think you're doing too badly."

"No complaints."

"Is anyone following us?" Hope asked.

Tyler checked all the mirrors. A couple cars were in the distance behind them, but neither did anything when he changed lanes, sped up, and slowed down. "Doesn't look like it."

"Where are you headed?"

"I actually want to get a few things from my house," Tyler said. "Having met your friends, I think I need to prepare a little better."

"They're not my friends," Hope said.

"Good. They don't deserve the title."

"You all right?"

"Sure. Why wouldn't I be?"

"Pop kept pointing a gun at you when he didn't need to."

"Not my first rodeo," Tyler told her. "None of them *needed* to point a gun at me, but yeah, he kept it up way too long. Maybe he won't make the same mistake again."

"I wasn't sure what was going to happen there."

"I was going to beat his ass if he kept swinging at me."

"You're not a Green Beret here, Tyler. Not to these guys. You're a guy I know who spent some pretty pedestrian years in the Air Force and knows how to fix cars."

"We called it 'the Chair Force' in my day," Tyler said. "Any years spent there are pedestrian."

Hope chuckled. "Your inter-service rivalries aside, I think it went well. The real test will be the first car you work on that we use in the field."

"When do you think it'll be?"

"I don't know," Hope said. "Probably soon. Jobs have been getting more frequent of late. We've gone from one a month up to three or four."

"Pretty major escalation."

"Yeah. No clue why. Chains doesn't tell us anything like that. Hell, I don't even know if the big boss man tells him."

"I'll be ready."

"Make sure you are. The Bureau's timeline means we probably only have two more jobs to bring them down unless I can show we're making significant progress."

"No pressure, though," Tyler said. "I'll talk to you later." He ended the call and headed back toward Baltimore. After confirming several times he hadn't sprouted a tail on the highway, Tyler turned into his neighborhood. He left the Crown Vic in his driveway and went inside for some supplies. In hindsight, he probably should have brought everything the first time. Tyler packed two pistols, a double-barreled model, and ammo for all the firearms into one duffel, and stuffed a few security measures into a smaller bag.

He drove back to Hagerstown, cruising through a Burger King as he neared his complex. Back at the apartment, Tyler made sure he could access a weapon whenever he needed one. The gang didn't know where he lived, but he couldn't count on this to remain true. As he ate his dinner, he also set up a couple basic security cameras to link to his phone. One went just inside the door, and the other provided a good view of anyone coming up the stairs. The final component was a Howler at the front door. If anyone breached it, the device would live up to its name.

You're not paranoid if they're really after you.

When he finished, Tyler threw his trash away and made sure the cameras worked. He didn't test the Howler. If the gang kicked in the door, they would get to experience it firsthand.

CHAINS CROSSED his arms and surveyed the space.

They'd worked out of this abandoned industrial complex for months. He didn't even know what purpose this building had served in its earlier days. The necessary equipment appeared, and operations worked better than ever. Felicity pulled double duty for a time while slowed things down. They needed cars which were more capable in their stock configurations to avoid piling too much on her plate. Now, they could go back to the way things were.

Presuming Floyd or Tyler—or whatever he went by— proved reliable.

"What do we know about this guy?" Connor demanded.

"We know he's a bit of a prick," Pop said. It took the older guy a few minutes, but he found all the parts and reassembled his gun. "Next time I point this at him, he's catching a bullet."

"You're too goddamn trigger happy," Chains said. Pop fell silent and began a studious examination of the concrete floor. "The bossman has noticed, too. You can't keep leaving bodies behind us. This group and what we do is too important to get caught because some yokel cop has a hard-on to catch a killer."

"No one would miss this son of a bitch," Pop grumbled.

"Maybe. Maybe not. To your question, Connor, we don't know too much. This ain't exactly a job where I can ask someone to apply online and upload their latest résumé. Felicity said he's done good work. Ten years in the Air Force fixing helicopters, and he's worked a bunch of mechanic jobs since."

"He moves around a lot?" Connor asked.

Chains shrugged. "How the hell would I know? Maybe he got used to military life. Every two or three years, you pack up and go somewhere else. He could be an asshole who wears out his welcome pretty quick." Pop bobbed his head but didn't say anything. "He did good work today under pressure. We need a new mechanic, he seems qualified, and he comes recommended."

"By our newest member." Connor frowned and crossed his arms. "We don't know a ton about Felicity either, do we?"

"Jesus, you want me to run background checks on these people?" Chains said. "What would I find in your file, *Aidan?*" Connor scowled at the use of his given name. Aidan McCloud became Connor among the group because of *Highlander,* even though he spelled his last name differently than Christopher Lambert's fictional immortal member of the MacLeod clan.

"He ain't wrong," Rock said. "We don't know very much about Felicity, and now we're taking her word on this new guy."

Chains put up his hands. "Look . . . I get what you're saying. Here's what I know. We've put our lives and freedom in Felicity's hands a bunch of times now. She's made some pretty daring escapes and outdriven cops on our tail along the way. She even picked up the slack on the grease monkey front. Point is she coulda turned us in a dozen times by now. Hell, all she'd need to do is drive bad enough for someone to catch her, and she never has. I'm not worried about her, the big man isn't, and none of you should be."

"All right," Connor said, though his tone suggested he remained unconvinced. "We'll see how this new guy does."

"If he sucks," Pop said, "I'm shooting him."

Chains sighed and shook his head. "Christ almighty, it's like herding cats with you lot sometimes. We'll have a job again soon. New target. New car. Different state. Why don't we focus on being ready and stop questioning everyone? If this Tyler shows he can't be trusted . . ." He spread his hands. ". . . We know how to solve the mechanic problem. They had to bury the last guy in five pieces."

The mention of the grisly event did not sate the other members' bloodlust. "Keep your phones handy, boys. I'll be in touch again soon. Until then, scatter." He left the facility, and the others followed suit.

14

———————

THE NEXT EVENING, A TEXT FROM CHAINS INTERRUPTED WHAT Hope wanted to be a quiet Friday night.

Meet at the spot. 8:30.

She finished her dinner. Like Tyler, Hope stayed in an apartment furnished—in both common senses of the word—by the Bureau. Hers was about ten minutes from his and in a more expensive area. It made for a nice upgrade compared to the dingy hotel she slept in the first few weeks. She wondered how much it cost to maintain places like these over time. Considering she'd be driving, Hope eschewed the glass of wine she'd been looking forward to. Maybe she'd still be in a good enough mood to drink it later. She might even need two.

Hope's Charger crunched on the gravel near the industrial site two minutes before the appointed time. Even then, she was the last to arrive. "Nice of you to join us," Connor said when she walked in—and after his eyes scanned her hips and chest.

"I'm still early," Hope said.

Chains took out his phone. He held it close to his body and turned so no one could see what he did. A moment later, a voice came through its speaker. "Is everyone there?" The leader. His voice sounded distorted as if passing through a device which electronically modified the output. Hope realized she'd never heard his unaltered speech.

"We're here," Chains confirmed. "Me, Connor, Rock, Pop, and Felicity."

"Where's the new mechanic?"

"We'll get him soon."

"Good. He doesn't need to be here for this part. The less he knows, the better. I'd hate to hear you gentlemen were forced to draw and quarter another man." Hope shuddered at the casual reference to such a brutal act of violence—and murder.

"Do we have another job coming up?" Chains asked.

"Yes," the main man said. "I've been impressed with the operations of late, so I'm okay with a more aggressive schedule than we used to run. Let's keep this one clean, though. No casualties if there's any possible way to avoid them." Pop frowned but held his tongue. "I mean it. Murder charges hit considerably harder than stealing a carload of shit."

"Speaking of stealing . . ."

"Yes. You want to know the target. It'll be a check-cashing joint in Virginia. Big volume. They still do payday loans and those sorts of things. We have someone who knows the operation. I want to hit it next week."

"We'll make sure the car is ready," Chains said. "We already have one waiting for our new grease monkey to work his magic on." One thing the group did well was never using the same car twice. Law enforcement couldn't look for a particular vehicle because it was different each time. After every successful job, someone drove the car via back roads to a remote area and set it on fire.

"Good job finding someone, Felicity," the boss said. "I was impressed with your ability to do double duty. I'm sure you're happier with an easier workload."

"Thanks," Hope said. "I am. It allows me to focus on the actual getaway."

"It's your most important work. I don't have anything else for tonight, people. We'll talk again next week." The call ended. Hope always searched for something in the voice—cadence, a pronunciation, anything she could key on—and came up empty each time. The faceless gang leader would remain unidentified for now.

"You heard the man," Chains said. "Enjoy your weekend. Our new mechanic probably won't."

Connor chuckled. Hope wondered exactly what lay in store for Tyler.

～

Tyler pulled the Crown Vic to a stop outside the building the gang used as its meeting spot and garage.

He saw Hope's Charger, a well-worn pickup truck, and one other car, a Mustang at least a decade old. "Felicity," he said to himself, remembering Hope's moniker with the group. Tyler walked inside to find the woman and Connor standing near a vehicle Tyler hadn't seen in years. "A Dodge Aries?"

"Yup." Connor tossed him the keys, and Tyler caught them.

"What the hell is this thing doing here?"

"It's our next getaway car," Connor said.

Tyler laughed. "Are the police on bikes? Tricycles?"

"They won't expect something like this to be speeding away."

"Probably because none of these K-cars have been 'speeding' in a long time," Tyler said. "You want to get away from the cops who drive cars designed for pursuit. To accomplish this, you dredge up a thirty-year-old heap no one would have ever called fast. You can time these blasted things to sixty with a sundial."

Connor jerked his head toward a counter on the far wall. "There's an envelope with some cash over there. You ever been to a junkyard?"

"Sure."

"Buy some better parts, then. You got seven grand to turn this baby into something we can use to get away from the law. Any tool you need should already be here." He patted the hood a few times. For a car of about three decades old, the silver Aries remained in pretty good shape.

"It's going to need a whole new engine and transmission for starters," Tyler said. "Probably some suspension work."

"So do it."

"How am I supposed to get those parts back here?"

"Use the truck," Connor said. "Keys are in the big red toolbox."

"Fine. I can get it all here. None of those things will over-come the limitations of the platform. This old buggy is front-wheel-drive. You ever heard of wheel hop? Torque steer?" Hope frowned. Tyler figured she knew the terms—and as the driver, she would need to deal with them on the road if the group went ahead with this ridiculous plan.

"He has a point, Connor," she said. "Rear or all-wheel-drive are worlds better for making a getaway."

"This is what we got." Connor shrugged. "Consider it a test. Maybe for the both of you."

"You're willing to go to jail over a stupid test?"

"We ain't going to jail," Connor said. "Either this car is going to do the job, or we say goodbye to a second mechanic." Hope started to say something, but Connor put up a hand to cut her off. "You want to cry about it, Felicity, go ahead. You're pretty new, too. Maybe you can help your boyfriend here get the car ready."

"He's not my boyfriend," Hope said.

"I don't really give a shit," Connor said. He looked at his watch. "It's Friday night. You have until this time Monday to finish. Either Felicity thinks this is a car she can use, or you catch a bullet. Clear?" Tyler didn't respond. Connor reached behind himself and pulled a pistol from his waistband. He kept it at his side. "If there's something you're confused about, I can go ahead and shoot you now. We'll find another grease monkey to keep us on schedule."

"I'm good," Tyler said. He watched Connor's hand. If the gun came up, Tyler would act. His undercover identity—and Hope's case—be damned. Like in the jewelry store, he wasn't about to stand still and be a target.

"All right." Connor put the gun away. "Seventy-two hours." He walked out of the area.

"Prick," Tyler muttered when the Mustang roared to life and pulled away with a screech of the tires.

"You gonna want some help?" Hope asked.

"Maybe. Let's see what parts I can find first."

"Sorry, Tyler. I didn't know he was going to be such an ass."

"If he brought the gun up, I would've fed it to him. It might've ruined your assignment, but no way I was going to let him get me in his sights." Tyler snorted. "He's almost as bad as the old guy."

She nodded. "I'm glad things didn't escalate."

Tyler wasn't sure he agreed, but he had more pressing things to deal with in the near future.

15

Saturday morning, Tyler went for an early run. It allowed him to explore the area around his new digs and look for obvious vulnerabilities and ambush points. He didn't find anything out of the ordinary or unexpected. Urban areas weren't designed for people who scanned for threats like Tyler did, and any day he spent in a city reinforced this idea.

After a shower and breakfast, he started calling junkyards by 0800. The largest in the area—about twenty minutes away —had the biggest inventory and the highest prices, and the guy who answered the phone said he had several truckloads of engines and transmissions. Tyler drove to the garage and measured the area he had to work with on the Aries. It could handle more than its stock motor but not most V8s. A naturally aspirated V6—even newer models peaked a little over 300 horses—wouldn't provide the power to evade law enforcement. Tyler needed something turbocharged.

He swapped his Crown Vic for the pickup and headed north. The truck was a couple generations old. It had power seats, locks, and windows but not much else. There was no rear cab, and this allowed for a longer bed. It reminded Tyler of the time when trucks were built and used for their capabilities. Nowadays, they sat four or five people, had interiors rivaling those of the luxury brands, and carried price tags to match.

The junkyard was a sprawling place, a graveyard of metal, glass, and hope. Many vehicles got rear-ended or sideswiped hard enough to bend the frames and total them. These accidents forced the owner into a different car but usually left the powertrain in good shape. Tyler found the man he'd spoken to, and the fellow led him to an area of totaled cars but intact engines.

The only one really fitting the bill came from a ten-year-old Audi S5 convertible. It was a V6 and supercharged rather than turbocharged, but both provided extra shove and would serve the same purpose. Someone else had already scavenged the transmission, so Tyler hunted around until he found another automatic which could handle the power. It would be a little extra work to get the units to play nicely, but the Aries only needed to work for a short while.

Back at the garage, Tyler spent a few hours getting the old Dodge on the lift and removing all the relevant parts. It was a cool spring day, and he left the bay door open, but the work still made him sweat. He enjoyed it even though he toiled away for a bunch of criminals. Under normal circumstances, he'd sabotage the car, but nothing about the current circumstances would be considered normal.

After eating lunch, Tyler stepped outside away from the prying eyes of the group's cameras. He called FBI supervisory special agent Roland Johnson. "Didn't expect to hear from you again," Johnson said after introductions.

"I didn't expect to call you again," Tyler told him. "I presume you've heard the news."

"I have. Hope doesn't work for me directly, but her case has taken her into my jurisdiction." Johnson ran the Pittsburgh field office, and his area included parts of West

Virginia as well. "I wasn't sure what I thought about her bringing you in at first, honestly. I still remember the militia mess."

"I remember solving a problem for you."

"Not exactly the way I would have done it," Johnson said, "but I guess you did."

"What can you tell me about Hope?"

"We had . . . well, high hopes for her when she came into the Bureau. For whatever reason, she's never quite gotten there. She's not bad at her job or anything, but I don't think I'd rate her above average. There's plenty of untapped potential there, but she's running out of time to show it."

"I guess rounding up these assholes would give her a . . . ?" Tyler trailed off. He couldn't say "gold star" because FBI agents who received those did so in memoriam for dying in the line of duty. "High marks on her personnel review?"

"More or less. She needs a win." Johnson sighed. "It's why I was leery when I heard she'd pulled you in. I don't think a string of dead bodies is going to advance her career."

"You think I'm gonna go off the rails and kill everyone?"

"I think I've seen your handiwork, Tyler. Impressive, to be sure, but I think shooting people is Plan A, B, and C for you, and you rarely ever get down to Plan D."

"If the clowns you dispatched to West Virginia are any indication, you need my help."

"I know they gave you a raw deal at first, but—"

"At first?" Tyler broke in. "They might have taken me to a goddamn black site if you didn't get involved. My objections to those idiots aside, Hope seems different. Better. I think she wants to make a difference and get her career back on track."

"And you're happy to help her do it," Johnson said.

"I was at the jewelry store when the crew hit it. They didn't need to shoot anyone. Somebody needs to take these guys down."

"Hope's a good-looking woman."

"I noticed. You're also not the first person who's pointed it out. I'm going to guess the FBI's power structure is mostly men?"

"Mostly," Johnson admitted.

"Maybe you should stop assuming only the attractive agents can find people willing to help them."

"Maybe I could. Anyway, I agree with you on taking this crew down. Perhaps you can try to leave someone alive this time."

"I'm supporting Hope," Tyler said, "but I'll tell you this . . . if it comes down to me or them, I'll send flowers."

"Understood." They ended the call, and Tyler thought about the installation of the new powertrain as he walked back inside. It was really a two-person job. He wanted to call Ortiz but also didn't want to expose his employee to the robbery ring. Ditto Smitty. The other qualified mechanics Tyler knew all had Army backgrounds, and if anyone in the gang watched their cameras, they might start to check identities and make connections.

It left Hope as the best option, so Tyler texted her.

WITH HOPE'S HELP, Tyler got the engine and transmission swapped out by Sunday evening.

Removing them from the truck proved a challenge. Normally, this would be at least a two-person job. Instead, Tyler used a chain like a pulley and got the heavy parts onto a wheeled dolly to move them around. The engine fit with maybe an inch to spare, so Tyler and Hope did most of their work on it before welding some new mounts.

Getting it to work with the six-speed automatic coming from another vehicle took a few hours of labor to make the connections. Tyler adjusted a few parts and even used the facility's machining capabilities to fashion a new one. It took him back to the days of working on tanks and Humvees when he enjoyed a full garage and a healthy Army budget—before the era of increasing operations and shrinking budget room made scavenging for parts a necessity.

Another trip to the junkyard provided a better and sportier exhaust, and Tyler also found some suspension parts in good condition. He couldn't overcome the limitations of front-wheel drive when it came to putting the power down, but he could try to mitigate them. Lowering the chassis height and cranking everything tighter would make for a stiffer ride, but it would also help Hope deal with the inevitable wheel hop of taking off from a dead stop.

By Sunday evening, Tyler felt like he'd sweated enough to lose five pounds, and the getaway car was basically ready. It needed a test drive and some final tweaks, but he and Hope got it as far as they could. "Time to see how she handles," Hope said. Tyler climbed in beside her. The interior was plain, spartan, and cheap—all hallmarks of American auto makers' outputs from this era.

The engine turned over and revved eagerly when Hope pushed in the accelerator. Shifting to Drive sounded a little clunky and notchy, but they couldn't make it any smoother considering the disparate parts of the powertrain. She eased the Aries down the long road and stopped at the end where it connected to a street. "Let's see how we do." She grinned at Tyler and mashed the gas.

The front tires screeched, and the steering wheel jerked in Hope's hands. She held it steady, however, and after the initial burst of torque, things got easier. The supercharger whined as the RPMs climbed, and the modified Aries drove pretty well. Hope maintained speed coming up to a couple curves. The stiffer suspension prevented most body roll, and the car responded with alacrity when she got back on the throttle.

"Not bad," she said. "It'll never be confused for a sports car, but I can work with this."

"I hope you can get away from the cops with it," Tyler said.

"Most of them can't drive like I do. I take more risks. They're trained to keep pursuits safe."

"You won't be able to evade a helicopter, though."

She shrugged. "We'll do our best."

"What happens if you get caught?" Tyler wanted to know.

"The Bureau would get me out at some point," Hope said. "I have to be arrested to sell it. The problem is we don't think the guys would talk. They won't give up the big man, and he'll simply recruit a few more assholes and get back to work. It's why I'm still embedded versus rounding them up."

After testing the K-car a little more, Hope turned it around and pulled it back into the garage. "It feels good," she said. "I can't imagine Dodge ever dreamed one of these things going so fast. Nice work . . . *Floyd*."

"I don't go by John," Tyler said. "I would never go by something like Floyd." Hope grinned. "I wish we could dyno this thing. The engine is good for over three hundred horsepower and torque. We might be getting a little more with the exhaust but not much. I really want to add a limited-slip diff, but it would take hours of toil and trouble to make one fit on here."

"You have any money left?" Hope asked.

"Some."

"You can probably buy a tuner for the ECU." Engine control units were a part of modern engines, and the right bit of hardware could tweak the settings to open up more performance options.

"I'll see what's out there," Tyler said. "I basically only have tomorrow, so it's gotta be something in stock at a store."

"I think you have a winner here." Hope patted the steering wheel which remained unchanged. It was definitely designed for an eighty-year-old driver and not someone who wanted to turn it aggressively. "A few tweaks tomorrow, and the gang will be happy."

"Maybe this'll be the last car I need to modify."

Hope offered an optimistic smile. "Maybe."

16

─────────

Monday afternoon, Tyler felt the car was ready for prime time.

He found a place about forty-five minutes away which sold a device allowing him to tweak the ECU settings. It ended up being a good thing thanks to the different transmission. Tyler made a few adjustments to account for the new exhaust and to eke out a little more horsepower and torque. Without a dynamometer, he couldn't get precise figures, but the reinvented Aries now had the necessary shove to get things done.

The whole setup felt a little jury-rigged, but it didn't need to work long-term. As long as everything made it through the next few days intact, someone would find the burning hulk on the side of a road in parts unknown. Tyler felt a little bummed about some of his best mechanical handiwork going up in flames in under a week, but such was the assignment he'd agreed to undertake.

He kept an eye on the cameras installed throughout the facility. None of them emitted a telltale red light, but he presumed they all worked, and the group had the ability to watch. The equipment looked recent—much newer than the building itself. In case the surveillance gear also captured sound, Tyler stepped outside if he needed to use the phone or if he and Hope chatted about anything other than installing an engine. So long as Chains and crew spied on him at work, he couldn't bring in anyone like Ortiz who could help with all aspects of the mission.

With the car ready, Tyler took it for a test drive. Everything felt right when he sat in the passenger's seat, but there was nothing quite like getting a turn at the wheel. Like Hope did the previous evening, Tyler eased the Aries down the access road and then punched it when the tires hit county asphalt. They screeched, and the front end proved unruly under a heavy load of torque, but Tyler soon got it under control. If the police spun out in rear-drive cars, no harm done. If they drove all-wheel-drive SUVs, however, Hope would be in for a challenge.

The transmission lacked a manual mode, and the Dodge predated paddle shifters by several automotive generations. Still, the six-speed gearbox capably handled an engine it was never designed to work with. Upshifts were quick enough. Downshifts required some heavy throttle input. Not sporty by any stretch, but it should be good enough.

Tyler pushed the Dodge through some curves. The suspension held up well. He did a 180 around the same area Hope did and drove back to the garage. The gang would be coming to inspect everything soon. Connor, his biggest critic, needed to be happy with the results. If he weren't, the man was completely unreasonable. Tyler wondered how the meetup would go. He had no plans to stand around and let Connor make threats and draw a pistol again.

~

HOPE STOOD SILENTLY and watched as Connor walked around the Aries and rapped on the hood.

His knuckles made metallic *thunks*. "I dunno." He ran his hand down the metal. "Looks pretty much the same."

"Want to see what's underneath?" Tyler offered.

"Maybe."

"You know how to count cylinders?"

Connor glowered and crossed his arms while Hope turned to hide her smirk. "We don't need you to be a smartass."

"Maybe not," Tyler said, "but if I were a dumbass, this heap you found me wouldn't work. It's good to go. I can't dyno it, but it's a little over the original horsepower and torque numbers. This is a reliable supercharged engine. Felicity and I both drove it."

"What did you think, Felicity?" Chains asked before Connor could say anything.

"Like Tyler said, it's good to go. Rides well. Fast enough. It's front-wheel-drive, so there's some wheel hop, but we can't avoid that."

"Not even for a hotshot mechanic like you?" Connor said, getting close to Tyler.

"With another day and more cash, maybe," Tyler said. "I took it out, too, after Felicity did. An experienced driver will be able to handle it."

"I think it's great," Chains said. "The car still looks unassuming. No one's going to expect a thirty-year-old Dodge sedan to be the getaway vehicle. We might be able to avoid police pursuit entirely." He shrugged. "If not, I think we'll be able to outrun them."

"They might wipe out anyway if they have rear-wheel-drive," Pop offered.

Tyler grimaced, and Chains must have noticed because he asked, "You don't think so?"

"I'm not sure," Tyler said. "In theory, yes, a rear-drive car could fishtail if pushed aggressively." He inclined his head toward Hope. "I doubt most cops are expert wheelmen. The thing is modern cars have traction and stability control systems. They'll minimize the back end sliding out. It depends on how new or old the vehicles are."

Connor took a step forward and got in Tyler's face. Hope held her breath and started scanning the other guys for weapons in advance of a possible throwdown. "Anyone ever tell you you're a wet blanket?" Connor demanded.

"Anyone ever tell you you're under-prepared?"

"The hell do you mean?"

"You don't red team this stuff? Sure, you guys have a really good driver, but at the end of the day, you can't presume everyone who responds is a Keystone Kop. Some of them are going to be good behind the wheel. They might roll up in something all-wheel-drive. Lots of departments use SUVs now, especially in areas where there's bad weather in the winter. If you're not taking these things into account, you might as well walk out of here and turn yourself in now because you're going to get caught eventually."

"You learn all this shit in the Air Force?"

"Mostly. Sometimes, I needed to learn the hard way."

Connor snorted and took a small step back. He then exploded into action, throwing a hard punch into Tyler's gut. Hope winced as Tyler folded in half and ended up on one knee. "Here's another lesson the hard way, then. Don't mouth off to me. You're just a mechanic. We can replace you."

Chains stepped between them and urged Connor backward. Rock helped Tyler regain his feet. He seemed all right. Hope tried to catch his eye, but he wasn't looking at her. "Enough infighting," Chains said. "We plan for law enforcement, Tyler, and we don't presume them to be incompetent. We just think we're better in terms of prep and execution. So far, we've been right, but we're not resting on our laurels . . . are we, Connor?" Connor mumbled something, so Chains repeated his question with more volume. "Are we, Connor?"

"No," he said, and his expression suggested he'd chewed an entire lemon before answering.

"Good. Thanks for modifying the car, Tyler."

"It'd better work," Connor said, jabbing his finger in Tyler's direction. "If we get caught, you're dead."

"Worry about your own skin if you get caught," Tyler said.

Hope released the breath she'd been holding. This had become a more volatile situation than she expected. Maybe this would be the last operation.

17

TUESDAY MORNING, EVERYONE GATHERED AGAIN AT THE makeshift garage.

Hope saw someone she didn't recognize. A mousy man with thinning hair in a cheap suit shifted his weight from left to right as the four members of the gang surrounded him. Tyler stood off to the side watching while trying to appear uninterested. "Good, everyone's here," Chains said. He pointed to the stranger. "Daryl has some intel for us on our target."

"I . . . I work for a competitor," he said in a nasal tone. "We've tried to acquire the place you're going after, but they won't sell."

"You own the other place?" Tyler asked, and all eyes turned to him.

"No."

"What's your role?"

"Assistant manager."

"Let's say the other outfit agrees to sell to yours. What do you get out of this?"

Daryl shrugged. "Money."

"He's not giving us the intel out of the kindness of his heart," Chains said.

"Last year, your target started doing payday loans. We . . . think they're kind of shady, but they're lucrative. It means they need more money on hand than you might expect from a normal check cashing joint."

"And?" Connor prompted.

"And their shipment of cash comes tomorrow morning."

Chains spread his hands. "See? I knew this would work. Daryl's also told us about police response times, and we verified his numbers." Rock nodded, and Hope took that to mean he did the research. "You can go, Daryl. Don't want you to be late or anything."

"Thanks," Daryl said. He left the garage, and a minute later, a Honda Civic Hope couldn't see past the other cars when she arrived headed down the access road.

"You heard the man," Chains said. "Tomorrow morning, Commonwealth Check Cashing gets an infusion of money. They need more than before to support payday loans." He shrugged. "If you want to think of this as stopping someone's predatory business model, be my guest. This time, we're just after cash. They shouldn't have any goods in the store."

"Is there a guard?" Tyler wanted to know.

"You ask too many questions for a man who ain't coming along," Connor said.

"It's one you should ask, too."

"I did," Chains said. "There is a guard. Typical rent-a-cop type. Someone puts a gun on him, and he'll stand in the corner and cry. We won't have any problems with him."

"What about the alarm?" Hope said.

"They have one, of course. Daryl didn't know the inner workings, but he said employees can activate the one at his place without being obvious. It might not be someone pushing a big button. We should presume they'll use it."

Pop crossed his arms. "What about the cops?"

"I got this one," Rock said. "The dweeb gave us response times. The nearest station is six minutes away at pace. This time of day, you'll find cars all around, so some will be closer than the station. We should have three minutes before anyone rolls up. Four, tops. I checked the numbers. You can find a lot of shit by asking on the dark web."

"What about traffic?" Tyler put in.

"What about it?"

"You might have info on police response, but it doesn't tell you everything. Places like this are on main roads, right?" A few of the guys nodded. "It means you have more cross streets and thus more possible escape routes. It also means you can run into more traffic. Cops are generally predictable in situations like this. The soccer mom in a Forester pulling out of a McDonald's is an unknown."

"We know we can't control everything," Chains said. "When variables like those come up, we trust Felicity to do what she does."

Hope smiled. "I got you guys."

"You going to drive the route ahead of time?" Tyler asked. "Google Maps only tells you so much."

"We'll be all right," Chains said. Hope liked Tyler's idea. It was good to get a feel for the streets. The group used a GPS they took from car to car to help with their getaways, but there was nothing like knowing the asphalt. Even if the group didn't want to make a dry run, Hope figured she could go on her own. The more she was around Tyler, the more she liked the way he thought. Bringing him in had been a smart play.

Now, they needed to deal with the other four guys and the elusive mastermind.

~

TYLER FIXED himself a simple dinner and sat on the couch to eat it.

The apartment came with a decent TV and a cable package, so he browsed the channels for something to watch. It was late enough for the local news to be over. Tyler turned on the national news for a few minutes, found it depressing and annoying in equal measures, and kept searching. He eventually came across an episode of *Top Gear* he'd never seen and left it on.

He finished his chicken breast, salad, and rice, and one episode turned into another. Tyler thought about the events of the morning. He and Hope turned the Aries—a car no one would ever accuse of being fast—into something able to evade pursuit. The gang's lack of preparation bothered Tyler. They conducted operations more often and didn't put in the necessary time to plan properly. It was a recipe for eventual failure, and while the group getting arrested could only be a good thing, Tyler doubted any of the men would narc on their leader.

Tyler walked into the bedroom long enough to retrieve a sketch pad and colored pencil set. He didn't bring his easel, but he still wanted to get things out of his head. Following his PTSD diagnosis, it took three shrinks to find a program he felt actually helped him. Tyler remembered scoffing when he heard about it. He was no artist regardless of the tool or medium. Once he started focusing on results over skill, however, he found sitting down with his watercolors helped him work through and process more than expected. He'd kept the program up ever since.

The sketch pad didn't offer as many square inches, but he'd make do. Tyler used a black pencil to draw the outline of a large building which mostly filled the page. He added two cars and then a few human figures—six in total by the time he finished the last one. He then added a seventh, drawing a disembodied face inside a rectangle representing a laptop screen. Because the leader's identity remained the great unknown in the operation, Tyler added a question mark where his face should have been.

He'd finished adding colors and other elements to identify the other figures when a knock at the door snapped him out of the zone. He opened the coffee table drawer, removed a Sig Sauer 9MM, and stalked toward the entrance. "It's Felicity," came a voice from the other side as he drew closer. Tyler looked through the peephole, confirmed Hope was alone, and opened up. She walked in, and he locked the door behind them. "Expecting someone else?" she asked, inclining her head toward the gun.

"You never know how good your Uber Eats driver is going to be," Tyler said.

Hope grinned and headed into the apartment. It wasn't a particularly warm day, but she wore a red tank top and tight jeans. They hugged every curve of her body, and she looked absolutely terrific. Hope dropped onto the couch and pointed at the sketch pad as Tyler walked up. "What's this?" She picked it up and studied the drawing. "You're an artist?"

Tyler snorted. "Hardly. I'm better with my watercolors."

"Okay, anyone who says, 'I'm better with my watercolors' has to be at least a little bit of an artist."

"It's a therapeutic program."

"PTSD?" she asked.

Tyler nodded. "Yeah. Took me a while to actually go and get the diagnosis. I guess I knew what the shrink would tell me, and I didn't want to hear it."

"Look, if this is too much, you can—"

"I'm fine, Hope. It was ten years ago, and I'd just finished my fourth combat deployment and accused my colonel of being a war criminal. Which he was, the bastard. My marriage had disintegrated, and my ex-wife kept trying to turn our daughter against me. You might say I had a lot going on even on top of all the compounds I raided and people I shot for Uncle Sam."

"Sounds like it." She pointed to two figures standing apart from the other group. One sported long blonde hair. "I take it this is us?"

"Yeah."

She smiled, and when she set the sketch pad down, she leaned closer to Tyler in the process. He inhaled her scent—fresh shampoo and soap with some sort of sweet perfume. She glanced at him and their eyes locked. Her mouth opened slightly before she exhaled and sat back on the couch. "I . . . I drove to the site today," she said. "Chains might have Google Earth, but I trust seeing a place myself."

"Good," Tyler said. "What did you think?"

"I was there a few hours after we will be tomorrow, so the traffic is different. I think it's doable. I made sure to check out side streets, easy ways off the main drag, and all that. Some train tracks run nearby. I got a schedule. If we time it right, I can head there and try to lose the cops when a train rolls by."

"You'll really be putting our car to the test."

"I trust it," Hope said. "It had two solid mechanics. We work well together."

Tyler nodded, and the last few minutes got his brain thinking of other ways he and Hope might go well together. Pleasant as those thoughts may have been, he pushed them aside. The two of them had a job to carry out. The mission came first. "I presume you'll let me know how tomorrow went after it's over?"

"Yeah. Although, if you see something on the news about a crew getting busted for robbing a check cashing joint, you'll know it was us."

"I can't see it happening." Tyler waved a hand. "Pop might be a wild card, but the group works well together. Plus, you'll be able to out-drive the police."

"Let's hope so." Her eyes briefly locked with Tyler's again before she stood and cleared her throat. "Anyway . . . I just wanted to say thanks. You've been really good on the job so far. I think we'll be able to wrap things up before long." She smiled and headed for the door. "See you later, Tyler."

"Be careful tomorrow," he said. Tyler watched with some interest as Hope walked away and down the stairs. When she left, Tyler checked the area and locked up again behind her. He wondered how many more times he would question exactly what he got himself into when he agreed to help Hope Raines.

18

Chains clenched and unclenched his fists in the passenger's seat.

Felicity drove the crew into Virginia. She seemed a little less chatty than usual, but no one spoke much on the drive south. Getting to Front Royal would take a little over an hour. The group originally sought targets deeper into Virginia, but Felicity pointed out how few roads they could take to get away once outside of city limits. Their routes would be predictable—and manned by police. Front Royal was big enough to feature businesses like a check-cashing joint, small enough to be undermanned against professionals, and located near a bunch of roadways big and small.

They took I-81 most of the way down, but Chains knew their route back would be different. Felicity plotted a bunch of options. The Aries came out way too early to have a GPS, but their driver brought a separate unit with her. As they drove farther into Virginia, Felicity guided the car from I-81 South onto I-66 East. "Not far now, boys," Chains said. He half-turned in the seat. Pop, Connor, and Rock crammed into the back. They sat shoulder to shoulder, and none looked happy about the arrangements. This car was smaller than the one they'd used last time. Being the man in charge of this crew meant Chains got to ride up front.

It also got him closer to Felicity, though she'd never expressed a whit of interest in any of the guys. Chains wondered about her relationship to their new mechanic. The two clearly knew each other, but how well? Security footage from the weekend showed her helping him work on the Aries but the nature of their interactions stopped there. "Five minutes," she said.

"Pop, you're going to be the lookout today," Chains said.

"What the hell?" the older man protested.

"Stop shooting people, and maybe you'll earn a spot back inside. For now, I want you helping Felicity keep an eye on the response. Take the police radio with you." Pop grunted and picked up the handheld device. "Between the two of you, we should know when the pigs are getting close. The rest of you will be with me. We want to get as much cash as possible. Expect a silent alarm to go off, but if you see someone making an obvious move to activate one, stop them. As far as we know, there's one guard, and he should be easy to control. Let's get in and out with no goddamn casualties this time."

"You got it," Rock said, and Connor nodded his assent.

A few minutes later, they cruised down North Royal Avenue. Houses lined the road at first, but the farther they got into town, the more the structures shifted to business. A yoga studio stood on the right, and Chains watched with interest as a few young women walked in. He saw their quarry a couple blocks later. Felicity took a couple side streets to go around the block and leave the Aries pointing in the right direction for a getaway. She curbed the car about fifty feet past the check cashing place. "Hurry up, boys."

Chains and the rest of the crew slipped their masks into place and climbed out. They didn't encounter anyone on the way in. Pop remained on the sidewalk while the other three walked in. Chains carried his favorite weapon—a Remington pump action shotgun he'd never needed to use—while the other two came in with pistols. "You assholes know what time it is," he said to the employees. Rock stood in front of the security guard while Connor trained his weapon on the three workers behind the counter. The lone customer—an old, skinny black man—cowered and backed toward the wall. "Fill the bags." He tossed three sacks across the counter.

Commonwealth Check Cashing was a rectangular building more wide than deep. A long counter separated the customers from staff, and the bulletproof glass opened enough at each station to allow transactions to happen. A single door to the back area of the place remained closed. The group would be visible to anyone walking past the long front window, but some things couldn't be helped. "Cops will come," one of the employees said. He looked to be a guy in his thirties, and he wore a Polo shirt over pressed chinos.

"Thanks for explaining how law enforcement works," Chains said. "Now shut up and fill the bag."

"We don't need to . . . ugh!" Chains ended the guy's protest by ramming the butt of the shotgun into his mouth. The guy fell back and covered his face, blood leaking from between his fingers.

"Anybody else want to have a conversation?" Chains barked. The other employee grabbed a bag and stuffed cash in it. "Hurry up."

"Keep your hands where I can see them," Rock ordered the guard. Both women behind the counter worked on adding money to the bags. Chains took a quick glance at his watch. They'd been inside for two and a half minutes. He didn't want to spend any longer than two additional minutes inside. Felicity hadn't hit the horn yet, so they should be all right.

"Keep going," Chains told the workers as they finished one bag. The man he'd whacked in the face stayed down and quiet. Whatever fight he thought he had in him spilled out with his blood. Maybe his dental bill would be a reminder how dumb it was to try and argue with someone holding a weapon.

"Stop reaching," Rock said, and he reversed his grip on the gun, battering the guard with the end of it. When the man fell to a crouch and tried to cover his head, Rock beat him a few more times until he lay prostrate.

One of the women filling the bags began crying. "Shut up," Chains said. "It'll go faster if you stop crying. You want us gone? Work quicker." The security guard was breathing, though he lay unmoving on the floor. At least the group didn't add another casualty to their count this time. The intel they'd gotten had been solid. Commonwealth Check Cashing was awash in money, and they kept enough at the counter to indicate they expected a raft of business today.

After this, the owner would need to tamp down his expectations.

"What do you have?" Connor said to the lone customer.

"T . . . take it," the man said, holding out an envelope. "It ain't much."

Connor rifled through it and fired it back at him. The envelope bounced off his face and landed on the carpeted floor. "Keep your pittance." A second full bag joined the first, and the crying woman worked on the third. Felicity sounded the Aries's horn. Chains looked at his watch. He wanted another fifteen to thirty seconds, but they'd have a good haul here already. Rock and Connor each grabbed a full bag, and a quick order from Chains compelled the woman to hand over the final one. She'd stuffed it maybe sixty percent of the way.

The trio rolled out, Chains hopping into the front seat, and the other two filing in the back. Felicity hit the gas, and the front tires spun but grabbed asphalt quickly, and they were on their way before the doors even slammed shut.

19

———

THE RED AND BLUE LIGHTS APPEARED AS SMALL PINPRICKS IN the rearview mirror.

Hope knew they would remain there—in addition to growing in number and getting closer—unless she could do her job as the getaway driver. She blew through a red light, narrowly avoiding someone in an SUV, and kept going up North Royal Avenue. Past downtown, it split, continuing north to an eventual dead end. Around a ninety-degree turn, West 14th Street would connect to Route 522.

Hope glanced at the primitive digital clock mounted into the Aries' basic and plastic-riddled dashboard. She'd taken care to set it to the correct time. A train would roll through in three minutes, and at her current pace, she would be a little more ahead of it than she wanted.

"Why are you easing off the throttle?" Pop asked from the backseat.

"Part of the plan," she told him. The lights grew a little closer, and two more pairs joined them.

The chase was on in earnest now.

"We'd better not get caught," Connor said.

"Got way too much cash here," Rock said, his hand going

into one of the bags and coming out gripping a wad of large bills.

"Put that shit away," Chains ordered. Rock moved all three sacks to the rear footwell, infringing on everyone's space. "We don't need to advertise what we did."

Instead of taking the left onto 14th, Hope stayed straight an extra block before swinging a hard turn onto 15th. Past a Motel 6, it joined Route 522 North. One of the police cars followed her on the brief detour. The other two held steady. The Aries handled the sudden changes of direction well despite the inherent limitations of its setup. She and Tyler dropped the ride height a third of an inch, redid some of the suspension components, and added structural bracing where they could. It was definitely a less comfortable cruiser, but it took curves and turns at speed much better now.

The automatic transmission remained a limiting factor. It was fine but probably not a great match for the supercharged V6 under the hood. A more modern dual-clutch model—or even a better torque converter version like a ZF—would have been up to the task. The one Tyler found got the job done, but it didn't downshift with urgency.

"You know they're closer, right?" Chains warned.

"Yep," Hope replied.

"Did you really want them to be?"

"Yep."

"I hope this is part of your plan."

"Yep."

She could hear the rumble of the train now as they crossed the south fork of the Shenandoah River. The tracks lay this side of a campground and another major intersection. As if on cue, flashing lights let cars know the road would be closed while the train zipped by.

"Jesus Christ," Connor said. "We're going to try and race a train?"

"We're going to race a train and *win*," Hope said. She

watched its approach and did another check of the mirror. The closest among the trio of police vehicles remained about three car lengths back. Perfect. The locomotive whistled and honked as the crossbar began dropping. Hope fed the Aeries more gas. It didn't downshift, but this ended up all right. The supercharger whined as the RPMs climbed.

The Dodge made it in the nick of time. The onrushing train screamed from the left. The car bumped across the track, and a rush of air gave it a little nudge forward as they cleared two seconds ahead of certain death. The police had no way around the sudden obstruction. They would need to wait for over a hundred cars to go down the tracks.

By then, the group would be gone.

"I THINK I need to change my shorts," Pop said once they were all back inside the makeshift garage.

Hope smiled. She'd taken a direct route to get ahead of the police while they waited for the train, and then a circuitous one back into Maryland. After a few turns, they stayed on Route 11, which ran beside I-81 North. Far fewer cars drove the state road, and they never saw a cop or heard about one being nearby on the scanner. Her left leg bobbed for a while, making her glad they didn't choose a car with a manual. Once the adrenaline rush wore off, Hope felt normal again. As much as she wanted to take these guys down, she'd have to admit enjoying these spirited drives. Route 11 conveniently continued into Maryland and got them back to the Hagerstown area. "I ain't washing them for you, old man," she said.

Rock and Connor counted the cash. Hope saw a few hundreds in the pile, but there were bills of every denomination. At two full bags and maybe two-thirds of another, they would have a nice haul. "I think this was the riskiest escape yet," Chains said. He popped the top on a bottle of beer and held a second longneck toward Hope. She shook her head. "You knew when the train was coming?"

"Yeah," she said. "I looked it up. Also checked out its previous stops this morning. It was running on time."

"What if it had been late?"

"I would have improvised."

"If it came through early," Connor said, "we might've been screwed."

"I had a contingency plan for that," Hope said. She could have gone off the road to the left across a large field. The challenge would be finding a way to rejoin a major road. Trees prevented easy access to the closest one. She probably would have been forced to drive across the grass, pick up Dodson Lane, and take it back to either Route 522 or 637. She'd been a little surprised none of the police made the attempt. Among the three responding vehicles, the Explorer might have pulled it off.

Chains started a call, and their absent leader's electronically distorted voice came through a second later. "Excellent work, everyone. This sounds like a great haul."

"It was," Chains said. "No issues. No casualties. It was an adventurous getaway, but Felicity is a hell of a driver."

"I know she is." Hope wondered about this. She'd never met Chains' boss, so any experience the man had with her driving came from word of mouth.

"We're still counting the money," Chains said. "I'll deposit your share shortly."

"Excellent," the main man said. "Enjoy a little free time, everyone. Let's reconvene next week."

Again in a week. The jobs continued to be closer together than they were a couple months before. The increased frequency led to higher chances of getting caught. Less time to prepare meant Hope needed to go off-book and scout a location and its roads by herself. In the past, the whole crew would make the drive, check out the area, and decide on the right routes together.

The call ended, and the guys got back to counting. About twenty minutes later—and with the help of a couple machines bank tellers used—they arrived at a total: just shy of sixty grand. "The jewelry store will end up making us more," Chains said, "but it'll take longer because of the fence's work and his cut. Here, we have money we can use today."

"Don't spend it all on Viagra, Pop!" Connor said, and he and Rock dissolved into laughter.

"Screw you guys," Pop grumbled. "I've never needed it with either of your moms." They all laughed now. Hope rolled her eyes. No matter how old they got, almost all men were simply overgrown boys.

Chains set a portion aside and fired up his laptop again. He'd be reserving a sum to send the leader his cut, transferring money to the man's account and then depositing cash to cover the outlay. She worked her way closer while feigning interest in their haul. No one really paid attention as she surveilled the screen. She couldn't see any of the credentials Chains entered when logging in, but she did spy the account number he chose as the destination: 9145883209 at Eastern Regional Bank.

Once he finished moving money around, Chains counted out two stacks and gave them to Hope. "One's for you, Felicity," he explained. "Excellent driving today, and I think going to scout ahead helped. You were really prepared."

"Thanks," she said, smiling to cover the absurdity of getting an impromptu performance review from a criminal.

"The second stack is for Tyler. I was skeptical of the car, but he really made it work. He's your friend. You brought him in, so you take him his cut."

"I will."

"Make sure he'll be ready to go when we need to work on another vehicle."

"I will," Hope said again.

20

———

A KNOCK AT THE DOOR PULLED TYLER'S HEAD OUT OF THE fridge.

He'd been assessing his dinner options. Today had been uneventful. He'd passed the time with a couple exercise sessions to keep sharp—and then a shower because keeping the edge keen worked up a sweat. Between the drive to and from Hagerstown and his cover identity, Tyler wished he could spend some time at the shop. Smitty and Ortiz probably needed a hand.

As with the previous night, Tyler carried his pistol to the door, and as with the previous night, Hope stood on the other side. He let her in. She carried a paper bag and smiled. "I have your cut," she said in a singsong voice.

"How did it go?" he asked, checking the outside and locking the door.

"The car was great. No issues. We got away clean. I managed to spot an account number Chains used to transfer money to the big man, so we'll see what comes of that."

"Great." He moved to the sliding door and pulled back the curtain enough to peek out.

"What are you doing?"

"Sounds like today was a success," Tyler said. "People tend to celebrate those . . . maybe let their guard down a little. It would be smart for the gang to follow you."

"I wasn't followed, Tyler," Hope said. "I've been good at driving and spotting tails long before I became a fed."

"Good. Speaking of fed, I haven't eaten yet. I was looking over my options when you knocked."

"Let's get some delivery." She smiled again, and the wattage brightened the room. Tyler imagined Hope could convince him of a great many things simply by flashing her killer smile at the end. "I know a couple places. You won't need the gun for the Uber Eats drivers around here."

Tyler chuckled. "You never know."

Hope took out her phone. After a moment, she asked, "You trust me?"

"Sure."

"All right. I'll get us something." A minute and a bunch of screen tapping later, she put her cell away. "You got any beer in the fridge?"

"There was some in there already." Tyler dropped onto the couch. For being a pretty basic sofa, it felt plusher and more comfortable than some more expensive models he'd sat on over the years. Hope carried a couple bottles into the living room, handed one to Tyler, and sat beside him to kick off her sneakers. He noticed the closeness between them but didn't say anything.

Hope clinked her bottle to his and said, "To a successful operation."

"Cheers." Tyler took a long pull of the amber liquid and asked, "How much is in the bag?"

"Enough."

"Do I get to keep it?"

"I don't know, actually. I've never used someone else on a job before. I guess you'd count as a consultant or informant."

"I guess it won't hurt if I hang onto it until you get an answer."

"Could take a while." Hope shrugged. "These things move at government speed."

"I kinda hope our dinner doesn't."

Hope pulled her phone out long enough to check something. "Forty minutes. You gonna make it?"

"Probably. Tell me about the getaway. I want to hear how the car did considering we turned a beater into something much more."

"It was *so* great," she said, turning a little toward Tyler and tucking her feet under her. "A little wheel hop, but we knew there would be. I managed to start driving before the cops got really close. My goal was to use a train as cover. I'd checked out the schedule and confirmed they were running on time this morning. As long as I let the police get close enough, they'd have to wait at the junction while we kept going." Her left hand clenched and unclenched as she recounted the story. "I even had to back off the throttle a little to let them get within a few lengths. Then, I slammed the gas and zoomed across the tracks a second or two ahead of the train. It was *amazing*." Her left knee bobbed, and her hand rested on Tyler's shoulder.

He glanced at it and then looked at Hope. Her eyes bore into his. "Glad it all worked—" Tyler got cut off by Hope leaning down and kissing him hard. She still smelled of soap, shampoo, and flowers, and the scents were on her skin, in her hair, and then all around him. Hope pulled Tyler's shirt over his head and then did the same with her own. When he saw the black lace bra, Tyler wrapped his arms around Hope and stood. She put her legs around him as he walked down the hall, and they tumbled onto the bed a moment later.

After a while, Tyler lay on his back with Hope beside him. Her head rested on his chest, and a few of her dyed blonde locks landed on his face. "I feel like I heard a knock at the door a few minutes ago," Tyler said. He felt even hungrier now.

"Me, too," she said, and she turned her head to face him. "I'm very glad you didn't try to get up and answer the door."

"I don't think you would have let me."

"Definitely not." She swung her left leg over Tyler and climbed atop him. "The food's been sitting out there a while."

"At least twenty minutes," Tyler said.

"We're going to need to heat it up anyway."

"Can't eat a cold dinner."

"Some more time won't hurt, then," Hope said, and before Tyler could agree, she kissed him again.

Hope woke up early and slipped quietly out of the bed.

Tyler remained asleep. She got her clothes back on, smiled at his lightly snoring form, and left the room. Sitting on the couch, she put her shoes back on. Going to bed with Tyler had never been part of her plan until it happened. Recounting the escape got her adrenaline flowing again, and then he was right there, and they'd worked together on the car, and it just sort of happened.

And it might happen again, she thought, and the brief musing made her smile. So what if it did? She and Tyler were adults, and whatever arrangement they worked under while he helped her didn't preclude anything else. She opened the door, made sure the bottom lock was still engaged, and closed up as quietly as she could. Once outside, Hope scanned for people and vehicles which didn't belong. She found none, climbed into her FBI-issued Charger, and drove away.

As she approached her own place, she got a text. It came on her Bureau phone which she kept in a hidden compartment carved out of the console. Hope looked at the message. *Need an update. Let's meet for breakfast. -PZ*

"Shit," she muttered. With a deadline over her head, the Baltimore office wanted to exert more control of the operation even though Hope technically didn't report to them. She fired back a suggested place and time, got an affirmative response, and went into her apartment to shower and put on clean clothes. Twenty minutes later, she emerged wearing jeans and flannel over one of her favorite automotive T-shirts.

Hope pulled into the Central Maryland Diner after a ten-minute drive. She chose it because its slow service and lack of a drive-through meant the place rarely drew a crowd early in the morning. Commuters couldn't afford the inevitable delays no matter how good the food. When she walked in, a bell above the door chimed, and the man she expected to meet looked up and offered a small wave.

Special Agent Patrick Zellhoefer was average in just about every way—height, weight, appearance, and—in Hope's opinion—quality of work. His blond hair would need a cut soon, though the mustache looked more under control. He gave a tight smile when Hope dropped onto the booth opposite him. Of the twenty or so tables scattered throughout the interior, only two others saw customers sitting at them. "Morning."

"Hi."

"You weren't followed?" he asked.

Hope scoffed. "And here I thought we might have a nice friendly breakfast, Patrick."

He put his hands up as a waitress approached. She was middle-aged with curly red hair, and her heavy-lidded expression suggested she needed a couple more hours of sleep. Hope sympathized and stifled a yawn. She didn't expect such an *active* night with John Tyler. "A pair of coffees," Patrick said when the server asked what they wanted.

"I'll have scrambled eggs, sausage, and wheat toast," Hope said.

"Make it two."

The waitress nodded and walked away. "Why am I meeting you?" Hope wanted to know.

"Agent Hess is taking a bigger interest in this operation."

"Not enough of one to come himself, though."

"Think of me as your handler."

Hope rolled her eyes. "Let's get this straight. I'm not a spy. You're my colleague. You don't work for me, and I don't work for you. If Jason wants to take the reins, he can damn well show up himself to do it."

The waitress returned with a mug of hot coffee for each of them. Hope added two tiny containers of cream, stirred her hot drink, and sipped it. Adequate. Patrick used three sugars and creamers each before finding the drink to his liking. "I'm not trying to be your boss," he said. "Hess wants to be in the loop, and he asked me to meet with you. I live closer than he does."

"So you're my geographically convenient liaison?"

"Pretty much."

"Great."

"You got anything for me?" When Hope sipped her java rather than answer, Patrick added, "Progress can add to your clock, Hope."

"You know about the job yesterday?" she asked after a moment.

"Yeah."

"I saw one of the guys use an account number to advance the leader his cut of the haul."

"You remember it?" Patrick said.

"Of course." He opened a note-taking app on his phone, and she recited the number and bank information, adding, "They might have it go to a dummy corporation in Shangri-La for all I know. Hopefully, someone at the Bureau can make sense of it."

"We'll do our best." Patrick put his phone away. "Thanks."

Hope grunted, and the server returned with their identical breakfasts. After eyeing both plates, Hope determined hers held a little more egg. "I hope it's enough to add some time to the clock," she said. "We can't hit double zeroes now." Especially not on her career, which Hope understood was tied to the outcome of her long assignment. She figured Patrick knew it, too.

"I think you'll be all right," he said.

"I'd better be."

21

———

Late Thursday morning, Tyler headed to the industrial site.

When he woke up a bit after eight, Hope was gone. He'd showered and eaten a leisurely breakfast before figuring out what he wanted to do today. Just because he might not get another vehicle for a week or two didn't mean he should sit on his hands and not investigate. When he arrived, the Aries was already gone. One of the crew must have taken it somewhere and set it on fire already. It was almost a shame—Tyler and Hope did some damned good work on the car.

Armed with a small notepad and pen, Tyler took down the address. He called Lexi, who answered quickly. "Everything okay, Dad?"

"Sure. I'm just doing a little nosing around." He remained outside to avoid the cameras and potential microphones throughout the interior. "If I send you some stuff, can you try and run down whoever's registered as the owner, lessee, or whatever?"

"I'll try."

"You have my laptop handy?" When Tyler left his job at Patriot Security almost three years ago, he took and kept the computer they'd issued him. Lexi understood its interesting capabilities far better than he ever could.

"I do," she said.

"Good. Let's start with this address." He rattled it off, and she asked him to hang on while she booted up the machine and got logged in. He repeated it once she was ready.

"Hmm," she said. "Some LLC with a weird name. Registered out of state."

"I had a feeling there would be a sophisticated knot to untangle here," Tyler said. "Whatever else these pricks might be, they're careful. They don't make obvious mistakes."

"You want me to try and run down who's really behind this LLC?"

"I guess, but I don't know what you'll find. Don't spend too much time on it. I'm going to record some serial numbers inside. The lift, major tools . . . those kinds of things. It'd be nice to see if they're registered to anyone we can run down."

"Look at you trying to be an investigator," she said. "You'll be in FBI boot camp before long."

Tyler snorted. "My boot camp days are ancient history."

"I don't know. A pretty agent might change your mind."

"She won't."

Lexi chuckled. "Whatever you say, Dad. Send me what you get, and I'll see if I can run anything down."

"Thanks, kiddo." Tyler ended the call and walked inside. Common tools would be impossible to trace or establish ownership, but major things like the mechanical lift as well as some other parts scattered about would carry serial numbers. As before, Tyler didn't expect much to come from this, but he wanted to try. Hope couldn't do this without looking nosy. She was the driver. As the mechanic, Tyler could provide an easy excuse. Someone in the group would likely be watching him, after all.

He moved around the area in a logical progression, starting with the lift and working his way around counterclockwise from there. By the time he finished, he'd recorded eight serial numbers. Tyler walked outside, texted all of them to Lexi, and ventured out for a quick lunch nearby. He wanted to return and wait. If one of the crew watched, thoroughness would demand he come in person and see what the hell the new guy was doing.

His seasickness meant Tyler had never enjoyed fishing, but he understood the concept of baiting a hook.

A LITTLE WHILE after Tyler finished lunch, he heard a vehicle approaching.

When you went fishing, sometimes you reeled something in. Rock stepped out of a Camaro and headed inside. "What are you doing here?" he demanded.

"Checking the place out," Tyler said.

"Why?" His eyes narrowed. "What are you up to?"

"I plan to strip this place for parts and sell them to feed my meth habit."

Rock recoiled. "Seriously?"

"Of course not. I wanted to take a closer look at your setup here. It's really nice. Giving me some ideas in case I ever get to open my own shop."

Rock walked the perimeter, checking in some toolboxes. He nodded when he finished, apparently satisfied Tyler hadn't taken anything. "Seemed kind of funny is all."

Tyler shrugged. "I have a key. Didn't think I needed to check in with anyone before I came here."

"Might be nice if you do," Rock said. "This ain't only a place for you to work."

"Understood."

"You get your cut from Felicity?"

"She dropped it off."

"She tell you about the next job?"

"No." Tyler wondered if Hope knew the group's plans. Maybe they came up with something while she wasn't around. If they were freezing her out, what did it mean for the investigation?

"We don't know for sure when it'll be yet," Rock said. "I'd figure next week sometime. You're gonna need to be ready when we need you."

"I will be."

"How's your job situation?"

"Flexible," Tyler said.

"And your morality?"

"At least as flexible."

"Good. Remember . . . you're on a job-to-job basis with us. The last mechanic didn't work out and we needed to move on. The situation didn't end well for him. I don't think you want to see a repeat."

"Definitely not."

"All right." Rock looked around the large interior. "Turn the lights off when you leave."

"Roger."

He walked out and fired up his Camaro. An idea came to Tyler. Hope possessed incomplete knowledge on the gang members and almost none on their elusive leader. If he followed Rock, Tyler might be able to learn more about him. From there, the dominoes could fall in any number of ways. He dashed off a quick text to her as Rock headed down the long access road. *Following Rock from the garage. Will report when I can.*

Tyler made sure to turn off the lights and secure the doors. Rock headed to the left at the junction with the street. Tyler climbed into the Crown Vic and hustled it down the lengthy path. Hope replied. *Be careful. They don't trust you fully yet.* Tyler realized they never would. There wasn't enough time. He and Hope were going to dismantle the group. In the meantime, he knew how to tail someone without being obvious, though being the lone operator on county roads made the process more complicated than an urban gig with multiple available vehicles.

Still, he would manage, and they might even learn something to accelerate Hope's timeline.

22

Despite the inherent limitations of following someone in the current circumstances, Tyler managed to pull it off.

He realized another potential handicap worked against him: he drove a Crown Vic, a car used by police and other law enforcement agencies for years. Any shady character with decent countersurveillance skills would have spotted the car in his rearview and felt a tingle in the back of his neck. Rock offered no indication he knew Tyler tailed him. When he could, Tyler did things like get over a lane, but he spent time on narrow county roads hoping for the best.

After about fifteen minutes, Rock turned right onto a network of side streets. Tyler accelerated, took the next one, and doubled back. None of the houses had garages. The silver Camaro would be obvious. Sure enough, Rock pulled into a driveway a bit past the cross street Tyler had taken. After waiting for the man to go into his Cape Cod style house, Tyler made a left, turned around, and parked where he could keep Rock's place in easy view.

He sat low in the seat and waited. Tyler realized his lone means of taking photos was his burner phone. They'd need to be good enough for Hope and her FBI contacts. Nothing happened for a while. Twenty minutes turned into forty and then an hour. After about ninety minutes total, another vehicle arrived. Tyler didn't recognize the GMC Yukon. He wondered if it was a government SUV until two goonish types got out. They were both big and brawny with short hair and beady eyes.

When they weren't looking at him, Tyler snapped a couple pictures. The two large guys walked up to Rock's door. He opened for them and smiled—an event Tyler hoped the phone's camera captured well. While he certainly wasn't much of a photographer, his own mobile boasted of a sharper camera with clearer zoom. Maybe Hope's coworkers could digitally enhance the output. Tyler considered Photoshop to be one small step below sorcery.

While his vantage point offered him a good look at Rock's front door, Tyler couldn't see into the house. He didn't have direct line of sight through a window, and even if he did, Rock and his two brutish guests could be behind a wall somewhere. Tyler checked his mirrors, climbed out of the Crown Vic, and got closer. Blinds obstructed all but one window, and Tyler only saw an empty room through it. He got back into the Ford, started it, and drove to another street in the neighborhood. When he'd curbed the car again, he texted the photos to Hope.

Rock has some friends who could have just stepped off the football field. You seen these guys before?

I'm busy right now. Can you come by later? Maybe we can look into them then.

Hope added an address in the next text. Tyler checked it out, and it resolved to an apartment complex which looked quite a bit nicer than his. She was the agent, after all, so if they both stayed in FBI-funded accommodations, she should get the better end of it. Tyler sent a reply telling Hope he'd come by in a couple hours. He circled back to Rock's house, saw nothing had changed, and drove away.

TYLER PARKED in one of the designated guest spots at Hope's building.

The exterior was cleaner and more modern than his. Metal joined the brick for a more pleasing facade. A larger grass field—this one including a small playground—surrounded the two closest buildings. Tyler walked up the four steps to the large green front door. His initial impression of the large metal door was it could stop a couple bullets if necessary. Tyler pressed the button for Hope's unit, and she buzzed him in a moment later. He headed up one flight of stairs and knocked.

Hope looked terrific when she opened the door. She wore a T-shirt over a pair of gym shorts, and she smiled when she saw Tyler. "Come in." He followed, and she locked up behind them. "I got your pictures." She headed into the kitchen, and Tyler watched her brief jaunt with appreciation and interest. "Want anything?"

"Yes."

She chuckled, and her grin told Tyler she knew he checked her out. "I meant to drink."

"Oh. Water's fine for now." Inside, the layout of Hope's apartment was similar to Tyler's, though being on the opposite side of the building meant everything was basically flipped. Whoever furnished this unit shopped at a nicer store than the person tasked with outfitting Tyler's place. Hope had a leather couch and recliner, a bigger TV, and dark brown vinyl flooring. As with Tyler's, nothing hung from the walls. He always felt the lack of personalization made safehouses obvious to anyone who bothered looking for details.

Hope returned with two bottles of water, and the two of them sat on the couch. Despite the typical squeaks when plopping onto leather furniture, it felt softer and much nicer than Tyler's temporary sofa. "Someone must have shopped for this place with a gold card," he said.

"It's a safehouse . . . or safe apartment, I guess." She shrugged. "I know the Bureau rents yours, but it's not the same. The bean counters could explain it."

"I try to avoid talking to them whenever I can."

"Me, too." She took out her phone. "I got your pictures. I've never seen those two guys before."

"You don't sound surprised about Rock hanging out with a couple guys who just graduated from legbreaker school."

"I've heard the guys talking about people they know. The kind who could help do particular jobs if we needed it."

"Does the FBI know these two?"

Hope shook her head. "No. I uploaded the pics to my laptop and checked. Whoever they are, they're not in the system."

"You log on from here?" Tyler asked.

"I can. I use a VPN. Most of the time, I try to go to a field site nearby. No one would peg it as an FBI place. It's just easier. I don't need someone coming by and seeing my work laptop connected to a federal network."

"Do the guys try to drop in on you?"

"No," Hope said. "I make sure they don't follow me. I try not to go to places where I might run into them. If one of them got enterprising and started looking for assets in the name of Felicity Snow, they won't find much."

"Including this apartment," Tyler pointed out.

"I was subletting, and my roommate is out of the country for a long time." Tyler frowned. "Come on. All I have to do is bat my eyelashes at those Neanderthals, and they'd probably believe anything with a whiff of plausibility.'

"Do you know much about them?"

"It's taken a while," Hope said, "but yeah. I know who the main four are. Chains' real name is Charlie, Lou Rocchio is

Rock, Pete Warner is Pop, and Aidan McCloud goes by Connor."

"There can be only one," Tyler said. Hope's brows knitted. "*Highlander*. Connor MacLeod was the main character in the movie. He was trying to eliminate the other immortals and be the last one standing. Maybe I'm lucky he doesn't carry a sword."

"If you say so."

"I guess it was before your time."

"But not yours," Hope said, giving Tyler a gentle elbow in the side. "Anyway, we still don't know who gives these jerks their orders. I caught Chains transferring money and managed to see the account number, but it was a dead end."

"Overseas?"

"Shell corporations, though it wouldn't surprise me if the funds diverted to the Cayman Islands somewhere along the way."

Anyone who used a foreign account did so because those governments didn't knuckle under when the US government came in demanding answers and info. "I guess we're still on the case, then." Hope bobbed her head. "Your timeline improve?"

"Don't know yet."

"I guess we'd better try and crack it quickly, then."

"Yeah," she said, "we'd better."

23

AIDAN MCCLOUD STILL DIDN'T TRUST THE NEW MECHANIC.

He'd done good work on the Aries. For something the group picked up as an old beater, Tyler took it and made it into a vehicle Felicity could use to outrun the cops. She helped, and this made him wonder about their relationship. What else were they doing together when they weren't working for the gang? Aidan scowled at the idea. He thought he'd made progress with Felicity. She was standoffish toward him at first but warmed up over the last couple months. Given some more time, he knew he could get her into bed.

The new guy complicated things.

It was another reason not to trust this Tyler. Something seemed a little off about him. Aidan felt he'd run into the man before but could never make the connection. It always gnawed at him whenever he and Tyler shared a space. The group took care of their last mechanic when he'd proven to be untrustworthy. They could do the same to Tyler. The modern spin on drawing and quartering had been Aidan's idea, and he smiled at the idea of Tyler chained to four cars waiting to rip him apart.

Aidan spent a long day at his job and pulled up to the industrial site in the evening. He unlocked the place and went inside. Everything looked like it did the last time he was here. Aidan unlocked the office—Tyler didn't have a key to this little room—and sat at the small desk. A desktop PC and monitor rested atop it, and the group used the computer to access the facility's security system.

Aidan logged in, opened the app, and found the folder for the current day. At midnight, the program would send footage to the cloud for storage. He started playback, and views from each of the nine cameras filled the screen. Nothing happened for a while until Tyler appeared.

Why did he come today? They didn't have a confirmed new job yet let alone a vehicle for him to work on. Adian leaned closer and watched the new guy. He walked around the interior and seemed to be writing things down after he looked at some of the major parts and tools. What the hell was he doing?

Aidan called Rock. "Yeah, I know he was there," the other man said. "I checked it out."

"You checked it out?"

"Yeah. I think he was straight with me."

"What did Tyler tell you?"

"He wanted to know the kinds of parts to get in case he wanted to open his own place someday."

"You didn't think it was suspicious?" Aidan asked.

"Seemed plausible," Rock said. "We got a nice setup here. I could see a mechanic wanting to duplicate it."

"He could have been recording serial numbers and trying to trace ownership."

Rock scoffed. "I doubt it. The guy's legit, Connor. Why are you so leery of him? You think he's got an in with Felicity?"

"No," Aidan said even though Rock was correct. "You're probably right. Forget about it." He ended the call.

His suspicions remained, however, and not solely because

of his interest in Felicity. Chains needed to know what went on today.

~

"I'm telling you . . . this guy seems shady."

Chains' sigh hissed in Aidan's ear. "I hear you. I do. I'm just not seeing it."

"Look, he—"

"Did he do a good job on the Aries?" Chains broke in.

"Yeah," Aidan admitted.

"He turned a car which had never been fast into something we used to make a damn good getaway."

"Maybe he's just building our trust for when he betrays us."

"Like I told you . . . not seeing it."

"You know he was snooping around the garage?" Aidan demanded.

After a couple seconds of silence, Chains asked, "What do you mean 'snooping around'?"

"He didn't need to come in. There's nothing for him to work on. But here he was . . . walking around and writing things down."

"You have the footage?"

"Sure."

"Send it to me," Chains said.

"Hang on." Aidan used the app to generate a sharable link and emailed it to Chains. "You should have it now. Rock said he knew about it and confronted Tyler."

"What did Tyler say?"

"He was getting ideas for what he might want when he opened his own shop."

"I'll watch what you sent and call you back." Chains hung up. Aidan set his phone down and waited. He didn't know how the other man would react. Chains ran things day to day even though he still took orders from the leader. Aidan had never met the big boss, but he knew Chains spoke for him.

Most of the time, at least. Aidan wondered if today would change anything.

A few minutes later, Chains called back. "What do you think?" Aidan said.

"I don't think we can call him shady based on this."

"Anything seem off about this new guy to you?"

"Like what?" Chains wanted to know.

"I can't say for sure. Something just . . . don't seem right. I also got the feeling I've seen this guy someplace, but I have no idea where."

"He's Felicity's friend."

"Yeah. And?"

"And you've been trying to get into her pants since she joined us."

Aidan snorted. "Tell me you wouldn't sleep with her."

"Of course I would. I'm just not following her around with my tongue hanging out. You're probably thinking Tyler has some sort of existing relationship with Felicity, you don't know what it is, and it's bothering you."

"So what if it is?" Aidan said.

"Think with the bigger head," Chains told him. "Rock's explanation seems valid. I know you won't let this go, though, so here's what we can do. Keep an eye on him. Thanks to Rock dropping in on him, Tyler knows the garage has cameras. He'll be careful, but if something's up, he might still make a mistake."

"And if he's working against us?"

"Then we kill him," Chains said. "Slowly and painfully. The last day of his life will also feel like the longest."

"What about Felicity?" Aidan said.

"What about her?"

"You mentioned they might already have some kind of relationship. What if she's dirty, too?"

"Same answer. We kill them both, and we enjoy it."

"We ain't killing Felicity before I get to have some fun with her," Aidan said. "She don't need to be willing."

"Whatever," Chains said. "She'll end up dead either way."

Aidan smiled as he ended the call.

24

―――――

FRIDAY MORNING, TYLER WENT FOR A TWO-MILE RUN NEAR HIS apartment.

When he returned, he worked through a series of push-ups, crunches, and body weight squats. A shower and a set of clean clothes later, Tyler was cooking breakfast when his burner buzzed. Chains sent a simple message. *Meet at the garage in 1 hour.* A moment later, Hope called. "I guess you got the same summons?" Tyler said.

"Yeah."

"Any idea what it's about?"

"Not a clue," Hope said. "Whatever it is, they're not telling me shit."

Tyler wondered if this was the fallout of him going to the garage and snooping around. Hope knew a little of what he did but not all of it. Might as well bring her up to speed. "You know I was at the garage yesterday."

"I was wondering why you went."

"To do a little investigating," he said while stirring his scrambled eggs. "Major components like the lift have serial numbers. Those can be traced."

"Funny," Hope said in a tone indicating she found nothing about this the least bit humorous, "I don't recall getting an inventory list from you. Just a message about you following Rock and pictures of a couple goons."

"I may have omitted a few details."

"And serial numbers."

"They didn't go anywhere. I had someone check, but I'll send you the list anyway."

"You're not an investigator, Tyler."

"I'm aware," he said. The eggs finished cooking, so Tyler used the spatula to put them on a plate.

"Are you cooking?" Hope wanted to know.

"Yeah. Why, you hungry?"

"No, I just ate."

"If you hadn't hurried out of here the other morning," Tyler said, "I would have made breakfast for you."

"Thanks. I'll settle for finding out what the hell Chains wants. See you there." She ended the call. Tyler ate his breakfast and left for the industrial facility. He arrived a few minutes before the appointed hour to find Hope's car and two others already there. Inside, Chains and Connor waited with Hope.

"Good," Chains said, "we have everyone we need now."

"What's going on?" Tyler asked.

"We're doing another job soon. Because actual recon worked out well last time, the four of us are going to do it again."

"Why do you need me? I'm just the mechanic."

"You seem to have no trouble offering opinions," Chains said.

Connor crossed his arms and smirked. "Besides . . . we can draw on your long career of distinguished flyboy service."

"Sure," Tyler said. "Get a jet . . . or at least a chopper. Either will make things easier."

Connor remained stone-faced, but Chains grinned. "We'll need to plan and execute this from the ground, I'm afraid," he said. "Let's go. Felicity, you drive Tyler's car."

IT TOOK ABOUT two hours to get from the Hagerstown area to a part of West Virginia Tyler had never been to before. Though he didn't go on the last heist, this place fit Hope's description of the Virginia town they hit—large enough to have some major roads and businesses but small enough to have a minor-league police force. The best of both worlds from the gang's perspective.

"There it is," Chains said, pointing to a building coming up. "On the left there."

The largest building Tyler could see featured a large marquee showing *DOUG'S PAWN EMPORIUM*. "A pawn shop?" he said.

"The biggest one around."

"Just because Doug thinks he's running an emporium doesn't mean it's worth a lot."

"You learn this in the Air Force?" Connor asked from the back seat beside Tyler.

"Critical thinking? Yes. You might try applying some, Connor. Life will be a little easier when you do."

Before the younger man could answer, Chains broke in. "Enough from you two. Look around. This is a state road. Plenty of side streets. Lots of ways to get out of here and eventually work our way back to Maryland."

"No train tracks around, though," Hope pointed out.

"I guess you'll have to outrun the law the old-fashioned way."

"I'm up for it." Her smile almost made Tyler do the same.

"It's the biggest place for several counties," Chains said.

"They handle a lot of volume and get a few . . . interesting items here and there. Doug basically buys anything because he knows he can sell it. He doesn't run a big crew. We're going to hit it when one of the other guys is off. Two men inside instead of three."

"You must have some inside info," Tyler said.

"I've got my sources."

"Are we driving by the place?"

"Sure. Felicity, let's take a tour of the parking lot and the streets nearby."

"You got it," Hope said. She swung the Crown Vic through a U-turn about a block past the shop. A sidewalk ran along the road, but there was no shoulder. Hope would need to pull into the lot. The emporium had its own. A pedestrian walking by, however, represented a variable outside of anyone's control. While it might only create a delay of a few seconds, even a small sliver of time mattered when evading pursuit.

The aged and choppy asphalt allowed for at least two dozen vehicles to park between its faded yellow lines. The spaces closest to the door were reserved for cars with handicapped plates. Parking would be another crapshoot unless the crew stole a handicapped plate or parking placard. If the place happened to be unusually busy when the crew arrived to rob it, Hope would need to leave their getaway vehicle farther from the exit. As Tyler wondered about a rear door, Chains said, "Let's drive around."

The rear of the building did not allow for easy access back to the street, though a desperate driver could cross the sidewalk and hop the curb. Survivable from the vehicle's perspective if done well. An unmarked red door bisected the brick facade in the back. A dumpster stood against the wall to the right. There were no parking lines back here, but Tyler spotted a camera about ten feet up in the overhang from the roof. It was pretty small and well-hidden. Whoever set it there picked a very good spot. "Looks like it might be easier to wait here," Tyler said.

"No way back to the main road," Chains pointed out.

"Getting over the curb isn't bad. So long as the car doesn't ride too low, it should be fine."

"Your department," Connor said.

"I'm aware how the division of labor works around here," Tyler said. Connor seethed but remained quiet.

"I like the idea of leaving from back here," Chains said. "The one piece of intel we're missing is how to get there from inside. Most of these shops have a counter, and you can't just walk to the rear."

"You'll have guns. I don't think Doug will put up much of a fight if he's there alone."

"Pawn shop owners tend to be armed," Connor said.

Chains nodded. "We'll have to hope Pop doesn't kill him. He might need to be the lookout again. The rest of us will deal with the owner, customers, and getting the take." Hope turned around and drove back to the other side of the building. No one else mentioned the camera, and Tyler decided to keep quiet about it. Maybe Floyd T. Rayford wasn't as observant.

"I think we can do it," Hope said. She got back onto the road and turned off on a side street. As she drove parallel to the main drag, other roads offered paths away from the pawn shop. Her GPS showed most of them intersecting with another state route. While Hope would have her share of options for the initial getaway, the number of escape routes out of the county itself would be smaller. Still, she'd done this before, and Tyler felt confident she could outdrive the local cops.

"You don't see any possible hangups, Tyler?" Connor said. "Drawing on your vast experience and all."

Tyler wanted to mention possible personnel shortfalls,

but he also couldn't risk his position in the group. As much as Connor needed to be put in his place, it would have to happen later. "So long as your intel on the place is good," he said, "I don't see a problem."

"Just what I was hoping to hear," Chains said.

25

<hr>

THE NEXT MORNING WAS SATURDAY, BUT TYLER DIDN'T GET TO sleep in.

A text from Chains woke him just after seven. *Be at the garage at 9.* He got out of bed, changed into athletic attire, and headed out for a two-mile run. He wore his last pair of workout clothes, so he would need to test the apartment's stackable washer and dryer afterward. They looked to be reasonably new and in working order at least. When he returned, Tyler worked on pushups, body weight squats, and several attacking and blocking routines.

As usual, the sharper edges of his personality didn't prove endearing to those around him. Pop was hostile toward him initially, though Chains stepped in before the situation could escalate. Connor remained skeptical from the start. Tyler wondered how long it would be before one of them made a move. He wasn't trying to piss anyone off, but he also didn't come here to make friends. So long as the gang members ended up in jail or the ground, they could think what they wanted.

After showering and putting on clean clothes, Tyler drove through a McDonald's on his way to the industrial site. He could tolerate their weak coffee for a single day. By the time he arrived, he'd finished his breakfast sandwich and two hash browns. A couple other cars sat outside. Once in the garage, Tyler spotted a vehicle much like the one the FBI loaned him. This one was a black Mercury Grand Marquis—basically the same car but with a few more pretensions of luxury. It fell short of the Lincoln Town Car there, and Tyler figured this one car was a good representation of why Ford folded Mercury years ago.

"Our new ride," Chains said. Connor sat on the hood of it, his arms crossed as he stared at Tyler. "What do you think?"

"Not bad," Tyler said. "Rear-wheel drive. Big engine even if it's going for ride quality over power. I can work with this."

"Good," Connor said. "You're on a job-to-job basis with us. Don't forget it."

Tyler swallowed his sarcastic reply. Floyd T. Rayford may not run his mouth quite so confidently considering his less distinguished career. "Sure," he said instead.

"There's cash in an envelope under the passenger's seat," Chains told him. "You've seen our target. You think this is a good vehicle for it?"

Something a little smaller would have worked better, but with the right modifications, Hope could make this Grand Marquis handle in a way Mercury never intended. The V8 under the hood was a good starting point for a getaway car. "It'll work. There's enough of these on the road to blend in, too."

"You drive one," Connor said.

Tyler shrugged. "Ford version, but yeah. I didn't have a ton of better options in my budget."

"Maybe you can upgrade."

"Maybe I will," Tyler said. "Something in the muscle car space."

"Stick with us," Chains said. "You can buy whatever kind

of ride you want after a few more jobs." He looked at his watch. "Can you finish by Tuesday night?"

"We don't ask him." Connor jabbed his finger toward Tyler. "This asshole works for us. We tell him when we need it done, and he either complies or catches a bullet."

"Charming," Tyler said, unable and unwilling to hold back now. "You have a real future in HR if this whole robbery thing doesn't work out."

"Screw you." Connor took a step forward but stopped when Chains cleared his throat.

"Let's not do this. Connor, I hear you, but things take time. I feel Tuesday is reasonable. We don't want a rush job. Tyler, what do you think?"

"This needs some serious work, but I can do it by then."

"Good. We'll leave you to it." He clapped Connor on the shoulder and pointed toward the door. They left, but Connor turned and spared a final glower for Tyler on his way out. Once they were gone, Tyler checked out the car. It was in good shape. A few spots of rust on the underbody when he did a quick check but nothing out of line. The exhaust looked pretty rough, but he planned to replace it anyway. The envelope held eight grand this time.

The junkyard awaited again.

~

AFTER A LONG SATURDAY catching up with a bunch of bureaucracy, Hope dropped by Tyler's apartment.

He was sweaty when he came to the door, and even his black T-shirt showed dirt and oil. "Someone was busy today," she said as he checked outside the door and locked it behind her.

"I have a new car to work on," he said. "A Grand Marquis."

"At least it's rear-drive this time. You gonna need help with it?"

"At some point, yes," Tyler said. "I have an idea there, but I really need a shower first. I was about to get in when you knocked."

"I'll hang out and wait." Hope smiled and sat on the couch. Tyler walked down the hall. Water ran a short while later, and it stopped after about ten minutes. Tyler soon emerged wearing jeans and another black T-shirt. Despite being on the job a while, his hair remained blond, but he would need a touch-up if they went much longer. "Looks like you got quite a bit done today," she said when he sat beside her on the sofa.

"I went to a junkyard and got a better engine," he said.

"The stock one is good."

Tyler waffled his hand. "Yeah, but it's not really designed for power, and wringing more out of it would require something like a supercharger. I was able to find a twenty-seventeen Mustang which got rear-ended hard enough to total it. The powertrain was fine. Five-liters, over four hundred horses, and a six-speed automatic designed more for sport than for retired dentists to cruise around."

"You get it installed?"

"Not yet. I had to drive farther to a different place. Got the old engine dropped. I'll get back to it tomorrow."

"I didn't expect you to work so hard," Hope said. "Thanks for sticking it out."

"It's fine." Tyler shrugged. "I don't have to do many things like this at my shop. We're more into maintenance and smaller repairs versus wholesale changes. It's cool to get my hands really dirty again."

"The rest of you was pretty dirty, too." She held her nose for emphasis. "P-U."

"I'm clean now."

She smiled. "So you are." Hope leaned over and kissed

Tyler but pulled back before they went too far down that admittedly pleasurable road. "What was your idea about this car?"

"I'll probably need some help with it again," he said. "It's a lot for one person to do."

"I can work with you."

Tyler shook his head. "No. I want you to say you're stuck with your real job. What does the group think Felicity does for work?"

"Admin assistant for an accountant."

"Maybe you're spending the weekend getting a jump on tax season, then. Whatever the reason, you can't come in. I have someone I want to bring in."

Hope gave Tyler a gentle elbow in the ribs. "Is she hot?"

"No. In fact, he's much uglier than you."

"One of the guys from your shop?"

"Yeah. Ortiz. He . . . helped me on some of the militia stuff."

"I didn't know that," Hope admitted.

"I kept him out of it," Tyler said. "Besides, I had him play a support role. No one who saw him survived to tell the FBI or anybody else."

"You think he's up for it?"

"He's always willing to lend a hand. I can have him help me work on the car. It'll need a suspension overhaul, and he's better there than I am. Once we're done, I can ask him to keep an eye on the target. This time, I know where it is ahead of time."

"All right." Hope nodded. "It's a good idea. I've had to work at irregular hours for the group, so I can always tell them my boss is cracking down."

"Speaking of bosses," Tyler said, "how quickly is our clock running out?"

"I think getting some info bought us a little time. It's not indefinite, though. We'll have this job and maybe another unless we really bust something open."

"Does the increasing frequency concern anyone you report to?"

Hope leaned back against the cushion and looked at the ceiling. It still carried the popcorn effect which went out of style years ago. "If it does, no one's ever told me. It certainly concerns me. Pop can be trigger-happy."

"The big boss must be getting desperate." Tyler frowned. "Maybe he wants to hit a certain amount of money. Maybe he's dying and feeling some urgency."

"We need to feel it, too."

"I know," Tyler said. "Let's see if we can sink them after this job."

"Yeah." Hope bobbed her head in agreement. "Let's."

26

ON SUNDAY, TYLER LAID THE GROUNDWORK FOR BRINGING IN
Ortiz by mentioning it to Chains.

When the man predictably asked about bringing Felicity
in, Tyler said she was unavailable.

I don't know. We don't like strangers
knowing our business.

He wouldn't know. I'd tell him I'm fixing a car
and need a hand.

You trust this guy?

Sure.

Serve with him?

Yes.

He going to be a narc?

No. I'm not going to tell him why I'm doing
this.

Won't he ask?

I'll say it's a car I've wanted to work on for a while and the garage is my cousin's. He's not going to go digging.

I'll let you know.

While Chains deliberated—and probably checked with the elusive big boss—Tyler kept going on the Grand Marquis. Working by himself, the deadline would be a challenge if he made all the changes he wanted to. In addition to the engine and transmission, he needed to replace the exhaust, fine-tune the power output, and stiffen the suspension. Mercury never built the car with speed and performance in mind, though the police versions of its cousin the Crown Vic at least introduced the possibilities.

Tyler finished his lunch Sunday afternoon when Chains called. "You gotta be sure about this guy."

"I am," Tyler reiterated.

"You definitely trust him?"

"A hundred percent."

"He take a bullet for you or something?"

"More or less. Lost part of his leg in a training accident. Should've been me." Tyler knew an IED injured Ortiz, but putting a personal spin on it created trust between the two men. Even a non-veteran like Chains could understand it.

Chains remained silent other than his breathing for a few seconds. "Fine. This time. Felicity better clear her goddamn schedule going forward. You want to pay this guy, it's coming out of your share."

"No problem," Tyler said. He'd planned to do this already. Ortiz was nice enough to volunteer his time and muscle, but Tyler felt better sharing some of his ill-gotten gains from the gang's take.

"Just get the car done," Chains said before breaking the connection.

Tyler texted Ortiz next.

Got a job for you. Need your help on a car . . . and maybe a few extracurricular things.

When do you want me, boss?

Tomorrow morning.

All right. I'm not scheduled at the shop.

I'll text you the coordinates. Obviously this is eyes-only. Thanks.

He didn't want to expose Ortiz to the gang. The man lacked a cover story, though they could work out the basics of one in case it mattered. Still, Tyler felt bad imposing too much on Ortiz's willingness to help out. Assisting with the car and keeping an eye on the pawn shop would be enough —even if Ortiz wanted to do more.

~

MONDAY MORNING, Tyler watched another car come up the driveway.

As he got closer, he realized Ortiz was driving. Tyler walked forward to meet the man as he climbed out. They shook hands. "Thanks for coming."

"Sure thing, boss."

"Whose car?"

"My aunt's," Ortiz said. It was a blue late-model Camry in good condition. "She doesn't drive it much. Her last name is different, too, so even if someone looks at it, they won't get it back to me."

"Officer thinking," Tyler said. He lowered his voice. "There are cameras inside. The gang knows you're coming, but I didn't tell them much else. It's possible we might get a visitor or two."

"They got mikes in there?" Ortiz asked.

"I can't tell. Best to whisper once we're inside."

"Looks like a nice setup from the outside."

Tyler grinned. "These guys might be robbers and assholes, but they've definitely assembled a nice garage. Once they're all dead or in jail, I'm coming back and taking some of their shit."

"I'll be sure to bring my truck then," Ortiz said. They walked in, and Ortiz looked around with wide eyes. "This is nice." He offered an appreciative nod. "I could get used to working here."

"It's not bad . . . but don't." Tyler swept his hand to cover the Grand Marquis. "The prior car they had me do was an Aries."

"Seriously?"

"Yeah. This still needs some work, but it's miles better."

"What do you want me to do?"

"The suspension," Tyler said. "It was designed to be soft and pillowy. We need it to be tight and aggressive. If it's stiff enough to the point of being uncomfortable, so be it. No one's using this car long term."

"All right," Ortiz said. He walked to the open hood and peered inside. "This doesn't look like the original engine."

"It's not, though if I had to guess, I'd say they're related." Tyler jutted his chin toward the Mercury. "From a Mustang about eight years old. Similar size but a lot more power."

"Transmission, too?"

"Six-speed, yeah. They went to ten gears a year or two later. I think this one will do better."

"All right. I'll get to work." While Ortiz slid under the car, Tyler made sure the powertrain mounts were solid. He'd thought about replacing the Mercury's on-the-column shifter for the more conventional console-based version coming from the Mustang but decided to leave it alone. People expected the former in something like a Grand Marquis. The more the car blended in and looked like a typical example of its make and model, the better for Hope.

A few hours later, the pair paused for lunch. Ortiz brought back a couple footlong subs and two bags of chips from Subway. They ate outside on the dilapidated picnic table near where everyone parked. "How's the shop?" Tyler wanted to know, still keeping his voice low.

"Good. Not too busy. Jake's picking up a little of the slack."

"Is Smitty cranky about what's going on?"

Ortiz chuckled. "He's pretty much cranky all the time. For a guy who's so good with the customers, he can be a grouch."

"He probably thinks I'm imposing on him." Tyler felt the same way sometimes. Smitty was a damned good mechanic and way better at talking to people than Tyler. These factors made the man's own shop a success before he came to work for Tyler. He was also a pretty strait-laced guy, which meant Smitty didn't care much for some of Tyler's knight-errant work—as his ex-girlfriend Sara used to call it. Even with Jake pitching in, Tyler wondered if he needed to hire another mechanic. It might mollify his best employee.

"He'll be all right," Ortiz said.

"Even with you out here helping me?"

Ortiz shrugged. "Maybe he'll complain a little, but he'll get by."

"Yeah," Tyler said. "We should finish the car tomorrow. Once we do, I want you to keep an eye on the target. At least for a day. Go in if you can but don't be obvious you're checking the place out."

"I got it, boss."

If Ortiz could get some good intel from a visit, it might help Hope. Part of Tyler wanted the path to the back door to be long and fraught with messy stock and stacks of boxes. If the crew got jammed up, maybe Hope would cut her losses and get out of there. The FBI could still swoop in and try to get the crew to turn on their leader. It was the best outcome for everyone, which is why Tyler didn't expect it to happen.

27

After they finished for the day, Ortiz drove back home. Under normal circumstances, Tyler would have offered him the sleeper sofa, but he didn't need anyone in the gang driving by and seeing Ortiz's car in the lot. By now, Tyler figured out they knew where his fake persona lived. Keeping them guessing about the rest was the better play, and Ortiz didn't mind the extra round trip.

After dinner, Tyler picked up his sketch book and pencils. They were a far cry from his easel, high-quality paper, and watercolors at home. He'd upgraded his supplies years ago when he learned to stop caring how the outputs looked. Tyler also realized only a poor craftsman blames his tools, so he replaced all the basic and starter equipment he owned with better versions. His eyes watered at the price, but he could see the results on the rich grains of the sheets.

Tyler sat on the couch and opened the book to the second page. He picked up a black pencil, closed his eyes, and took a deep breath. The VA shrink who put him on the therapeutic painting program told him he couldn't force it. It was better to try and clear his mind and let the ideas come. His brain would decide what it needed to expel onto the parchment.

While it sounded like bunk at the time, it turned out to be true.

His hand moved, and the outline of a long, squat building appeared, covering most of the paper's width. A few cars squeezed in on one side. Inside the open bay door, bodies lay strewn on the floor. Tyler reached for a red pencil and colored in some blood effects. When he'd finished and snapped back out of the zone, he looked at his handiwork and frowned.

"Interpreting dreams is bullshit," he remembered telling the shrink. "Why should I think making sense of what I paint is any different?"

All of his skeptical moments and comments about the program—the question he recalled now was but a single one on a long list—dissolved once he learned it really worked. To her credit, the doctor was always patient with him. Everything she explained turned out to be true, and now, figuring out what he put on the page was a regular part of the process. Even Lexi did it when she saw his output.

Tyler understood most of it. The building was the industrial site the gang used as a garage. Most of the bodies were men, but one—with a few squiggles of red hair—clearly represented Hope and her natural color. He blew out a deep breath. Failing meant the group would kill him, but they could go further and presume Hope brought him in deliberately. Connor already seemed to harbor a few ideas in this regard. One bad job, and all he needed to do was plant the idea in Chains' mind.

As much as Tyler wanted the men to fail, he needed to do what he could to make sure their jobs succeeded. Both Tyler's and Hope's lives depended on it. Between them, the job required both to stay alive and figure out a way to bring down Chains and company. Tyler looked at the paper. The result of failure lay before him.

He couldn't allow it to happen.

CHAINS WENT over the upcoming job with the group's leader during a video call.

As usual, the boss was in a nondescript room, and Chains couldn't even tell if he stood or sat. Mediocre lighting kept him partially in shadow. Chains only knew the man as Barbell, a nickname he apparently earned after using one to beat a fellow inmate to death after an incident in prison. The boss was older than the rest of the crew—even older than Pop—and Chains guessed him to be about sixty. Reddish-blond hair mixed with gray hung down to his shoulders, and his goatee was almost all gray. "Have you been into the shop?" he wanted to know.

"We're avoiding going in," Chains said. "We have intel on the layout. It's solid. We've been there, driven the roads, spent time in the parking lot. We know the terrain."

"How's the car for this one?"

"Coming along. We got a Grand Marquis."

"Better than some old Dodge."

Chains chuckled. "Connor's idea. He doesn't like the new mechanic and wanted to see how good the guy was."

"He sounds capable," Barbell said. "I'm not sure I like the idea of risking everyone's freedom simply because Connor doesn't like the guy."

"It all worked out," Chains said.

"This time." Barbell paused, blew out a deep breath, and frowned. "How's the new mechanic doing?"

"Good so far."

"No incidents?"

"He's a little bit of a prick, but we don't need him to have a winning personality." Chains pondered a few standoffs and other incidents with Tyler. "Seems a little too confident in himself for a mediocre Air Force career. The guy's bounced around since he got out of the service."

"Is Felicity working with him?" Barbell asked.

"She did on the Aries. Not this one. He brought in some guy he knows." Chains put up a hand before Barbell could object. "We kept an eye on them. Cameras didn't catch anything weird, and the mikes didn't pick up any shady conversations. Seems like one guy helping another."

"Someone else from the military?"

"I think so. The guy walks a little funny. I think he has a prosthetic leg."

"I don't care as long as the car works," Barbell said. "It's something of an odd arrangement, though. Why wasn't Felicity able to help?"

"Something at her day job. She's missed some time for us and couldn't get away." Barbell grunted. "You were right about her. She's been great."

"I figured she would be. A woman trying to make it in a space dominated by men is going to work hard and bust her ass."

"It's a pretty nice ass, too," Chains said.

"Let's focus on the job," Barbell said, a little annoyance creeping into his tone. His mostly gray brows furrowed. "And your new mechanic."

"Connor still doesn't like him. Pop doesn't seem to, either, but he's salty around everyone."

"What do you want to do, Chains?"

"I think we need to test him."

"Test him how?" Barbell demanded.

"Find a couple guys to stop by the garage at night." He shrugged. "Let's see how Tyler does against them. Nothing in his background suggests he's super capable."

"You don't know. It's not like he uploaded his CV and references. The guy could have a black belt unrelated to his time in the military."

"Maybe we should find out," Chains said.

"I'll leave it up to you," Barbell told him after a short

pause. "Don't lose a good mechanic because a couple of the guys don't like him."

"I won't. I'll make sure the guys we find don't kill him."

"What if he kills them?"

Chains sighed. "Then he cleans up his mess . . . and we have a few more questions."

28

Tyler continued working on the car on Tuesday while Ortiz sat on the pawn shop.

He reported on his progress in the early afternoon. *Pretty easy to get away via the back. Nothing out of the ordinary here. Workers are armed but don't seem especially aware. Definitely not former military. There are cameras, but I don't know how good the system is.*

Tyler took a break and tapped a reply. *Thanks. Sounds like the crew will be able to get in and out easily.*

You want me to stick around? Maybe keep an eye on the place another day?

No. You've done enough. Thanks. I'll let you know if I need anything later.

When he'd nearly gotten the car finished to his satisfaction, Tyler heard another vehicle approach. Chains walked into the garage a moment later. He eyed Tyler up and down before approaching. "Looks like you're finished."

"She needs a test drive," Tyler said, "but I think we're basically there."

"Good." The other man ran his hands along the hood. "Looks nice. A little lower, maybe?"

"It is. Suspension mods. We needed a stiffer ride. This thing was built to make old people feel comfortable."

"You work on a lot of cars?"

Tyler shrugged. "Enough. The basics aren't much different than a helicopter. I don't need to worry about keeping this thing in the air at least."

Chains opened the door and sat behind the wheel, running his hands along it. "You work with Felicity much before?"

"Here and there. Enough for her to recommend me, I guess." Tyler realized Chains was pumping him for information and maybe trying to spot inconsistencies. While Tyler couldn't recall everything he'd told the group, he knew he would stick to the false identity Hope and the FBI made him.

"You overlap with her in the Air Force?" Chains asked.

Tyler didn't know much about Hope's false identity as Felicity. If they were supposed to serve together, however, he figured she would have told him. It was too important a detail to leave out. "I'm not aware of her service history," he said. "Besides, I coulda been in and out before she got there."

The de facto leader nodded. Tyler wondered if he'd passed some sort of test. "You rather fix cars or helicopters and jets?"

"Cars."

"Why?"

"Only have to worry about them in two dimensions," Tyler said. "Once you add in up and down, you have to sweat the takeoff and landing. Way too much can go wrong even if the craft is in good shape."

Chains climbed out and closed the door. "I look forward to hearing about how this baby performs."

"Me, too. Kind of sad it's basically a single-use ride."

Chains bobbed his head. "I guess it is."

"Anything else you want to know?" Tyler wondered.

When Chains frowned at him, Tyler added, "If you wanted my CV, you could make an online portal for uploads."

"Not exactly the way we operate," Chains said. "You going to let Felicity drive this thing later?"

"If she's up for it, sure. She might still be toiling away for her other boss." Chains let out a dry chuckle. "Everyone else have a job outside of this?"

"Some do." Chains offered nothing else. Tyler didn't want to press him for info and make the man suspicious. He was already here on a fact-finding mission. "Looks like you've done good work here. See you later, Tyler."

"Bye." Chains left the garage and drove away. Tyler stared at the Mercury and wondered if he passed the pop quiz.

TYLER TIGHTENED the exhaust on the Grand Marquis. He heard a rattle from the rear on the test drive. The new stainless steel system replaced the aging stock model, added some power thanks to increased efficiency, weighed less, and looked better. The car performed well when he took it out. The acceleration fell a little short of Mustang levels but far surpassed what the Grand Marquis could do with the factory configuration. The ride was stiff, and Tyler felt every bump and imperfection in the road, but turns and curves produced little body roll.

All told, he would call it a success.

Tyler wheeled himself out from under the car. Like the Aries, this represented some of his best work as a mechanic, and he did it in the service of criminals. Worse, the gang would torch the car if they finished the job successfully. A failure meant the cops would impound it. Either way, Tyler's handiwork would ultimately be for naught. He hadn't expected to feel salty about this when he agreed to take the gig, but he did.

Tires crunched on the service road outside. One of the gang must have come by to check out the car. Tyler wondered if anyone else would be grilling him, or if Chains' Q&A session was enough. Rather than someone he knew, two strangers walked through the open bay door. "Nice setup you got here," one of them said. Both were white, tall, and slender. Their stringy hair and general unkempt appearances made Tyler wonder if they were junkies looking for money or parts to sell. So far, neither produced a weapon. Tyler held a wrench, and his grip tightened on the Craftsman.

"This isn't a public garage," Tyler said.

"You want us to leave?"

"I think it's in your best interests."

"Yeah?" the other asked. His hair was longer and lighter, and his green eyes a fair bit more wild. He moved closer to Tyler. "Why's it in our best interests?"

Tyler remembered the cameras around the area, and he wondered if these two tweakers represented another test. He couldn't deploy his full skill on them. The group needed to think him capable but not much more. Floyd Tyler Rayford never received any special operations training, and nothing in the phony background suggested extreme proficiency in hand-to-hand. "Not much here you're interested in. No cash. All the good parts have serial numbers."

"You think we care about serial numbers?"

"I think you probably don't want to get arrested."

"Enough talk," the darker-haired man said. He took a few steps forward and pulled a long knife out of his waistband. "We're going to take what we want. If you get in the way, I cut you. You annoy me enough, you die." Tyler didn't say anything. Both men tried to glare at him but averted their eyes when he used his own thousand-yard stare in response. "You hearin' me, mister?"

"You want to wait?"

"What?"

"Do you want to wait?" Tyler repeated.

"For what?" the blond one asked.

"Maybe for you to pull a knife. A third guy to arrive." The two exchanged confused looks. "Anything."

"We ain't waiting for shit," the knife wielder said, and he stalked closer to Tyler.

29

———————

Lexi hurried out the door to meet T.J. for dinner.

The other woman proved cagey on the phone, but Lexi chose to put a positive spin on things. Why invite her out for another meal if the answer was no? Maybe there would be some more fact-finding and sizing up. Lexi wondered how many hurdles she would need to clear and realized the answer would be much higher if this particular opportunity didn't work out.

Lexi parked in the lot of a kabob place she'd never heard of in Greektown. She went inside and spotted T.J. in a booth. The other woman smiled and waved. Lexi did the same and stood in line behind one other person. Flatscreen TVs displayed the menu behind the counter, a definite step up from the big boards with plastic lettering she remembered from her youth. Lexi opted for a gyro with fries and a soda. She filled her cup at the fountain and joined T.J., who wore a green sweater over black jeans. "Thanks for coming," T.J. said.

"Of course," Lexi said. She plucked a couple napkins from a dispenser and set them under her cup. The table was cheap plastic but clean. The booth at least offered some padding.

The interior was pretty spartan, and framed pictures of Greek locations scattered on the walls tried to set the ambiance. "I figured it had to be a good update if you wanted to meet in person again. You could give me bad news on the phone or by text."

"You're right. My boss said he's open to having a summer intern."

Lexi clapped and drew the attention of everyone else in the restaurant. The place wasn't crowded, and everyone's attention returned to their food or dinner companions quickly. "Paid or unpaid? I'm all right with either."

"Paid," T.J. said. "C.T. went on some screed about unpaid internships only going to the children of rich assholes or something like that." She chuckled. "There are times I tune him out. You probably will, too."

"I guess we'll see," Lexi said. "I tune my dad out sometimes." Someone behind the counter shouted T.J.'s name, and she got up to collect her food. She returned with a gyro and fries on a tray. Lexi chuckled. "I got the same thing."

"Great minds think alike."

A moment later, the same voice barked out Lexi's name, and she retrieved her food. Both women ate in silence for a while. The gyro meat was terrific with just the right amount of spice. The mediocre fries got rescued by the tzatziki Lexi dipped them in. "C.T. wanted to know something," T.J. said after wiping her mouth. About a quarter of her food remained. "I'm curious, too. Have you decided what kind of investigator you want to be?"

Lexi sighed. She'd figured this question would come up at some point, and she still didn't have a definitive answer. "I haven't figured it all out yet. Part of me wants to work for a prosecutor, investigate criminals, and help put them away. The other part would prefer working for a defense attorney trying to keep the state from trampling innocent people. I've seen what can happen. My dad and I have both been on the wrong end of some of that shit, and I'd rather spare someone else the problem if I can."

T.J. nodded. "I know you've mentioned your dad before. It sounds like you've gotten involved in some of the things he does."

"He never tries to involve me," Lexi said. "It's the opposite, really. Over a year ago . . . before his shop opened . . . he took a gig for a friend. Protection detail for a pop singer. Alex Anne. You heard of her?"

T.J. nodded. "I like her music."

"Me, too. Anyway, despite my dad coming on, a bunch of traffickers kidnapped Alex Anne and almost killed her other security guy. Two men came after me on campus when it was clear my dad was closing in." She paused for a deep breath, remembering getting away from Ahmed and Scott inside a building and then running to her car at a dead sprint. "I had to shoot them both. It wasn't his fault. He was chasing the group down. It wasn't my fault, either. I wasn't about to let them grab me up."

"Of course," T.J. said.

"Cops have a hard time seeing these things in black and white. I know I did the right thing, but they still could have recommended the county prosecutor charge me. That's the kind of shit I'd want to stop. Good people who barely escape a bad situation shouldn't have to worry about the government kicking them while they're down."

"You're right." T.J. bobbed her head, and her blonde ponytail settled on her left shoulder. "I think those are the kinds of cases C.T. likes. He prefers taking on people who have power over others."

"I guess I'll like interning there, then," Lexi said.

"He did want me to ask about your father," T.J. said. "Your dad helped C.T. once when Rollins was out of town. You know Rollins, right?"

"Yes."

"One of C.T.'s acquaintances ended up getting shot. The guy went off the rails on a revenge campaign, but still . . . C.T. thought shooting Vinnie was unnecessary."

"Is he going to blame me for shit my dad did?"

"No," T.J. said, "but I think he wants to know how far the apple fell from the tree."

Lexi drank some soda while she contemplated her answer. "My mother is in jail for at least a couple more years. She's a grifter, and she finally got caught. My dad is a retired soldier who can't walk away from trouble and might have some interesting ideas about how to resolve problems. I'm the daughter of both." She shrugged. "I get some things from my dad and others from my mom. If you asked, I would tell you I think I'm less inclined to shoot someone than my dad is. He had to do too much of it overseas. I've only been put in bad spots a couple times."

"I'm not trying to judge you," T.J. said. "Or your father."

"Your boss might be."

"He wants to know what kind of employee you would be."

"A damn good one," Lexi said.

T.J. smiled. "That's what I'll tell him, then."

"HAVE IT YOUR WAY," Tyler said as the duo moved to flank him.

He wasn't worried about the unarmed man, instead keeping his focus on the one with the knife. Tyler disliked fighting people armed with bladed weapons. Amateurs were often unpredictable, and one random unlucky cut could nick an artery and end the fight—and perhaps a life—quickly. The blade was about four inches long, and the dark-haired tweaker swung it back and forth in a way which suggested he only knew how to use it for show.

"Leave, or I'll gut you," he said.

Tyler shrugged. "Get on with it, then."

The man swung the knife toward Tyler, who thrust his left arm up, slamming his palm into his enemy's wrist and deflecting the attack. At the same time, he jabbed the guy in the face with the business end of the wrench. A couple teeth rattled free of his gums, and the tweaker spun away with a hand to his mouth.

Tyler turned to face the other. "You hurt my friend," the fellow growled. Tyler blocked three wild strikes and countered with a hard punch to the solar plexus. The lighter-haired man backed away and gasped. As he followed up, Tyler remembered he couldn't look too proficient on camera. He would need to use the Army's common fighting techniques—they didn't differ much across the services—rather than the deadlier strikes he learned at Fort Bragg. Tyler kicked his foe hard in the midsection, folding him in half. A guttural roar from his six told Tyler the one with the knife was ready to get back into the fight.

Normally, he would try to use the two against one another, aiming for one idiot to maim or kill his friend with the blade. This was off the table today. Instead, Tyler grabbed the bent-over man by the collar and belt and shoved him hard toward the knife wielder's legs. The inevitable collision sent both spilling to the concrete but resulted in no slices or stab wounds. The knife clattered to the concrete. Tyler grabbed it while the junkies untangled themselves and placed it on the roof of the Grand Marquis.

"Gimme my knife back," the dark-haired one barked as he rose to unsteady feet.

"You want it?" Tyler beckoned him forward with a wave of his hand. "Come get it."

He did. Tyler turned two more wild punches aside, countered with a hard right of his own, and knocked the guy flat with a pair of elbow strikes. Even without much specialization, the services taught people about elbows and knees hitting harder than hands and feet. The other fool remained on all fours and groaned constantly. "Get out of here," Tyler said.

Both made it back to vertical after varying degrees of struggle. Their eyes eventually settled on Tyler, and they glared. He wondered if these two happened upon the garage or if someone gave them a significant hint. It could have been anyone in the gang. All of them seemed skeptical of Tyler to one level or another. "Whoever put you up to this, the tip wasn't worth it."

"Who said someone put us up to it?" the blond one asked.

Tyler shrugged. "Call it a hunch. Now get lost. If I see you again, I'm taking your knife and splitting you open from neck to crotch." They mumbled curses and other uncharitable remarks, but both headed toward the door and left. Once they were gone, Tyler threw the knife into the trash, sanitized his hands, and went back to putting the finishing touches on the Mercury.

30

———

It was Tuesday night, and Hope knew this was the deadline on the new car.

She texted Tyler to see if he'd finished. He said it needed a final test drive—preferably by her—but was otherwise good to go. A message from Chains popped up, telling her they would check out the new ride tomorrow. This meant they'd likely be doing the job on Thursday. Maybe she could gather more intel by then. She asked Tyler if he'd eaten dinner, and when he said no, she told him she would bring some by.

A bag of burgers, fries, and onion rings later, Hope neared Tyler's complex. She again checked the rearview for anyone tailing her, saw no one, and pulled into the lot. Tyler opened up a moment later, checked behind her like he always did, and locked the door once she was inside. "Smells greasy," he said. "I like it already."

Hope smiled, found yesterday's newspaper in the recycling bin, and spread it out across the table. She emptied the contents of the bag—two cheeseburgers, two orders of fries, and a cardboard basket of onion rings to share. "Still got beer?" she asked.

"I replenished."

Hope pulled two bottles from the fridge and set them on the table. Tyler joined her, and they started eating. "You think the car will come through?" she said.

He nodded. "This one is a much better platform than the Aries. It'll be all right."

"You learn anything with your friend helping out?"

"He sat on the pawn shop," Tyler said. "Even went inside once." When Hope frowned, Tyler added, "Don't worry. He's not sticking around. I wanted to know how easy it would be to get to the rear exit. Regardless of how many employees there are, it could have been a very indirect path. Turns out it's not."

"You were hoping it would be?"

"I'd like to see the gang get caught." Tyler shrugged. "The FBI would spring you. We'd only need one of them to give up their leader."

"I don't think it would work," Hope said around an onion ring. Staying in the paper bag for a few minutes robbed them of a little crunchiness, but they still tasted good, and the ranch dressing added a nice tangy note. "I'm pretty sure Chains is the only one who knows who the big boss really is."

"You don't have any idea?" Tyler asked.

"None. Never have. If I've talked to him, it's either been audio only or set up in a way I can't see his face."

"Does he sound familiar?"

Hope shook her head. "No. There's some kind of distortion on his voice. I can make out what he's saying, but they definitely put some kind of effect on it."

"Maybe he's Darth Vader." Hope snickered at Tyler's comment. "If Connor or Chains don't like the car, the main man might Force choke me over FaceTime."

"I find your lack of horsepower disturbing," Hope said in her best James Earl Jones, and they both laughed.

After a few more bites of food, Tyler said, "Two tweakers came to the garage tonight."

Hope's eyes widened. "Really? I didn't think anyone knew we used the place."

"Me, neither. Interestingly enough, Chains stopped by for a chat earlier in the day. I think he was trying to see if I knew my own backstory. Lots of questions. I wonder if they're on to me."

"If they are, I haven't heard."

"You brought me in. They wouldn't tell you."

"You want out?" Hope said.

"No. I sent the junkies packing. My suspicion is Chains told them to see if they could rough me up. Probably gave them drugs or enough money to buy a few days' supply."

Hope ate her last fry and leaned back as much as the wooden chair would allow. "We'll have to keep an eye on the guys. I don't want them to be suspicious of you."

"Or of you," Tyler said. "You joined more recently than the four pricks, right?"

"Yeah."

Tyler finished eating and wrapped all their trash in the newspaper. He collected it and tossed the whole thing in the trash. "Want another beer?"

"Sure."

Tyler drained the last of his and plucked two more bottles from the six-pack. He set Hope's in front of her and rejoined her at the table. "I think we're on the right track," he said. "If we keep it up . . . and maybe get a little lucky along the way . . . this might be the last job we get tangled up in."

"It would be nice." Hope took a long pull of her beer. "You'd have me out of your hair . . . which could go back to its normal color."

"Two colors, really. Don't forget the gray." They both grinned. "Besides, I'm not trying to get rid of you?"

"No?"

"No."

"Good." Hope stood, walked to Tyler's chair, and lowered

herself onto his lap. "I'm not trying to go anywhere." She put her arms around Tyler's neck and kissed him. "Except maybe down the hall."

"HOW MUCH DO you really know about the guys in the gang?" Tyler asked Hope as they lay next to one another.

She rolled onto her side and cocked an eyebrow at him. "I'm going to try not to be offended."

"What do you mean?"

"We just had sex, and now you want to chat about the boys?"

Tyler chuckled. "We can't share a cigarette in a non-smoking apartment. Consider it small talk."

Hope smiled. "All right. We know something about all of them. Not complete pictures yet. They're all careful. Masked up on operations. They don't spend a whole lot of money in showy ways. None has a really big social media presence."

"This isn't working. I'm starting to like them a little."

Hope swatted him on the shoulder. "Do you have an idea?"

"I followed Rock once and got those pictures of his two goonish friends," Tyler said. "What if I follow someone else?"

"We know their addresses," Hope said.

"People don't always go home," Tyler pointed out. "Maybe one of the guys has a girlfriend you don't know about. Or an old buddy who's a shady character and involved a truckload of bad stuff."

"Fair point. We don't know much about their friends and associates. I've wanted to do something like this, but I always get overruled."

"I get the feeling you don't get your highest marks in following orders."

"Very true," Hope said with a grin cute enough to make

Tyler want to kiss her. He refrained—for now. "I get my boss's objections, though. I'm a woman alone in a group of guys. It makes me easier to spot in the field."

"I can blend in a little better."

"Who do you want to tail?"

"I think we need to play it by ear," Tyler said. "Pop is on thin ice, so I think he's out. Not much value there. I'd like to get Chains, but I'll settle for Connor or Rock."

"You're just going to follow them from the garage?"

"I'll think of something. Rock doesn't hate me like Connor does, though none of the guys are exactly trying to be my buddy. Maybe I can persuade him to go out for a couple brews the night before a big job."

"You might be able to," Hope said. "Be careful."

"I will."

"You're going to try doing this tomorrow?"

"If I get a chance, yeah. Part of it will depend on who comes to do the car inspection."

"Let's hope it's not Connor, then. He might keep an eye out for you following him."

"I'll figure something out if he's the one."

Hope's hand rested on Tyler's cheek. "Try not to get caught."

"I've done this sort of thing before," he said, squeezing her hand.

"I know."

"You need to make sure you drive the car and give it your seal of approval."

"Yes, boss."

Tyler turned toward Hope, pushing her flat and rolling atop her while she giggled. "Give it the gas." He kissed her a few times. "Plenty of power." He kissed her neck, and she wrapped a hand in his short hair. "Make sure you take a few turns at speed."

"Right now," she said, "I'm not worried about going fast."

31

———

Wednesday morning, Tyler woke to find Hope gone.

He checked his phone. No messages from anyone in the group. Tyler got out of bed, stretched, and did a series of body-weight exercises. He then practiced strikes and kicks for about twenty minutes before hopping in the shower and making sure his hair still looked the right color. No word from anyone yet. Tyler made himself coffee and a simple breakfast. When he finished eating, Hope texted. *Just drove the car. It's great. I'll tell the guys all is good.* Tyler replied in the affirmative. With nothing else to do until someone reached out to him, he waited.

After breakfast, Chains sent a message. *We'll check out the car at the garage. Felicity says it's good. Be there at 3.* Tyler ate lunch at his apartment and then headed to the gang's workshop. He brought a pistol and meant to get there early in case Chains and the crew had something extracurricular planned. His Crown Vic drove up the access road just after two o'clock. No one else had arrived. The cameras inside would give away Tyler's presence but only if someone watched them.

He unlocked the door and went inside. A few overhead lights automatically came to life after detecting his motion.

Tyler slipped a few strong wrenches into his clothes where they would be within easy reach. The trusty M11 at the back of his waistband felt familiar. He doubted the guys would want to get into a shootout, but they'd already done a few things to surprise him.

At the appointed hour, one car neared. Rock walked inside, and Tyler mentally pumped his fist because Connor sat this one out. "You the evaluation crew?" Tyler asked.

"I am today." Rock walked around the exterior of the Grand Marquis. Other than its ride height, expanded grill, larger exhaust tips, and a cutout for heat extraction in the hood, it looked almost identical to the car it had been several days before. Someone who didn't know what to look for would think the Mercury to be a typical example of its make and model. Rock got down on all fours and checked the exhaust. He completed his circuit of the vehicle in a few minutes. It felt like a longer version of the walkaround a rental car employee does before handing over the keys.

"What do you think?"

"Looks good," Rock said. "How's she drive?"

"I think it's good. Felicity approved, too. If you want to take it out, the keys are under the driver's seat."

Rock thought about it and eventually nodded. "All right. I'm no hotshot driver, but I'll see what she's got." He climbed in, found the keys, and started the car. Thanks to its Mustang engine and aftermarket exhaust, the Mercury growled like a predator when the engine turned over. Rock revved it a few times, and the car's roar filled the area. He put it in gear and drove it out the open bay door. Tires squealed a moment later.

He returned after a short drive. "Damn good." Rock smiled and then frowned. Maybe he was supposed to play it down the middle and not praise the new guy. He left the keys where they were and climbed out. "I think it'll work."

"Good."

"I guess I'll see you for the next job?"

As much as Tyler wanted the man to walk out, the job demanded he make an effort to prevent it. "Want to get a couple beers?" he asked.

"Huh?"

"Beer. You drink it?"

"Yeah."

"I was thinking we could go and down a few," Tyler said, "in the same place at the same time."

"Last mechanic never wanted to drink with us."

Tyler shrugged. "You shouldn't have killed him if you valued his antisocial nature so much."

Rock spent several seconds with his brow furrowed before he spread his hands. "Why not? You know where the Main Street Tap House is?"

"No, but I'm going to guess it's on Main Street."

"It is. Meet me there at five."

"Will do," Tyler said. Rock left. Once the other man had gone, Tyler walked outside and texted Ortiz. *Might need your help again. Can you come back up here? I want to follow a guy and get some pics. Easier to do both if I'm not alone.* Ortiz said he was down to help, and Tyler sent him a pin with the bar's location and suggested he arrive a little after five if traffic allowed. Ortiz said he would do his best.

A FEW MINUTES BEFORE FIVE, Tyler walked into the tap room.

It looked like many he'd stepped into in his duty posts across the country. Dark wood floors and a similar color for the bar. Inconsistent overhead lighting. A mix of stools, tables, and booths, with some of the latter in rough shape. Unlike many other joints, however, this one displayed their beer menu on TVs, breaking down the variety by color and type. Tyler, never much of a beer snob, ordered a domestic he'd never heard of and took a seat on an empty stool near the end of the mahogany. It allowed him a view of the front door, and he wasn't exactly competing with a truckload of people for seats.

Rock joined him a few minutes later. He ordered something much darker. Ortiz stepped through the door at five after. He never looked in Tyler's direction, heading for the opposite side of the room and grabbing an open table. The two men could see each other easily. A waitress approached Ortiz. Rock took a long pull of his beer and looked at Tyler. "You ever want to join in on a job?"

"No."

"Really?"

"I had my share of excitement already," Tyler said. The place wasn't crowded yet, but he still kept his voice low and tried to talk in generalities. "What you guys do really can't compare to jumping out of a plane."

"I thought you were a mechanic," Rock said, his eyes narrowing.

"I was. Still am. It's kind of hard to avoid doing any jumps in the Air Force, though. Once I specialized, I basically stopped all the daredevil stuff." He shrugged. "Not much of an interest in doing it again."

"You a good shot?"

"Good enough." Tyler sipped his domestic brew while Rock took a bigger swig. If the other man kept gulping them down, Tyler didn't want to match him drink for drink. An empty glass remained on the bar to his right. When Rock turned to the left to scan the room, Tyler poured some of his drink into the other glass. "Besides . . . I thought one of the last guy's problems was too much ambition. I'm happy to stay in my lane and get paid for it."

"What about Connor?" Rock wanted to know.

"What about him?"

"He doesn't seem to like you much." Rock chugged the

last of his beer and signaled the bartender to bring them each a new one. Tyler finished his. He would need to slow down going forward, especially when the barkeep collected the unused glass to the right after dropping off new drinks.

"He treat everyone the same?" Tyler asked.

"Nah. Connor's all right." Another big swig. "I think he just doesn't like you."

"You can't please everyone." Tyler looked over the top of the bar onto the other side. A small prep sink was within reach and basically in front of the stool to his right. So long as Rock looked away and the bartender remained generally inattentive, Tyler could discreetly drain his beer without having to drink it all. He took a sip to keep up appearances. For his part, Ortiz nursed a soda.

"It might help to try, you know." Rock slammed back some more of the dark amber liquid. When he wasn't looking, Tyler poured about a third of his bottle into the sink and then downed a small amount. If he pretended to keep pace, Rock might go on talking.

"Not really my thing," Tyler said.

"It hurt you in the Air Force?"

"Probably. I knew I wasn't going to get promoted past a certain point, so I got out when I could."

"Makes sense," Rock said before polishing off another bottle. He again signaled the bartender for a fresh round. While the young man worked on the new drinks, Tyler dumped out most of his old one. Two fresh frosted longnecks appeared a moment later. After guzzling about a quarter of his third beer in twenty minutes, Rock asked, "You known Felicity long?"

Tyler wished he and Hope worked out a few more details of how their alternate personas knew one another. "Long enough for her to recommend me, I guess," he said. "I was out of the service when we met."

"You do much driving?"

"You mean like she does?" Rock bobbed his head. "Some, but she's better at it than I am."

"And you're a better mechanic than she is." It didn't sound like a question, but Tyler nodded anyway. "Works out pretty well, I guess." Rock again looked around the interior. A few more people had wandered in since Tyler arrived. He needed to wait for another bar patron to glance away before dumping out some of his latest brew. At a table, Ortiz ate an order of mozzarella sticks and kept an eye on Rock without being obvious.

"Seems to go well for everyone," Tyler said.

Rock belched and drank more beer. He couldn't stay much longer if he wanted to make it to the door in a straight line. Tyler caught Ortiz's eye and inclined his head toward the exit. Ortiz made no visible response, but he flagged down the waitress and gave the universal gesture for "bring me the check."

"I guess we'll see how well things go tomorrow," Rock said. He glanced at his watch. "Shit. I oughta go. Gotta be sharp for tomorrow. You got the check?"

Tyler smirked. "Sure. Hope you have a good day at work tomorrow."

"Yeah . . . thanks." Rock slammed the last swallow of beer, slid off the stool, and took a second to find his balance. Tyler considered calling the cops and reporting him for drunk driving. If the police managed to find him in time, Rock would be in trouble. They'd arrest him, and the crew would be down one man. The events which would follow represented a huge unknown. Would Chains and his boss call the job off? Would they power ahead with a diminished crew? Might they press Hope or Tyler into service to make up for Rock being absent? Too many variables. Instead, Tyler made sure Ortiz saw Rock leaving. He offered a slight nod and walked out not far behind his target.

Tyler settled up the tab and headed for the door, too.

32

———————

Ortiz fired up his truck. He watched as the guy Tyler referred to as Rock walked across the lot on unsteady feet. After chugging three beers in under a half-hour, the man was probably in no condition to drive. Ortiz wasn't here to call the cops, however. He would tail Rock and grab some photos. He started when the man approached his Camaro and climbed inside. Ortiz made sure to get the license plate, which was nicely illuminated thanks to the light Rock parked under.

Tyler exited the bar and hopped into a Crown Vic. When Rock pulled away, Ortiz backed out of his parking spot and followed the drunk from the lot. Rock drove slowly at first before getting on the gas, and another car passed Ortiz in this window. He let it happen. Being the second car back in the chain worked better for following someone. Attentive drivers might still spot the tail. Those who were already buzzed, however, would likely miss it.

Ortiz used his truck's built-in GPS to see where Rock might go. About a mile farther along, he turned off the main road onto a side street. It was part of a network on the map. Ortiz went one block past Rock's turn and made a left. He drove down a parallel avenue and spotted the Camaro between gaps in the houses. After a couple stop signs, Ortiz cut over and got behind Rock again. Just after the next intersection, the man slowed and made a right into a driveway.

The house was a boxy Cape Cod like many of the others near it. Beige siding needed a good power washing. Ortiz drove another few homes down, turned around in a driveway, and stopped on the other side of the street. He slumped low when Rock climbed out of the Camaro. It didn't matter. The guy would have missed a clown car in the driveway in his current condition. Ortiz snapped a few more pictures, making sure to include the house number and zooming in on the nearby street sign.

As Rock approached the entrance, the door opened, and an attractive dark-haired woman stood in the opening. She wore a thin nightgown and a smile. Always a winning combination in Ortiz's experience. Rock went inside, and the door closed behind them. Ortiz took another picture to ensure he had a clear shot of Rock's license plate. He started the truck and drove up the road. When he passed a Crown Vic, Tyler called. "Looks like you had no problems."

"It was easy, boss."

"Good. Send me what you got, and I'll share it with the FBI."

"A woman answered the door," Ortiz said. "I don't know if it's her house or his, but she was clearly expecting him."

"Did you get a photo of her?" Tyler asked.

"A couple. You should be able to see her face well enough to ID her. She wasn't wearing much. Make sure you tell your FBI friends I'm not a pervert."

Tyler chuckled. "I'll speak highly of your virtue. Thanks, Ortiz."

"You got it, boss."

Ortiz's drive back to Baltimore proved uneventful. He checked for people following him and saw no one. As he approached his house, he drove around the block and doubled back on himself twice. No one was there. Once he was inside, Ortiz sat in a recliner, removed his prosthetic lower left leg, and took stock of his photographic handiwork. He didn't care for a few but forwarded the rest to Tyler. A moment later, his boss responded with a thank-you text.

Now, it would be up to Tyler and his FBI contact to make the case. Ortiz wondered if they would need him again. Part of him hoped so.

～

JUST AFTER SUNRISE, Tyler met Hope for coffee.

She chose an out-of-the-way diner only regular customers and federal agents could find. Tyler arrived to find Hope already sitting in a booth nursing a white mug of coffee. Maybe a quarter of the seats were full, and the place already smelled of sizzling meat, toasting bread, and java. When he sat across from her, a middle-aged waitress arrived, set an identical mug down, and filled it from the pot. "Thank you," Tyler said.

"What'll ya have, hon?"

"What's she having?" He inclined his head toward Hope.

"She said she was waiting for you," the waitress told him.

"I'll take two scrambled eggs, bacon, home fries, and an English muffin," Hope said.

"Ditto," Tyler said.

When the woman walked away, Tyler took out his phone. "We followed Rock last night." He kept his voice low even though no one sat close to them.

"We?"

"Ortiz helped. I didn't want to run the chance of Rock spotting the Crown Vic. He slammed three beers in a half-hour. I probably could have tailed him in a bright pink hearse, and he would've been none the wiser."

Hope chuckled. "That's an amusing image."

"Speaking of images . . ." Tyler sent the photos Ortiz forwarded him to Hope. When her phone buzzed, she pulled it out to see them.

"Who's the woman?" she asked after scrolling through most of them.

"No idea. It's a different destination than the first time, but I'm not sure whose house it is. I figure you and your people know where he lives."

"We do, but I don't know the address offhand. He's not married, though."

"He seems to have a girlfriend, then," Tyler suggested. "Considering the way she was dressed answering the door in the early evening, I don't think they sat on the couch and read books all night."

"Good job getting a closeup," Hope said.

"Ortiz took the pictures. I let him take the lead tailing Rock. No one's seen his truck, and they're a little more common out here than in Baltimore."

"Nice." Hope slipped her phone away. "I'll send them along. With facial rec and all the databases we can tie into, we'll know who she is, who owns the house, and pretty much everything else." Her knee bobbed up and down.

"Nervous about today?"

"A little," she admitted. "I basically always am."

"You know you're a damn good driver."

Hope smiled. "Thanks. I just . . . I always imagine failing. We can't get away. The locals were too good or too smart. Before they move in to arrest us, Chains pulls out a gun and shoots me in the head." She closed her eyes and took a slow, deep breath.

"I don't think it would happen."

"I know."

"Pop's the trigger-happy one," Tyler said. He grinned when Hope kicked him in the shin under the table.

"Anyone ever tell you you're an ass?"

"At least once a week."

Hope rolled her eyes, and a smile spread across her face. "Thanks. I think I needed that."

"I need some breakfast." Tyler swigged some coffee, and when he set the mug down, the waitress appeared with two heaping plates. After she left, she came back a moment later to top off their coffees.

After wolfing down her eggs and a piece of bacon, Hope said, "I think we'll be okay today. Whoever picks the targets does a good job."

"You think Chains does it or the big boss?"

"I think it comes from the top."

"We're close," Tyler said. "I think we can wrap this up soon. With a little luck and some good research from your colleagues, this could be the last job."

"I hope so." She sipped her coffee. "Thanks, Tyler."

"I'm happy to bust these assholes, too."

"I'm . . . not sure what this means for my career."

"I expect it'll be something good," Tyler said.

"Yeah. It will. I guess . . . I don't know what field office I might get assigned to." She set her fork down and squeezed his hand.

"Do what's best for you." Tyler gave her hand a squeeze. "We're both adults, Hope. I like you, but I don't expect you to damage your career for me."

"I like you, too."

"Just don't let the teacher catch you passing me a note."

She pulled her hand back to keep eating. "I don't think my generation did that. We were already texting by high school." When Tyler frowned to do the math, she added, "I'm thirty-four."

"You must have started on a flip phone, then."

"I did. Still know all the alpha equivalents."

They both finished their plates, accepted coffee refills,

and drained the mugs. "I'm glad you could meet me this morning. It's nice to do this before a job."

"No problem," Tyler said. "I paid for Rock to drink last night, however, so you're picking up the tab for breakfast."

"I guess it's the least I can do." She grinned. "You're officially an unpaid consultant after all."

"We should all get paid after today."

"Fingers crossed," Hope said.

33

Hope climbed into the Grand Marquis.

She ran her hands over the steering wheel. Its leather was old and a little cracked in spots, but it still offered a good grip. The large four-spoke wheel better fit something designed for luxury than speed. She wished Tyler had found a smaller and more maneuverable model, but this would work for a single job. Chains joined her up front, and the other three hopped into the back, putting Pop in the middle. He grimaced when sitting shoulder to shoulder with Rock and Connor.

"I like this better than the Aries," Connor said. "Roomier back here."

"I hadn't noticed," Pop grumbled.

"Weapons check," Chains said. Everyone took out their guns and made sure they were loaded. "Now comms." They all slipped small earbuds in, and each person could hear one another. "Let's go, then." Hope pulled out of the garage. She really wanted this to be the last job. She even considered abandoning the guys inside once they'd passed the point of no return. It was a bad idea, however. They would probably shoot everyone inside, steal a car, and luck into an escape.

Then, she'd be no closer to bringing them in, and they'd all be literally gunning for her.

One more job.

The drive was uneventful. Despite a couple patches of traffic, the crew arrived in town when they wanted to. Doug's Pawn Emporium stood on the left as Hope drove past. She made a U-turn a little farther along and doubled back. Five cars sat in the lot. Too many. She kept going. Considering how trigger happy Pop got in the past, minimizing customers became a priority. Finding a time the place would be totally unoccupied save for employees was unrealistic, but Chains and the big boss wanted to control the variables as much as possible.

After a couple minutes, Hope swung the Mercury back around. This time, only two cars occupied the lot, so she pulled in and parked near the door. "All right," Chains said. "We can expect two employees. Maybe a couple customers. We get in, get the haul, and get out. Let's not shoot anyone." He glared at Pop for a moment. "Clear?"

"Yeah," the others said.

"Felicity is going to wait until we tell her to move to the back. Once she does, we'll run out, pile in, and go. Let's have a clean job." He put a balaclava over his face, and the other three guys followed suit. Hope waited in the car. The front windows allowed her to see into the store. One employee—presumably Doug—stood behind the large counter. His shoulder holster was obvious. He probably thought it made an effective deterrent—and it did against most people. The other guy stocked something on a shelf near the door. The boys would see him first when they walked in.

A few seconds later, they were all inside. Connor moved quickly to cover the second man, whacking him with the butt of a pistol and beating him a few more times once he lay out of Hope's field of view. Two customers lingered nearby, and weapons in their faces made them cower. The crew herded them near the fallen worker to keep everyone in the same area. Connor locked the door.

After reaching toward his weapon, Doug raised his hands. "Back away from the register!" Chains shouted, and his voice came through loud and clear over the comms channel. Doug did. Chains directed him to stand at the far end, and he continued to comply. While Chains, Rock, and Connor smashed the display cases and demanded money from the safe, Pop kept an eye on the second employee and the two customers. One of them asked to leave, promising not to tell anyone what happened. Pop barked at the man to be quiet. Hope wondered if putting him on crowd control was a mistake. If this ended in blood, the group would have plenty more to worry about than another robbery charge.

In addition, the pressure would mount on Hope to wrap things up quickly.

"Hurry," Chains told the others. Their bodies blocked most of Hope's view, but they shoved things into bags. "Doug, you're gonna open the safe." He shoved the proprietor along. "Let's go, and don't waste my goddamn time."

A car slowed, and Hope worried another customer would try to join the fracas and see what happened. Instead, the well-worn SUV turned into a fast food joint nearby. Hope let out a deep breath. "We need to move it along," she said. "No one's come into the lot yet, but a bunch of cars are driving close."

"Get out of the way!" Chains ordered. A whack and a grunt came over the channel. "I'm in the safe," he said a moment later. "Not as much as I wanted. Let's wrap this up. Grab anything valuable you can carry. Pop, help them out."

"What about the other guy?" he asked.

"Is he getting up?"

"He's woozy."

"Let him be, then. Felicity, head to the back in one minute."

"Roger that," Hope said. She'd kept the engine running and gave the parking lot another check. No one else pulled in or slowed. No activity in the mirrors. She put the transmission into reverse and started backing out when the sounds of a commotion came through her earpiece.

"Hey!" Pop shouted. "Stay down, you dumbass."

"What's going on?" Chains demanded.

"I said stay down!"

"Pop! Don't do anything stu—"

The sound of a gunshot rang over the communications line.

It was loud enough to make Hope wince. "Shit," she muttered, putting the Mercury in drive and speeding around the building to the rear. She had a feeling putting Pop on crowd control would come back to haunt the group. He should have strictly been on smash and grab duty. Now, a man was probably dead, and scrutiny on the group would only increase.

A cacophony of voices talked at once. Hope pulled the earpiece out as she waited near the back door.

34

———

The four guys ran out the back door.

Chains opened the front and climbed into the passenger's seat. The other three hurried into the rear. Once Connor made it inside, Hope hit the gas and pulled away. He shut the door and buckled himself in as she drove back around, cut off a car preparing to turn in, and gunned it onto the main road.

"Not a word about what happened in there," Chains ordered. "Not a goddamn word."

"Everybody all right?" Hope asked.

"Yeah," Connor said. He glared sideways at Pop, who sat in the middle. Rock wore a sour expression. It seemed everyone realized the gravity of the situation. They needed to do jobs without additional casualties, and now, another body went against their ledger. Even forgetting about the FBI, this would mean more heat from the locals. A bigger and deeper investigation. Police agencies across state lines would start talking to one another and comparing notes. They'd end up bringing the feds in.

"What a shitshow," she grumbled.

"Not now, Felicity," Chains said.

Hope looked in the mirror. A lone pair of flashing red and blue lights remained in the distance. So far, there had been a minimal police response. However, once the guys left, Doug either called the cops or hit the alarm. The customers probably dialed 9-1-1 if they got over the shock of seeing someone shot in front of them. Either way, she presumed the police knew what happened and where, and they would respond accordingly.

This was the part she liked.

Hope blazed through a red light at speed, drawing a wimpy horn of protest from an old Honda about to turn. The Mustang engine did well in this sedan. It put down more power than the stock motor, and the tweaks Tyler and Ortiz made to the exhaust and suspension allowed for a stiff but pretty compliant ride even over sixty. The speedometer blew past seventy as Hope checked the mirror again.

Two more black-and-whites joined the chase.

"We got a bigger pursuit now," Connor pointed out.

"No shit," Hope said. She slowed a little, taking a curve on screeching tires. At the next intersection, she braked hard and drifted into a smooth turn, getting back on the gas and straightening the car out for the short trip down a side road. In about 500 yards, she turned left onto another state street. The police were too far back to see what she'd done. Still, she gave the Grand Marquis more gas, and it complied. A light turned yellow, but Hope zoomed through doing eighty and still adding velocity.

On this road, she headed east-northeast until taking another. The plan was to stay off the highways, avoiding both heavier patrols and a much higher density of traffic cameras and license-plate detectors. The speed limits were lower on these narrower streets, but the posted rates were usually fifty and up unless within the limits of a town. Hope kept the speedometer near the far right of its travel, rarely dropping below seventy as she headed back toward their destination.

"HE WAS REACHING."

Pop stuck to his story about the pawn shop employee he shot.

"Any chance he might live?" Chains wanted to know. He leaned on a large table which held their weapons and bags of loot.

"Doubt it." Pop shrugged. "I shot the son of a bitch in the chest. Even if an ambulance got there right away, I doubt he made it."

Hope figured the same. Here was another dead body on the group's ledger thanks to their oldest—and least wisest—member. Younger guys like Connor and Rock were idiots sometimes, but they possessed more good operational sense. "Did you really have to shoot him?" Chains pressed.

"I told you . . . he was reaching."

"So shout him down. Kick the gun away. Pistol whip him. Connor already made him see stars. The guy probably couldn't have hit the back wall if we gave him time to line up a shot. He didn't need to die."

"It was my call."

"We'll see," Chains said, and he walked away, slipping his phone out of his pocket.

"You saw him reach, right?" Pop asked everyone else.

"Connor and I were filling our bags," Rock said. "I wasn't looking at him."

"I couldn't see him from outside," Hope said. "Once he fell, he was out of my view."

"You weren't right there," Pop said. "I know what I saw, and I know I made the right call."

"You understand the problem, don't you?" Hope said. "Robbery is one thing. Murder is quite another. We've hit multiple states, but the more bodies that you drop, the more incentive the various police departments have to start talking to one another. It's not a long trip from there to the goddamn FBI getting involved."

"You're making too much of it." Pop crossed his arms. "I don't go into these things looking to shoot anyone. If people sat still and did what we told them, no one would die."

Hope wandered away from the group to try and hear Chains. She figured he talked to his boss, and a cold feeling in her gut told her Pop's fate hung in the balance. "I'm tired of the bastard shooting people," she overheard. There was a pause as Chains—and Hope—needed to wait for the big boss to answer. "How many more? We already have too many bodies on the ledger. I'm sick of him." It sounded like Chains spoke the last four words through clenched teeth. Another short break. "Right. Yeah, I'll do it." Hope made her way back. Connor, Rock, and Pop all looked through the bags. If anyone noticed her drift ten feet and come back, they didn't say anything.

"You can't keep dropping bodies," Chains said. He again stood at the table, leaning down. Hope took up a spot at the far corner. "It's too much." He sighed. "Pop, we've talked about this."

"I told you," Pop protested, "the son of a bitch was reaching."

"And I told you there were other alternatives."

"So what? You're kicking me out?" Chains remained silent. The cold sensation in Hope's gut spread. Pop, undeterred, kept on talking. "I've done a lot for this group. You wouldn't have made all these hauls without me. We're a team, and you don't break up a winning team." When Chains again made no response, Pop asked, "You gonna say anything?"

Chains picked up a double-barreled shotgun, leveled it at Pop, and blew his skull apart with dual blasts.

Blood splattered on Hope as the mostly headless body collapsed to the concrete, and she couldn't help the scream.

"What the hell?" Connor said. Blood and other random bits covered his torso and Rock's.

"Let's clean this up," Chains said. "We need to bury him where no one's going to find him."

35

"WE GOTTA TORCH THE MERCURY, ANYWAY," CHAINS SAID. "Might as well do it with a body inside."

Pop's headless corpse now lay on a tarp Rock bought from a hardware store. He and Connor moved the body onto it and dragged it away. A little blood collected on the dark plasticky surface, but a bunch more remained on the concrete. Connor and Rock worked on cleaning it up—the latter had been smart enough to split his supply run between two different stores and pay cash for everything.

Felicity screamed when Chains shot Pop, and after a couple minutes of rapid breathing, she ran to the bathroom. When she came out, her arm, face, and hair remained wet, and a couple red spots lingered on her shirt. It was white, and Chains figured modesty must have prevented her from turning it sheer with a bunch of water. After a couple more moments spent collecting herself, she chipped in on the clean up. For as good a driver as she was, the last fifteen minutes reminded Chains how Felicity was just a woman as fragile as any other.

Despite the size of the area, the place took on the aromas of industrial cleaner and bleach. At least they overpowered the coppery smell of blood. Chains found a box fan in the office and set it up to blow air out the service bay door. After a few minutes, it helped a little. "Let's get everything in the car," Chains said.

"Everything?" Connor repeated.

"Yeah. We're setting the car on fire. We can burn Pop and everything we used to clean up the mess. Why throw it in the trash?"

"All right." Connor and Rock used sponges to clean up blood and other matter. Felicity worked a mop across a different area of the floor. She wrinkled her nose when squeezing red liquid in the bucket. Every five minutes, she dumped it out for fresh water and cleaner, and it didn't really help much. There was a lot of blood, and the nature of the shot meant its splatter covered a large area. The twelve-gauge did a number on Pop, who chose and deserved his fate.

Once the concrete floor looked clean, Chains ordered a final pass with bleach to be sure. When everyone finished, he said, "Let's load the car."

"Where are we putting the body?" Rock wanted to know.

"Across the backseat."

"What if we get pulled over?"

Chains shrugged. "Don't. Putting it in the trunk means it might not burn as much as we want. Wrap the tarp all the way around Pop, put him across the back, throw in all your dirty towels and rags, add the cleaners, and we're good."

"I don't want to be the one driving," Rock said, crossing his arms.

"I'm out," Felicity said. The others looked at her. "I drove us out of here, and I got blood and who the hell knows what else on me. I'm going home and taking a shower. You boys want to shoot each other, you get to deal with the fallout."

"Fine," Chains said, waving a hand. "Go ahead. We'll be in touch about the next job."

"You're just gonna let her go?" Rock said.

"I think you and Connor can handle it from here," Chains told him. "You know what needs to be done. Find a good place to set the car on fire. One of you drive it, the other follow. This isn't our first rodeo, and it may not be the last." Barbell wanted Chains to take a good look at everyone, and he intended to. Instilling a little fear in them could be valuable. They'd all just seen Pop go from alive to missing his head in the span of a second. It wasn't as grisly as their last mechanic getting pulled apart, but Chains knew it carried the same impact.

Let them be afraid.

ALL DAY THURSDAY, Tyler wondered how the job went.

When he didn't hear from Hope, he grew worried. He couldn't reach out to her without potentially making the others in the group suspicious, however, so he waited and checked his phone periodically. In the evening, Hope finally made contact, sending a short text saying it had been a shitty day, and she was on her way to his place. Tyler wondered what the first part meant, and he remained curious ten minutes later when she knocked on the door.

"We got away clean," Hope said once Tyler locked the door behind her.

"Good."

"Pop's dead."

Tyler frowned. "Can't say I'm sorry, but it does come as a surprise."

"It's a whole story." She sighed, walked to the couch, and plopped down heavily. Tyler sat beside her, and Hope leaned into him. "The job went okay at first. Two employees, two customers. Easy to control. One of the guys beat the other worker, so he wasn't looking to get back into the fight. We were almost done when I hear a gunshot. Pop killed the guy. Tried to say he was reaching."

"Another body," Tyler said, shaking his head. "I'm sure it didn't sit well with Chains."

"Or his boss," Hope said. "The two had a chat once we were back. I tried to overhear it but didn't get much. Anyway, Chains comes back, grabs a shotgun, and blows Pop's head off in front of us." Hope rubbed her arm.

"Were you standing nearby?"

"Close enough to get blood and other shit on me, yeah." She nestled into him more. "It was gross. I've been an agent for twelve years, so I've seen a few things. Felicity, though, is just a hotshot driver, so I screamed and played up how freaked out I was."

"Smart call," Tyler said.

"We all cleaned up the mess, but it meant Connor and Rock had to take Pop to be a part of the car-be-que. I got out of it."

"You know where they went?"

"I think so," she said. "Heard them talking about a couple spots when they were loading the car. Before I left, I told my contact in the Bureau. If it checks out, it's another murder charge to add to the ledger."

"I wonder if the forensic teams will be able to get anything," Tyler said.

"I don't know." Hope slipped her phone out of her pocket. "Those pictures you sent of Rock ended up working, too. The woman popped on facial rec. Her name is Monica Lilly. Rock doesn't have a major online presence, but they're connected on Facebook and Instagram."

"She's his girlfriend?"

"They're not married."

"She have any priors?" Tyler asked.

"Nothing big. A DUI from a decade ago. I doubt she has

anything to do with the crew. If Rock is smart, he's kept her in the dark."

"Does all this get you more time on the clock?"

"It should," Hope said. "Between the burned-out Mercury with Pop's body, whatever intel we can gather from that scene, and this new info on Rock and his lady friend, I think we're making progress." She sighed. "We're going to need to deal with Pop killing the pawn shop employee. Police agencies will talk and realize they need to call us."

"We'll get these guys." Tyler slipped his arm around Hope, who squeezed his forearm and offered a small smile. "Things are falling into place."

"I think they need to fall a little faster," Hope said.

As if on cue, Tyler's burner buzzed. "I'm being summoned to the garage."

"Chains?"

"Yeah."

"Want me to go with you?"

"He didn't tell me to come alone, but I think it's implied."

"How about I linger nearby?"

"Sure," Tyler said.

"You can give me a signal if it looks like the shit is getting too close to the fan."

"All right."

Hope frowned and asked, "What's the signal going to be."

Tyler stood and grinned. "Believe me, if shit happens, you'll know it when you see it."

36

CHAINS STUDIED TYLER AS THE MAN WALKED IN.

He didn't seem like much. Not too tall. Not too big. He kept himself in good shape, but he clearly didn't go to the gym every day. Still, he was fit for a guy either pushing fifty or on the wrong side of it. The blond hair must have been a dye job at his age, but some guys couldn't let go of the way they used to look. Even past the glasses, however, Chains couldn't meet Tyler's stare. For a guy who didn't serve with distinction, he picked up a killer's eyes somewhere along the way.

"Everyone else go home?" Tyler asked.

"Yeah."

"Job go okay?"

"You talk to Felicity?" Chains said.

"No." Tyler shook his head. "Once it got later and I didn't hear from her, I got . . . well, not worried. Concerned."

Chains didn't know whether to believe this. Felicity seemed rattled by Pop's execution. She could have confided in her buddy Tyler, or she might have gone home, internalized everything, and hit the bottle. For now—and considering Tyler gave none of the classic signs of deception—he took the man at his word. "The getaway was clean."

"What about in the shop?"

"Less clean." Chains crossed his arms. He wanted to see if Tyler would push it. If he got too inquisitive, maybe it meant he was something other than what he let on. Instead, the man scratched his head and shrugged. "You're the boss. I'm just the mechanic. I figure you'd tell me if it was important."

"Pop won't be riding with us anymore."

"All right," Tyler said. He didn't follow up with a question.

"Did you like him much?" Chains wanted to know.

"Not really. He held a gun on me when he didn't need to. Connor's just kind of a dick in general, but Pop seemed to have some issues."

"Yeah." Chains bobbed his head. "I guess he did. Anyway, it'll be the three of us plus Felicity on jobs for the time being." He reached into his back pocket and produced an envelope. Tyler caught the toss. "There's your cut. Good job."

"You torch this one, too?"

"Yeah . . . why?"

"Just kind of a shame to have some of my best work go up in flames."

"I guess it is," Chains said. "Let the cash console you. Thanks for stopping by tonight. I'll be in touch when we're ready for another gig."

"Sure," Tyler said. He held up the envelope and added, "Thanks" before pocketing it. Outside, his Ford fired up and headed down the gravelly access road. Chains took out his phone and dialed a number.

"He's leaving now. Crown Vic."

"You want to know where he goes?" the other guy asked.

"Yeah."

"Anything else? Should we rough him up?"

"No," Chains said. "Just follow for now. Let me know when you got him."

After a moment, the reply came. "We got him."

Tyler spotted the tail right away.

On some level, he expected it. Chains didn't come across as guarded or skeptical during their brief meeting, and he should have been both after the day's events. Tyler got the impression he was being sized up, but this happened almost all the time when men who were not—and knew they would never be—friends found themselves in each other's company.

Sending someone to follow Tyler made sense.

The car pulled out from the shoulder after Tyler turned left when the access road met the actual street. The driver kept the headlights off at first, but the silver color didn't exactly blend into the surrounding gloom. The two-lane county road with its absence of illumination meant the headlights came on in short order. Tyler eyed the car in the rearview. The guy behind the wheel took a phone away from his face. Probably the confirmation call from Chains. He shared a quick word with his passenger. Both their faces were shrouded in the poor lighting of the cabin, but they looked white.

Tyler again butted up against what his alter ego should know and be able to do. If he lost his pursuers, would it make Chains suspicious about the real capabilities of Floyd Tyler Rayford? In the end, he figured he could let them linger back there a while. There weren't a ton of places to turn off the main drag yet, so any sudden turns would arouse suspicion in even the most moronic of chasers.

As he drew closer to a curve, Tyler applied the brakes sooner than he needed to. The car behind him crept nearer his rear bumper. It allowed him to read the first three characters of the license plate in the rearview mirror. Four to go. A short distance later, the road bent in the other direction. Tyler did the same thing and discerned the next two. If he wanted to be obvious about what he did, he probably could have gotten all seven on the first try, but if the pair behind him remained in the dark, they'd probably be happy to just cruise along without incident.

A third curve got him the final two. Civilization lay a short distance ahead, and the cross streets would allow Tyler to evade the guys behind him. His Crown Vic wasn't built for speed, but neither was their Kia sedan. When it came down to it, the Ford put out more ponies, so Tyler liked his chances. He eased off the gas approaching a green light, and it turned yellow before he neared the intersection. As it flipped to red, Tyler hit the gas and made a right turn on screeching tires. The back end slid out a little, but a quick steering correction got the big Ford pointed in the right direction again.

The Kia needed to wait for another car to move through before rejoining the chase. Tyler pressed the accelerator and took a left at speed. He didn't really know where he was going, but getting away from the tail was the priority. A couple sudden turns later, he cruised along alone. To be safe, he flipped the headlights off. The Ford lapped up a long straightaway. No other vehicle appeared behind him. Tyler put the lights back on and worked his way back toward his apartment.

He didn't see the Kia again. When he got inside, he called Hope but didn't get an answer. After a few minutes, he tried her again and got the same result. He dialed Lexi next. "Kind of late, isn't it, Dad?"

"If you're going to bed at ten-fifteen, you must not feel well."

She chuckled. "Fine. You got me. What's up?"

"You have the Patriot laptop?"

"Sure. Give me a minute to turn it on." She set the phone down and picked it up again after a brief pause. "Everything all right?"

"Yeah," Tyler said. "I just had a couple clowns following me, and I wanted you to run the plate."

"Couldn't your FBI girlfriend do that for you?"

"She's not my girlfriend." Tyler frowned at hearing the defensiveness in his own voice, but he continued before Lexi could get a word in. "Besides, I tried. She's not picking up."

"Maybe she's in bed."

I doubt it, Tyler thought. He'd learned a few things about Hope's sleeping habits since they started working together—and especially on the occasions they'd shared a bed. "Either way, I can't reach her, so I'd like you to run it for me."

"All right," Lexi said. Her voice changed a little. She must have moved the phone to hold it between her shoulder and ear. "Go ahead."

"Maryland tag, bravo seven three sierra yankee two two."

"Got it." Keys tapped over the connection. "Are we talking about a Kia Optima?"

"Some sort of Kia sedan, yes." They used their own car and didn't even bother swapping on another plate. Stupid.

"Registered to a Brian Mott of Hancock, Maryland. Want me to look him up?"

"If it won't keep you up past your bedtime," Tyler said.

"I'll survive," she said. "One prior for assault. Not a big online presence. I'll send you a link to his profile so you can check him out."

"Thanks, kiddo. Love you."

"Love you, too, Dad. Be safe."

"I will." Tyler used his laptop to follow the Facebook link. Mott kept the bulk of his profile locked down to people he wasn't acquainted with, but Tyler spotted Aidan McCloud on the rather short list of friends. Tyler put all he'd learned into a text to Hope. He figured it would either buy the investigation a little more time or move it closer to completion.

Either worked for him.

37

———

CHAINS HEARD FROM MOTT SOONER THAN HE EXPECTED, AND he figured the news wouldn't be good.

"He got away."

"What happened?"

"Guy's a good driver," Mott said. "Didn't seem like he knew we were there, but he must've. As soon as we hit a bunch of lights, he started making turns and cutting other cars off. There wasn't a ton of traffic, but I lost him somewhere."

"I get the feeling you were overmatched," Chains said. He wondered anew about the increasingly mysterious Floyd Tyler Rayford. A man who didn't have a particularly long or illustrious Air Force career beat the hell out of two guys and lost a tail he must have known was there from the jump. Some things didn't add up.

"Charlie? You want me to do anything else?"

"I'll let you know tomorrow." Chains ended the call. He drank a few beers before going to sleep. When he woke up the next morning, he didn't feel refreshed. Annoyance lingered in the back of his head. Tyler's story didn't match what Chains and others had seen, and the whole mess pointed to Felicity. She recommended him. Said they knew each other. Now, despite her daredevil driving, Chains questioned her loyalty to the group.

After a shower and breakfast to clear his head, he called Mott again. "I want you to follow someone else."

"Who?"

"Our driver. Her name is Felicity. I'll send you her address."

"Will she make me right away, too?" Mott asked.

"I don't know," Chains said. "If she does, let's just say I'll have some additional questions, and she might not want to hear them."

"You want me to get a tracker and put it on her car?"

"Not yet. It's not simply where she goes. I want to know what she does. Who's she talking to? It might matter."

"Dude, I'm not a private detective."

"No," Chains acknowledged, "but you need the work, and I think you can pull it off against most people."

"Sorry about last night."

"Forget it. I'll deal with Tyler another time. Right now, let's shift our focus to Felicity."

"I thought work was going well for you," Mott said. "Why the suspicion?"

"Some bad things have happened recently. An . . . incident in the field meant we had to let someone go unexpectedly. It's time to question everyone, and it starts with the newest folks. I have less time with them, so I also have less trust built up."

"All right. Send me the info, and I'm on it."

"Will do," Chains said, and he ended the call. He found Felicity's info and texted it to Mott. For the first time, he thought about what might happen if the driver wasn't who she claimed. What if she was a cop? Or—worse—a fed? It probably meant Tyler came from a similar background. The group would need to deal with them, and while the idea of tying limbs to cars and pulling two more people apart appealed to Chains on a visceral level, he knew this would be different.

Barbell would want to be involved personally.

~

HOPE WORKED her cover job from home.

She'd taken enough accounting classes in college to fake being a bookkeeper, so the Bureau assigned her—as Felicity Snow—to do it for a local small business. This way, if the robbery gang managed to check her references, Felicity would have a job. It was part-time and didn't require her to commit to a lot of hours. The arrangement left her mostly available for the group except on the occasions she oversold her workload.

Whatever her qualifications, a few hours of spreadsheet work threatened to make Hope's eyes cross. "I need a better cover job next time," she muttered to her empty apartment. If things didn't resolve in her favor, there would be no next time. She might remain an FBI employee, but they would relegate her to a desk job in a shitty location. Quitting would be a good career move at that point.

Hope's phone buzzed. She picked up her burner before realizing the vibration came from her Bureau issue. Patrick Zelhoeffer texted.

> You good to talk?

> Yeah. Working at home. What's up?

> You sent in some good info. We've built more connections. Think we could make a move soon. Hess is more optimistic than I've seen him in a while.

> I'm not sure I've ever seen him smile.

It's pretty rare. :) I want to meet and go over
a few operational things.

How about tomorrow morning?

Sounds good. Usual spot?

Sure. 0900?

See you then.

Hope set her phone down. Thinking of a professional peer as her handler felt weird—and like something out of a Cold War spy movie—but with a little good fortune, the arrangement would end soon. Patrick could go back to kissing Hess's ass, and Hope could pick her next field office. She finished what she was working on and left her chair to look out the window. The sun was close to finishing its descent, and orange light spread from the horizon. On a normal Friday night, Hope would wrap up her week and wonder what she could get into on Saturday and Sunday. Tonight, she would drink a little wine and wish an early Saturday meeting with Patrick to go well.

Hope scanned the parking lot. She knew most of the cars and residents by this point. The only vehicle she'd never seen before was a late-model Kia sedan. It sat in a marked spot. Maybe someone got a new ride. The car appeared empty. Hope kept an eye on it for a few minutes, but nothing changed. She moved away from the window, walked into the kitchen, and allowed herself to feel optimistic that this assignment was coming to an end.

38

———

TYLER WAS OUT OF BED AND EXERCISING ON SATURDAY MORNING when the text came in. Chains wanted him at the garage in an hour. Tyler glanced at his watch—0735. He finished his pushups, crunches, and squats. If he stayed on this job much longer, he would need a third bottle of hair dye and a kettlebell. Once he'd worked up a good sweat, Tyler showered and got dressed. He drove through a McDonald's on the way to the industrial site, polishing off his sandwich and two hash browns as he pulled onto the access road. He would need a cup of stronger coffee later.

Chains was already inside the large open space when Tyler walked through the door. The man stood in front of a crew cab pickup. "This is our next getaway vehicle."

"Planning an off-road escape?" Tyler asked.

"What if I am? We can't always use a sedan."

Tyler shrugged. "An SUV would work. They're the most common vehicle type on the road today. Best for blending in."

Chains crossed his arms. "Yeah . . . I don't see us outrunning the cops in a goddamn CR-V." He jerked his thumb toward the truck. "You'll need to work on this. It's got an eight-cylinder engine at least. I'm sure you can change some things to make it more capable."

"What's my deadline?"

"No rush on this one. We're not doing a job next week."

"Don't want to go in the field down a man?" Tyler said.

"Part of it."

"What's the other part?"

"None of your goddamn business," Chains said. "You're here to take the cars we give you and modify them to outrun the police. If I wanted someone to ask questions, I'd bring in a reporter."

Tyler put up his hands. "All right. I didn't mean any harm." Chains' sour expression didn't waver. He'd never been the warm and fuzzy type, but the man seemed more on edge today than usual. Maybe Pop's unexpected exit from the team weighed on everyone.

"Let's call it ten days," Chains said. He tossed Tyler an envelope of cash. "I'll let you know more once we figure out what and where our next job is gonna be."

"You got it."

Chains grunted and walked out. After he left, Tyler inspected the truck. It was a GMC model and probably about ten years old. A quick check under the hood showed the V8 Chains promised. Like with the Grand Marquis, this engine didn't get installed to make the pickup go zero to sixty in four seconds. It allowed the vehicle to haul and tow good-sized loads. Given enough time—and Tyler had plenty—he could make this work.

If Hope's people did their jobs, this gig wouldn't last another ten days. Tyler locked the garage and left. Hopefully, he'd be back home and working at his own shop early in the coming week.

HOPE MET Patrick at the Central Maryland Diner again. Even on the weekends, the service remained slow but friendly, and the crowds stayed small. Hope wondered how the place managed to keep the lights on. Most of the staff was older than her and closer to her parents' age. Maybe it had been here a while, and the proprietors actually owned the place free and clear. Regardless, she wouldn't need to worry about it much longer.

Patrick already sat in a booth when Hope arrived. She slid in opposite him. "Morning," he said, showing a collegial smile.

"Good morning," she said automatically.

A waitress who must have been twice Hope's age approached with a mug and a coffee pot. She filled the cup for Hope and topped off Patrick's. They both ordered the same things—toast, bacon, eggs, and home fries—before the woman walked away again. Hope's seat allowed her to see through the large window at the front. A normal amount of traffic for a Saturday morning zoomed by in both directions, but no other cars stopped and turned in.

Hope sipped her hot coffee and said, "So Hess is optimistic? I never thought I'd see the day."

"It doesn't happen often."

"Sounds like he thinks we can wrap this up soon."

Patrick nodded. "He does. He's already talked to the US Attorney. More than once, in fact."

"And?" Hope prodded him.

"AUSA is ready to bring charges against everyone. She just wants one more damning bit of evidence."

"The robbery and multiple murders aren't enough?"

"I'm just the messenger." Patrick shrugged. "I swore off trying to figure out how lawyers think a long time ago." When Hope remained silent, he added, "Is there anything else?"

"Pop," she said.

"What?"

Hope made sure she lowered her voice even though no one sat near them. "Chains killed one of the gang members. He went by Pop because he was the oldest. He was also the most trigger-happy. I think he shot everyone who died on the jobs . . . including the pawn shop robbery. Chains talked to the big boss. I tried to overhear at least one end of the conversation, but I really couldn't. When he came back, he grabbed a shotgun, and that was it." A shudder crawled along Hope's spine as she remembered the boom and belch from both barrels, blood splattering on her, and Pop's mostly headless body collapsing to the floor.

"You as a witness is a good thing," Patrick said. "Your sworn testimony will help. A body would help more."

"I know."

"Did they bury him?"

Hope shook her head as the waitress approached, dropped off their food, and left again. She looked at her plate and wondered if she could eat anything. Remembering the gory details of Pop's execution sapped her appetite. "Car-be-que," she said after a moment, frowning at her bacon.

"You know where?"

"Not exactly, but I can come up with some ideas. You could compare it to anything that's been reported. Locals might have already found it."

"All right," Patrick said around a bite of toast. "Send me your list."

"I will."

They both ate for a few minutes—Hope reluctantly at first until hunger took over—before Patrick spoke again. "Maybe this'll be my last trip to Hagerstown."

"Too country for you?"

"Too far," he said. "I like working in and around Baltimore. Ninety minutes for coffee and a so-so breakfast kinda sucks."

"You can complain about the miles when you go for SSA."

Patrick chuckled and raised his mug. "Fair enough. I guess you'll be moving along after this?"

"Probably. I need a change."

"Well, good luck to you."

"Let's put a wrap on this one before we break out the confetti," Hope said.

39

———————

Chains' phone buzzed with a call from Brian Mott.

"You have something for me?" he demanded.

"We're still tailing the girl."

"And?"

"She's meeting some guy for breakfast in a diner."

"I'm going to send you a picture." Chains found a good capture of Tyler's face from the garage's security cameras and texted it to Mott. "Is this the guy she's eating with?"

"No," Mott said. "This guy's younger."

Chains frowned. As far as he knew, Felicity didn't have a boyfriend. As often as Connor and Rock hit on her, she'd had plenty of chances to mention it—for all the good it would have done her with those two. "Describe this guy."

"You want us to go in?"

"No. I don't want her to see you in case we need to take action later. Where are you?"

"Across the street," Mott said. "Old tire shop closed for repairs. We got binoculars, but we gotta be careful not to use them when a load of cars are going by. Don't want to attract attention."

"Fine," Chains said, rolling his eyes. "Have you been able to get a good look at him?"

"More or less. He's blond, probably twenty years younger than the guy you showed me." Mott paused. "Seeing him again, I'd guess he's a cop. He has the look about him."

"Shit," Chains muttered. This didn't mean Felicity's breakfast companion was actually in law enforcement, but like most criminals, Mott possessed a good sense for sniffing out cops. "I'll need to confirm who he is."

"How?" Mott wanted to know.

"Don't worry about it. I have my ways. Can you get a good picture from where you are now?"

"No. We just have our phones."

"All right," Chains said. "Get closer, then. Park in the lot of wherever they are. Don't go in, and try not to be obvious for Christ's sake. I need a good photo of the guy she's with."

"Will do. I'll send you what we can get."

Chains pocketed his phone and stewed. If he presumed Felicity met with the police, was she one of them? If not, how did they get their hooks into her? Was she setting the gang up for failure this whole time? Chains took a deep breath and tried to stop badgering himself with so many questions. He got up and paced around his living room. A few minutes later, his phone vibrated again. Mott sent three photos, and all of them were clear enough to get an ID. When the man called a moment later, Chains said, "Good work."

"What's next?"

"Get out of there. I'll call you if I need you again. When this is all over, I'll make sure you get some money."

"Sounds good," Mott said, and he ended the call.

It was time to find out who Felicity and her mysterious breakfast companion really were.

A KNOCK at the apartment door stopped Tyler's food prep. He carried his pistol to the entryway. A single set of shadows showed in the small gap between the door and the thin carpet on the other side. He stood to the side as best he could while looking through the peephole. It was Hope. He swung the door open, and her eyes fell almost immediately to the gun in his left hand. "Expecting someone else?" she wondered.

"You never know. Chains sent a couple tweakers to test me . . . or whatever they were doing there."

"With Pop dead, I think he's going to be suspicious for a while. It's what he does."

After Hope walked in and Tyler locked up behind her, he asked, "Did the same thing happen when they killed the last mechanic?"

"More or less. I was still sort of new then, so I probably didn't see all of it. The guys changed a little, though. More sullen. Shiftier eyes." Hope dropped onto the living room couch. "I actually came by to give you some good news."

"I could use some," Tyler said as he sat beside her.

"I talked to a guy from the Bureau this morning." She chuckled. "He's calling himself my handler now. Whatever. Anyway, his boss is optimistic, and he's recommended charges to the US attorney. Seems like things will be moving quickly in the coming week."

"Excellent."

"You . . . don't seem convinced."

Tyler shrugged. "I've seen enough optimism evaporate. We heard good news coming out of Washington a truckload of times. By the time it got to Afghanistan, most of it melted. It never really translated to the men and women with their boots on the ground."

"You're cynical."

"I'm experienced."

Hope frowned. "I'm going to choose to believe the Bureau

on this one. I know they want to tie a pretty bow on this one, and I think we're getting close."

"I admire your optimism," Tyler said.

"Can you share it?" Hope asked.

"Maybe after another positive development."

"I think we'll see one soon."

"It would be nice," Tyler admitted. "The gang is continuing. Chains called me to the garage this morning. A crew cab pickup is the next getaway vehicle. Maybe they expect you to go off-roading for the next escape."

"Not ideal . . . I'm better on cement and asphalt." She leaned back and looked up at the ceiling. "I can see my career getting back on track. It's close."

"I hope it works out for you," Tyler said, and Hope smirked. "Sorry. It's kind of hard to avoid using your name in certain contexts."

"I think it's why my father named me Hope. People say it every single day." Hope shifted, putting her head on Tyler's shoulder and tucking her feet under her. "I'm glad I met you, Tyler."

"Me, too."

"You're just saying that because we're good in bed together."

He chuckled. "Well, it's on the list of reasons, sure. Someone needs to stop these guys. It's good we're doing it together."

"It is."

"You going to look me up when you get a tough case at your next field office?" Tyler said.

"Maybe. You up for a road trip if I do?"

"Maybe. What would be in it for me?"

Hope grabbed Tyler's hand and placed it on her thigh. She moved it up and smiled. "Take a guess."

40

Chains texted a contact he called on in dire circumstances. *Need to run a couple things by you. Can we meet?*

A few minutes later, a reply flashed on his screen. *Come to the house. Bring food and money.*

"The usual," Chains muttered. He drove through a Burger King, picked up enough food to feed himself and at least two other people, and headed into Frederick. His acquaintance lived in a small old house on the outskirts of downtown. Instead of the more common Victorian model, this was a compact rancher. Chains knocked on the door, and an electronic lock disengaged.

The living room was a mess when he walked in. He'd learned to get used to it. Pizza boxes, food wrappers, dirty dishes, and empty Mountain Dew cans lay strewn about the place. The house smelled like old food, must, and body odor —the latter growing stronger as Chains made a left and headed down the short corridor to the office.

A man sat at a desk with three monitors atop it, the one on the right oriented vertically for some reason. Chains didn't know his actual name. He only ever called the guy Cobra after a tattoo on his arm. Cobra looked to be in his thirties, was about six feet tall, and nearly as wide. He must have been four hundred pounds. Cobra's background was something of a mystery, but Chains knew he'd worked as a contractor for federal law enforcement agencies. This level of access plus a malleable morality made him a good man to know.

"Burger King," Cobra said in a nasal voice belying his massive frame. "I didn't know you cared."

"Me, either." Chains sat the larger bag and a big cup of sugary soda on one of the few empty spots on the desk. The office wasn't quite as messy as the living room, but this probably owed to its smaller square footage. Chains sat in a guest chair, tried to ignore the fact Cobra badly needed a shower, and opened his own bag of food. Aromas of the burger and fries masked the unpleasantness around him.

"What do you have for me?"

"A few people I'd like to know about." Chains took out his phone, found the photos, and sent them to a secure email address. "You should have them now."

After a couple mouse clicks, Cobra confirmed receipt. "You want me to run these in the order you sent them?"

"Sure." Chains took a bite of his Whopper and tried not to watch as Cobra crammed way too much of a chicken sandwich into his mouth.

"The blond guy is a fed," Cobra said after a moment.

"Like FBI?"

"Yeah. Special Agent Patrick Zellhoefer, assigned to the Baltimore field office. He works for SSA Jason Hess."

"Shit."

"I can see why you wouldn't want this guy around."

"What about the woman?" Chains asked.

Cobra picked up two chicken nuggets, shoved them into his mouth, and still managed to find room for a few fries. Chains averted his eyes and focused on his own dinner. After a minute, the fat man said, "No exact match. There's a close comp, though." He turned the vertical monitor around. "Meet

Special Agent Hope Raines." Chains studied the photo. The hair and eyes were different, but this woman otherwise looked like Felicity's twin.

"Another goddamn fed," Chains grumbled.

"Sounds like you have a personnel problem."

"We'll handle it. What about the last guy?"

Cobra spun the screen back around and worked the keyboard. He soon shook his head. "No match in any federal law enforcement database."

"So this guy's not a fed?"

"No." Cobra winced. "Jesus! He has a killer's eyes. My guess is he's ex-military. Probably special forces of some sort. They don't put guys with thousand-yard stares like this in the band."

"Can you get into those databases?" Chains wanted to know.

"Sure," Cobra said. "It'll take even more time and cost you some extra money. Maybe a lot depending how hard the process is."

"Forget it." Chains shook his head. "You've given me enough to act on. Cash is at the bottom of the bag."

"I saw it."

"Thanks." Chains stood and headed for the door.

"Until next time," Cobra said.

Chains walked away from the office. The smell of body odor lessened, but his mood didn't improve. Felicity—or Hope—or whatever her name was worked as a fed. She was in contact with at least one more. Her friend the mechanic probably had a different background than advertised. The gang was already down one member in Pop, but Chains knew more upheaval would soon be coming.

He understood what he needed to do.

Tyler locked the apartment door once Hope left.

He smiled as he closed up shop. When Hope first approached him about working with her, Tyler noticed her obvious beauty right away. He never expected the two of them to become lovers. After his relationship with Sara Morrison cratered a few months back, Tyler didn't look for anything new. He understood Hope needed to worry about her career first. They were having fun, and the whole thing made him feel younger again.

A short while later, as Tyler ate dinner, his phone vibrated. The number looked familiar, so he answered. "How's consulting?" SSA Roland Johnson asked.

"Doesn't pay very well," Tyler said. "I'm surprised you're calling. I keep hearing about the Baltimore field office."

"This group has caused problems in multiple states. I oversee the cases in some of them. We're all working together."

"One big happy FBI family."

Johnson chuckled. "You might be going a little far there, but everyone wants to see these guys go down."

"So do I."

"US attorney is pretty far down the road on warrants. I think the legal end of the case is going to end up moving very quickly."

"Good." When Tyler fell silent, Johnson didn't say anything. Tyler's normal tactic was to remain quiet and let the other person start rambling, but this didn't work against someone with the kind of training a supervisory special agent received. So Tyler added, "What are you calling to tell me?"

"I don't think we need you on this anymore," Johnson said.

"Your opinion is noted."

"And?"

"And Hope brought me in," Tyler said. "When she tells me I can walk, I'll go."

"Look, Tyler . . . we don't need civilians hanging around the investigation." Tyler chuckled. "What?"

"I'm sorry. Did I miss you becoming a commander in the Navy? Maybe Hope is a lieutenant now?" Johnson didn't say anything. "Everyone attached to this is a goddamn civilian, Roland."

"You know what I mean."

"Yes," Tyler said. "I'm not a fed, and you don't want me around when the shooting starts. Even though I'm probably better equipped to handle it than most of the people you might send."

"Little full of yourself, aren't you?"

"I'll let my service record speak for me."

Johnson sighed. "Here's the deal. I think we're close to wrapping this up. My guess is our criminal friends aren't going to go quietly. I can't guarantee your safety if you're still around."

"I'm well aware the FBI can't guarantee my safety. A few of the clowns in your employ gave me a first-hand demonstration last year."

"Take all the potshots you want, Tyler," Roland said. "I'm trying to let you exit gracefully with the thanks of the Bureau."

"I'll exit when Hope tells me she doesn't need me anymore," Tyler said. "Until then, if I need the FBI to protect me, I might as well open a bike shop at the beach." Johnson started to say something else, but Tyler ended the call. Gourmet meals like his hot dogs and potato salad couldn't wait. When he finished eating, he texted Hope. *Johnson just called me. Can't guarantee my safety, etc. I told him I'd be done when you dismissed me.*

She didn't reply.

41

———————

CHAINS CALLED BARBELL TO GIVE HIM THE BAD NEWS.

As usual, they talked over video with the group leader standing in shadow. Chains already knew what the man looked like and had met him several times. Normally, the extra precautions didn't bother him. Tonight, after everything he'd learned today, they did. "I didn't think we needed to chat for a few days," the boss said.

"This is important."

"What is it?"

"We have a big personnel problem," Chains said. "After the whole Pop situation, I've had some guys I know keep tabs on the group. Felicity had breakfast with a fed."

"You know he's a fed?"

"Yes. I had someone look into it. Patrick Something-or-other out of the Baltimore field office. He's not our only problem, though." Chains sighed. "It's Felicity."

"You found out she's a fed, too?"

"I did," Chains said. Barbell's phrasing made him frown. Did the other man know something he wasn't letting on? "She's FBI agent Hope Raines." Barbell lapsed into silence.

"My guess is she infiltrated our group to try and bring us down."

"What about the new mechanic?" Barbell demanded.

"Not a fed. As far as I can tell, he's ex-military, but my source's guess is the guy is underselling his experience."

"What the hell did you do to my robbery ring?" Barbell grunted. "This is some serious shit. How do you propose cleaning it up?"

"I was going to ask you."

"No." Barbell shook his head. "No. You got us into this mess. If you want me to resolve these problems, my first step is a bullet in your damned head. Still want me to take the lead?"

"No," Chains muttered.

"Good. Now, tell me how you're going to get us out of this."

"We round up this Hope and her friend, and we kill them."

"Not bad."

"She's a good-looking woman," Chains said. "Maybe the boys should have some fun with her first."

"Absolutely not," Barbell said.

"What?"

"You heard me. I want you to take Hope Raines alive. If she fights back and someone needs to punch her, so be it, but I will not stand for anyone violating her. Am I clear?"

"Sure," Chains said. This was a weird conversation. Barbell never shied away from violence or barbarism before. He loved seeing the gruesome videos and photos of the prior mechanic getting torn to pieces. Why draw a line with this traitorous woman? She was alone in a group of men. She knew the risks. "What about Tyler?"

"Bring him alive, too, if you can. I want to talk to them both before they die."

"Are we taking them to you?"

"Yes. I want them here tomorrow. If the feds are trying to bust us, they're less likely to work on weekends. If we dismantle their case and kill their agents before Monday, this whole thing might go away."

"You think it'll be so easy?" Chains asked.

"Maybe not. We might need to lay low for a while. Maybe relocate our operation to a different part of the country. The heat will die down at some point. You make sure they make it here. I'll take care of the rest."

"I will." Chains stared at his phone after Barbell broke the connection without saying anything else. For the first time since meeting the man, he found himself questioning his boss's wisdom.

HOPE COOKED a late meal at her cover apartment.

After staying in a motel the first couple weeks she'd worked the assignment, Hope had gotten used to this place. In some ways, it was nicer than her house. Home offered a little more space, but the apartment featured newer paint, updated appliances, and better furniture. It was almost a shame the Bureau wouldn't let her keep using it.

Hope dropped dry spaghetti noodles in a pot of boiling water. A smaller pan held her sauce. In her home kitchen, she liked to take the time and make it from scratch. Here, it came from a jar with a few shakes of spice added for extra flavor. She thought about sharing the meal with Tyler. She left his place to come back here and eat despite the fact they'd done dinner together before. The first time she jumped his bones, in fact, they left carry-out waiting in the hallway. Hope wondered how many dinners she and Tyler could share. Would he want to see her every day? She smiled at the thought. Hope liked Tyler and enjoyed his company— even out of the bedroom. It seemed silly, but as she stirred her marinara, she wondered if they might take a shot at having some semblance of a future together.

Once the pasta cooked for about eight minutes, she upended the pot into a strainer. Hope killed the burner the sauce still simmered on. She'd just gotten a plate down from a cabinet when someone knocked on the door. Maybe it was Tyler. Hope smiled at the possibility as she walked toward the peephole. The happiness didn't last, however. Rock stood on the other side. Hope opened the door. "Felicity," he said.

"What's going on, Rock? It's not like you to make a house call." She wished she'd brought a gun to answer his knock, but her silly wish that Tyler came by to eat dinner with her made her not think about it in the moment.

"I know." From the left, Chains and two other men barged in. Both strangers were big and brawny, and Hope thought they were Rock's friends Tyler caught on camera. Each grabbed one of her arms and steered her into the living room. Chains closed and locked the door.

"Hope Raines," he said. Hope didn't reply and fought to keep her expression neutral. "You've been lying to us."

"You've been killing people," she said. "Did you really think no one would notice?"

Chains slowly approached. As he stood before her, he ran the back of his hand over her face. Hope tried to recoil, but she could only move so much with the goon squad holding her in place. Chains took his hand away, drew it back, and punched her hard in the stomach. She bent in half as the blow blasted the air from her body. "You deceitful bitch," he growled near her ear. "You're lucky. If I had my way, I'd let these guys take you down the hall and come back for what's left of you in a few hours. Our leader doesn't like my approach, so I'm playing it his way. You give me any trouble, though, or if you scream, I have three guys who won't mind punching you until the lights go out. Maybe a little after, too. We clear?"

"Yeah," Hope croaked.

Chains punched her in the face anyway. "Get her out of here," he ordered. The beefy guys lifted Hope off her feet and carried her out the apartment door. She didn't know what her chances of surviving the next twenty-fours were, but the gang knew her real name and occupation.

She'd probably be dead soon.

42

Rough hands pushed Hope forward.

Once Chains, Rock, and company got her into the waiting van, one of the men put a black bag over her head. She couldn't see anything through it, and the guy tied it enough to prevent her from discerning much of value through the gap between the canvas and her neck. They left it on even when the vehicle stopped some twenty minutes later. Hope had tried to keep tabs of time and turns, but they changed direction so often that she lost track.

Two hands hoisted her in the air, carried her a short distance, and then threw her down. She landed on something soft. More rough fingers held her legs while someone else tied ropes around her ankles. She tried to resist when someone forced her arms over her head, but a punch to the face left her woozy and unable to fight back. Her wrists got bound like her ankles. The restraints weren't tight enough to cut off blood flow though they didn't miss by much. Hope could barely move, and metal rattled whenever she tried. She got the sinking feeling these brutes tied her to a bed. "Let me go!" she shrieked. Footsteps moved away, and a door slammed shut.

Hope tried to gulp in air, but the bag over her head made it difficult. She focused on slower breaths to calm herself. She was at an unknown place with Chains, Rock, and at least two others with ill intent. Her cover had been blown somehow. She wondered if Tyler was all right. Maybe Chains or Connor's natural suspicion led to them grabbing him, taking a power drill to his knees, and learning what they were really up against. They'd mercilessly killed the last mechanic. Torture was definitely in the toolbox.

As much as she cared for Tyler, Hope couldn't worry about him now. He was a capable operator. She needed to try and get herself free and take out these assholes. Moving her legs more than an inch or so proved impossible. Ditto her arms. She couldn't reach the knots for an attempt to untie them, and the canvas sack prevented her from seeing anything. Hope needed to raise and move her head occasionally to prevent the bag from settling and remaining across her nose and mouth.

An unknown time later, the door swung open with a quiet squeak and then closed again. A single set of footsteps approached. The bag came off Hope's face, and one of the guys she didn't know glared down at her. His eyes scanned her body, lingering on her hips and chest, and fear gripped her. She was in the most vulnerable position imaginable, and a large man who cared little for her well-being stood over her. "Who the hell are you?" she demanded in a raspy voice.

"Doesn't matter," the man said. He sat on the side of the bed, the outside of his hip against hers.

"Chains know you're in here?"

"Doesn't matter," he repeated and lifted her sweater to place a large hand on her stomach. Hope wanted to recoil, but her restraints kept her in place. "I don't take orders from his boss. What he don't know won't hurt him."

"I'll scream."

"I'll knock you out." His hand—which had come to rest just below her breasts—drew back and became a fist. "You don't need to be awake to give me what I want."

The door opened, and Chains moved into the room. "Get out," he barked.

"I was just—"

"Out!"

The guy glared at Hope, fixed Chains with a similar look, but finally stood. He left without a word. Chains closed the door again. "I know you're here against your will, but I don't want to see anything really bad happen to you."

"And they say chivalry is dead," Hope muttered.

"You want me to call him back in here?"

"I don't think your boss wants that."

"You're right." Chains nodded and sat where the other man did. He made no attempt to grope Hope, at least. "What he really wants is to know what he's up against."

"Just me."

"Who's your friend?"

"Tyler?"

"Yeah," Chains said. "Don't try to tell me he's just some ordinary mechanic you happened to know. I'm aware you've met with the FBI at least once and probably more. Is Tyler a fed, too?"

"No," Hope said.

"Who is he, then?"

She shrugged as much as the ropes holding her would permit. "Just some ordinary mechanic I happen to know."

Chains drew his hand back and punched Hope hard in the stomach. She wanted to curl up but couldn't move. "Do I need to remind you about Durant?"

Fighting to draw another breath, Hope could only shake her head.

"He overstepped," Chains said, ignoring Hope's silent

response. "We did a little research into how we might kill him. Even practiced some. Once he was all trussed up to the cars, we gave them a little gas. Tightened all the chains. Stretched his joints. Remember him screaming? He knew what was coming. Poor bastard probably had his shoulders and knees pop out before we all floored it and tore him apart." He made sure to look into Hope's eyes. "I really don't want to see the same thing happen to you."

"Piss off," Hope said.

"Have it your way." Chains stood. "We'll get Tyler one way or another, and you'll both go to see Barbell. If you tell me what I want to know, maybe your meeting with him won't be so unpleasant."

"Like I told you ... piss off."

Chains shrugged and left the room, slamming the door shut in his wake.

HOPE SOMEHOW MANAGED to get a little sleep. Rock or Chains untied her long enough to let her use the toilet, eat a granola bar, and drink some water. Then, it was back into bondage. They always brought one of the muscleheads with them for backup. Hope was determined not to cry. She woke up sometime Sunday morning.

Chains returned to the room. One of the goons waited outside. He wore the same black shirt and jeans as the day before. "Want to tell me anything today?" he asked, standing near the bed with his arms crossed.

"Besides 'piss off,' you mean?"

"Yes."

"No," Hope said.

"You and Tyler ... or whatever his name is ... did a good job fooling us. I tried to have him tailed a couple times, and he shook them. Sent a couple tweakers after him. I think he's more than you let on. I don't doubt the military angle, but my guess is he was in some kind of special forces. He wasn't just a grunt who got out at the first real chance." Hope remained silent. "I'm right, aren't I?"

"You think I'm going to help you capture him?"

"With the proper motivation," Chains said.

"You gonna hit me again? Does punching a tied-up woman make you feel like a big man?"

"As a matter of fact, it does." One step got him to the bed, and he punched her in the midsection again. Hope grunted in pain, and Chains hit her in the stomach again and again. By the end of the barrage, she struggled to breathe, and tears ran down her cheeks. "I could do this all day, but you can't." He moved closer and ran the outside of his hand over her cheek, wiping up some of the wetness. "You're a pretty woman, Hope. It'd be a shame to ruin this face."

"What's it matter?" Hope said. "You and your master are just going to kill me anyway."

"I don't know what's going to happen," Chains said, and Hope snorted. "I'm serious. I know he wants you alive and in mostly good condition. He told me the same for Tyler, too."

"Really?"

"Really. We're going to take him alive. If you tell us where he is, it'll go easier."

Hope pondered this. She didn't want to give up Tyler, but if Chains and crew spent hours looking for him, the instructions might be different. Barbell could tire of the delays and simply tell his men to torture and kill Tyler. Finding him sooner meant his survival was more likely. Besides, he might turn the tables and kill the crew. As much as she wanted to remain silent, she decided to roll the dice on taking Chains at his word and Tyler getting the best of whoever went to collect him. "Fine."

"Who the hell is he?" Chains demanded. "I want to know."

"He's a retired Green Beret."

"I figured as much. Now . . . where can I find the son of a bitch?"

43

———

By Sunday morning, Tyler grew concerned he didn't hear back from Hope.

He knew she sometimes needed to work her cover gig, and perhaps the demands of her actual FBI job caused her to be in the office working the case. She'd talked about the optimism from the Baltimore field office, and an AUSA being close to moving ahead with arrest warrants. Depending on where she was on an FBI campus, Hope's phone might be in a locker somewhere while she toiled away in a secret or top secret facility.

Still, Tyler was concerned.

A knock at the door gave him a moment of positivity. He wanted it to be Hope, but he carried a pistol to the door in case it wasn't. The sour face of Connor looked back from the other side of the peephole. "What do you want?" Tyler asked.

"Need to talk to you. Can I come in?"

"You can talk from there."

"It's pretty awkward," Connor said. Tyler agreed. He looked through the peephole again, saw only Connor, and relented. When he unlocked the door, Tyler kept the pistol held against his hip. "You don't need the piece." Connor remained in the doorway and finally advanced into the apartment.

As if on cue, he stepped to the side, and a massive man surged in behind him. Tyler tried to get the gun up, but he was a tick late, and the larger man swatted it away. He shoved Tyler back, and he rebounded off the wall of the entryway. Tyler ducked a haymaker which put a serious dent in the drywall. He stayed low and punched his bigger foe hard in the gut. Connor tried to grab him from behind, but Tyler's elbow connected with something solid, and Connor backed off. Tyler turned to face him.

Only then did he hear a third set of footsteps.

He turned, but Connor's other brutish friend was already on top of him. The third man through the door clobbered Tyler in the face. This time, after he bounced off the drywall, Tyler fell to the floor. Large boots kicked him in the ribs and drove the breath from his lungs. "Enough," Connor said, and both his lackeys backed away. Connor walked closer and crouched near Tyler. "I don't know who you really are, but your story is bullshit."

Tyler was outnumbered and over-matched physically. He hoped to keep the trio—especially Connor—talking long enough to come up with the second part of his plan. "It's a little embellished."

"No. It's bullshit. So is 'Felicity.'" He added air quotes when referring to Hope's cover identity, and Tyler frowned. "Yeah, we know who your girlfriend really is. The question is . . . who are you?" He leaned a little closer. When he did, one of the large goons moved with him. With the heat of the moment down to a simmer now, Tyler realized they were the pair he photographed the week before. Connor reached out and plucked the glasses from Tyler's face. He held them in front of his own. "Fake. Clear lenses." Connor tossed the spectacles aside and stared at Tyler. "You know what I think?"

"Can't wait to find out," Tyler said.

"I think we saw you at the jewelry store outside Baltimore. You were the one who helped the old man to the back and tried to help the employees get free. The dye job and glasses were good. You even made your voice a little different." Connor let out a dry chuckle. "Christ, I never wanted Pop to shoot people, but I wish he'd plugged you then. How the hell did you end up working with Felicity . . . or whoever she is?" Tyler remained silent.

"We grabbin' him?" one of the meatheads asked.

"In a second. Is Tyler even your name?"

"It is."

"Let me tell you how this is going to go, Tyler," Connor said. "I never really trusted you, and now I know I was right to be suspicious. Your girlfriend is with a couple of friends. They're already on the way north to meet the big boss. He wants to see you, too, and he told us to bring you alive. He didn't say anything about unharmed." Connor flashed a wolfish grin. "You come quietly, and we won't rough you up. You resist, and you'll regret it. Clear?"

Tyler didn't have a better option at the moment. Any of the three men around him could prevent him from regaining his feet, and he wasn't going to win a fight from the floor. Waiting represented the best play for now. Most operations were vulnerable in transport. He could try to get away then—when his captors would be less inclined to expect it. "Yeah. Clear."

"Good." Connor tossed handcuffs to one of the goons, who pulled Tyler to his feet with little effort. He slapped the metal restraints on but made the mistake of binding Tyler's hands in front of his body. Connor picked up the gun Tyler dropped a few minutes before. "Now, I want to be sure you don't give us any trouble on the ride." Before Tyler could say anything, Connor whacked him in the head with the butt of the pistol.

~

HOPE RODE with a bag over her head again.

As before, she didn't know where they were headed. This drive took much longer, however. After some initial slow going, whatever vehicle her captors used maintained highway speeds for quite a while. It felt like hours, but the bag blocked anything like signs, mile markers, or even the sun Hope might use for a frame of reference. Her hands were bound with rope behind her back. The feel of a leather seat was constant.

At some point, they took a right turn at speed, jostling Hope on the rear cushion. The vehicle slowed after this, however. They must have been back inside a town. An indeterminate time later, they took another right. The drive was slower now, and Hope heard the occasional other car on the road. At some point, the vehicle made a left, and the tires crunched over gravel and small stones. When the driver stopped, doors open, and rough hands yanked Hope from her seat.

She tried to look around, but the black sack and the man herding her inside didn't give her the chance. Once a door closed behind them, someone yanked the bag from Hope's head. She sucked in a deep breath and took in her surroundings. This place looked like another body shop and garage, though the parts suggested it catered to motorcycles as well as cars. It sat in the middle of a large lot covered with gravel. A few cars and bikes in varying states of repair stood outside. A large grassy field lay across the lot. Hope looked out the side window and saw train tracks to the north. She still had no viable clue where she was.

Chains and Rock waited nearby along with three other burly guys Hope had never seen before. "Where the hell are we?" she asked. No one answered right away, so she repeated the question.

"You'll find out soon enough," Chains said, his eyes coming to rest on a door which probably led to an office and the back of the shop.

"So . . . is this where your boss makes a dramatic entrance?"

"I don't think you're in a position to ask smart-assed questions," Rock said.

"Screw you," Hope said. She jabbed a finger in Chains' direction. "You listen to him no matter what. Guys like you are all about freedom until you find someone who shouts the orders you always wanted to follow anyway. You're pathetic." Rock scowled, rushed forward, and punched Hope hard in the midsection. With her wrists tied, she couldn't defend herself. The punch folded her in half, and once more she had to struggle to draw in her next breath.

"Take it easy, goddammit," Chains said in a harsh whisper. "He doesn't want us hurting her."

"Why?" Hope said when she could speak again. "You couldn't let the boys have their way with me. I had to come here alive. Now, you can't lay a hand on me. Why not? What am I missing?"

The door swung in, and a man's form filled the opening. The lighting behind him prevented Hope from getting a good look at his face, and he made no effort to come forward. "You're missing a lot, Hopester," a familiar voice from long ago said. "I'm very disappointed. How many times did I tell you I was placing all my hopes and dreams with you?"

Hope's mouth hung open as the man moved into the room. He was about sixty, tall, and still broad-shouldered. The long hair hanging down to his chest was a mix of coal gray and black. His eyes were cold—colder than she remembered—and whatever warmth his face held years ago was long gone now. Hope managed to croak only a single word.

"Dad?"

44

<hr>

L EXI TOOK TIME OUT FROM HOMEWORK ON A S UNDAY TO CALL her dad.

No answer. She waited a few minutes and tried again. Same result. She knew he still worked on the robbery ring case with the FBI agent. Lexi hoped he didn't find himself in hot water again. He couldn't turn away from it, even when it was someone else's kettle too close to the fire. She sent a text asking how he was and went back to her essay.

About an hour later, she still hadn't gotten a response. Lexi called Ortiz, and he picked up despite it being the weekend. "I haven't see him in a few days," Ortiz said when Lexi asked.

"Was he all right then?"

"Sure. We were working on tailing some guy to try and get more information. It's easier with a two-man crew."

"Did you get what you needed?" Lexi wanted to know.

"I think so. I took some photos, and your dad said he was going to send them to the FBI lady."

"I just get the feeling he's landed in the soup again."

Ortiz chuckled. "He does have a habit of it. Look, you

know he's good at what he does. Your dad hasn't found himself in a bad spot he can't get out of yet."

"Yet," Lexi repeated. How much longer would it remain true. He was fifty-two and would turn fifty-three soon. At some point, going against younger, stronger opponents who possessed a numerical advantage would be insurmountable even for a capable and experienced operator.

"I'm off today," Ortiz said. "I can drive up to Hagerstown and see if I run into him."

"Thanks, Ortiz, but we don't know if he's there. Maybe later if we still haven't heard anything."

"All right. Keep me in the loop."

"I will." Lexi ended the call. Smitty might have been a great mechanic who interfaced with the public way better than her dad did, but Ortiz was his best hire. He was good in the shop and willing to get his hands dirty when the situation called for it. Lexi put her phone away and tried to focus on her paper again. It worked, and she finished it about forty minutes later. Emily and Kim were out somewhere, so Lexi ate a quiet lunch and began filling out her schedule for the upcoming fall semester. She would take the summer off when it came to classes but filled in her pending internship with a smile. Others who had been in the criminal justice program since enrolling as freshmen might have a leg up on her, or they might have landed a sweeter and more prestigious summer gig with some fancy law firm.

Lexi liked her CV, and for the first time she could remember, she felt good about her career prospects.

ROLAND JOHNSON CALLED Hope to give her an update.

She didn't pick up. He tried again after waiting a few minutes. Still no answer, and the same happened with a text. "Shit," he grumbled. If the gang got wind of who Felicity

Snow really was, she would be in serious trouble. Johnson's next call went to Patrick Zellhoefer, and the younger agent picked up right away. "You've been working with Hope Raines, right?"

"Yes, sir. I'm sort of her handler."

Johnson rolled his eyes. He didn't have time for whatever spy fantasy Zellhoefer constructed. "I can't reach her. Have you heard from her recently?"

"We talked about the case yesterday."

"And?"

"And I think she was glad to hear things were moving toward the finish line," Zellhoefer said.

"I'm worried these assholes somehow learned who she really is. Did anyone see you together?"

"We met at a diner. It was never crowded."

"Still a possibility," Johnson said. "I want you to go by her apartment. See if she's there. If she's not, I want to know what the place looks like." When Zellhoefer didn't answer right away, Johnson added, "I know you usually take your orders from Hess. He and I are on the same level, and if this woman really is in trouble, I don't want to lose time dicking around with you. Understood?"

"I'll head over now, sir."

Johnson hung up. "Damn straight you will," he said to the empty fourth bedroom which served as his home office. He couldn't do anything except wait for the younger agent to call, and how far the man lived from Hagerstown—and how quickly he drove—was the main factor. Johnson returned to some work he wanted to catch up on. Just over an hour later, his phone rang.

"She's not here," Zellhoefer said.

"Tell me what you see."

"A few large sets of footprints in the carpet. They seem pretty fresh. Hang on." He fell silent for several seconds. "There's blood. Not a lot, but I can see it."

"I think we need to presume the group captured her." Johnson shook his head and swore internally. "There's one more thing you need to check on."

"Name it."

"Hope brought someone in," Johnson said. "She called him a consultant. I'd call him a wild card. He was posing as the group's new mechanic. I'll send you the address where he was staying. It's another Bureau apartment. I want you to check it out, too."

"Roger that," Zellhoefer said.

45

Tyler shook off the cobwebs as one of the goons shoved him toward a waiting SUV.

It was a GMC Yukon, the preferred vehicle of government agents and poseurs for years. Tyler stumbled en route to the large vehicle but managed to stay on his feet. Large hands pushed him inside, and the door slammed shut with a loud *thunk* behind him. It almost hit him in the head. Connor climbed into the passenger's seat. Tyler sat behind him. One of the muscleheads took the other half of the backseat, and the second one folded himself into the driver's chair.

"You have the address?" Connor said.

"Yeah," the driver said. He keyed it into the GPS, chose one of the three available color-coded routes on the screen, and they were underway. Tyler waited for the last vestiges of fog to lift. His hands were cuffed in front of him, so he could use them. The trio didn't buckle him in, but he could grab Connor's seatbelt and choke him. This would draw a response from the goon on the left. Tyler saw the butt end of a gun peeking out from a shoulder holster under the fellow's windbreaker.

The scenario wouldn't work. Tyler needed to wait for a

more strategic time to make his move. The navigation system showed the destination as Clairton, Pennsylvania, a town Tyler had never heard of. Two hours and forty-five minutes remained until they arrived. At some point, one of the guys would need to stop to take a leak or get something to eat. Tyler could try and seize the advantage then.

"Your girlfriend is already there," Connor said after looking at his phone. Tyler remained silent. "Nothing to say now? You gonna tell me she's not your girlfriend?"

"She isn't," Tyler finally said.

"Whatever. I'm pretty sure you were boning her. Close enough." He paused and let out a single dry chuckle. "I used to want to get with her bad. She's hot." Connor's head wagged. "She's a fed, though. The hell with her and the hell with you."

Tyler again remained silent. They got onto I-70 West. If Clairton were somewhere near Pittsburgh—which Tyler inferred based on all the driving to the west—they'd be riding the interstate for a while. Tyler needed the Yukon on smaller roads—or somewhere like a parking lot—to try and take control of the situation. "Where are we headed?" he asked after a few minutes.

"To see the boss," Connor said. "I don't think it's gonna go well for you and your girlfriend."

"Too bad we couldn't do nothing with her," the guy in the backseat with Tyler said.

"What?"

"Yeah." He shrugged. "Chains said she was off-limits. Couldn't even have any fun with her. Boss's orders. He wanted her alive and mostly unharmed."

"I guess he has his reasons," Connor said.

Tyler frowned and pondered what those reasons might be. Before he could say anything, the meathead next to him spoke up. "You hit it?"

"What?"

"The FBI lady. You hit it?"

"What are we, high school sophomores?"

The guy leaned to the right and punched Tyler in the face. His head nearly hit the window. Stars flashed in his vision, but the fog cleared faster than when he got whacked with the pistol. "I don't like you. When someone gives the order to kill you, I'm snapping your neck."

"How nice for you," Tyler said.

Silence ruled the day for a while. At some point, the driver needed to turn a large loop to remain on I-70 when it passed near a town. Tyler hoped they would stop at some point. As the highway trip resumed, the GPS showed around 94 miles remaining. After a while, Connor asked, "You comfortable back there, Tyler?"

"I'm all right."

He chuckled. "We'll make sure you're not once we're on a smaller road." The driver laughed as well. A short while later, an exit ramp on the right dumped them onto Pennsylvania state route 51. "There are some nice curves coming up."

Within a mile, Tyler realized what Connor had been talking about. The road veered left and then right again. Rather than applying the brake and navigating this stretch at a reasonable speed, the driver fed the big SUV more gas. He jerked the wheel to the left. The all-wheel-drive system prevented the tires from sliding out, but Tyler slammed hard into the door and window. The driver yanked the wheel in the other direction. This time, Tyler slid toward the goon sharing the rear seat with him. The man led with his shoulder, and the side of Tyler's skull bounced off it.

The three clowns shared a laugh as Tyler again tried to clear the cobwebs. He couldn't take many more blows to the head if he wanted to get out of his current predicament in one piece. This wasn't how he envisioned the transport going. No vulnerability presented itself yet. With the interstate behind them, Tyler would need to grab an opportunity soon

—even if it didn't seem like a great one. Beggars couldn't afford to be choosers when outmanned and outgunned.

At the next twisty segment in the road, the process repeated itself. Tyler saw the terrain change coming, so he was better prepared. He still rattled around and got bounced off the meathead next to him. "Comfortable now, Tyler?" Connor taunted. Tyler didn't respond. "You miserable prick. I'm gonna enjoy watching you die."

Tyler looked past Connor to the road ahead. More curves loomed. He would be ready this time. Another chance to turn the tide may not present itself. When the driver banked to the left, Tyler had already shifted in his seat. He leaned against the interior of the door and even angled his right shoe to press against the wall of the footwell. The driver jerked the wheel in the opposite direction.

Tyler pushed off the wall, using his own force to add to what physics provided him. He led with his elbow. The goon's eyes widened before Tyler's elbow took him flush in the face, and his head hit the glass. Tyler reached under the man's jacket and withdrew the pistol from the shoulder holster. A Glock. No conventional safety. Tyler shot the woozy meathead once in the chest.

The two up front were still staring out the windshield. Not everyone processed danger quickly. Tyler leaned against the mortally wounded man beside him and put three rounds into Connor's left side. He slumped in the seat, the belt preventing his body from toppling forward. The driver hit the brake, but Tyler was able to brace himself against the back of the seat. He shifted back to his original spot again, holding the Glock on the man in the captain's chair. The Yukon cruised along at thirty now. "Pull over."

"Or what?"

"Seriously? I just shot your friends, and you wonder what's going to happen?"

"Yeah."

"You can pull this damned rig onto the shoulder," Tyler said, "or I'll kill you and let the combination of friction and no throttle input bring it to a stop."

"You shoot me," the guy said, "and this thing might crash into a tree."

"I'll take my chances. You gonna do what I told you?"

The driver answered by speeding up. Tyler reached forward with the pistol and fired three shots into his ribs. The dying man's spasm jerked the wheel to the left, taking the Yukon off the road and into the grass. Trees lay ahead after a short rise. His foot must have slipped from the accelerator. Without any gas going to the engine, modern cars cut the throttle to save fuel. The GMC lost most of its speed as it went up the small hill, where it crested the top and came to rest about a foot from a large trunk.

Tyler got to work.

46

Roland Johnson's phone rang again a short while later. "Are you at the apartment we set up for Tyler?"

"I just got here," Patrick Zellhoefer said. "There's a Crown Vic in the lot. Looks like it came straight from the Bureau's excess lot."

"It probably did," Johnson said. "Tyler apparently wanted a car because he didn't want to risk his own. I take it you haven't been inside yet?"

"Heading there now. Hang on." Johnson heard the sounds of Zellhoefer walking and then fiddling with the lock a moment later. All FBI-owned apartments used one of a few different keys. It created a vulnerability if unauthorized people—through a compromised agent or one who went rogue—gained access. However, getting the specialized ring required several procedural and logistical hurdles someone at Johnson's level or above needed to navigate. "I'm in," the younger man said a moment later.

"What do you see?"

"Hope had the nicer place for sure." Muted footsteps came over the connection. "There's some drywall damage in the entryway."

"Recent?" Johnson asked.

"I don't work in construction, but probably. There are bits and dust on the floor nearby. Unless Tyler took a whack at it himself in frustration, I'm going to guess at least one person came here to grab him."

"More than one."

"How do you know?"

"I know Tyler," Johnson said. "He's a pain in the ass, but I'll take him against a random legbreaker any day. It must have been a crew. Two guys at least."

"Carpet's pretty worn in here," Zellhoefer said. "I can't really see a lot of impressions in it."

"Any blood?"

"No. I'm going to check the rest of the place." Johnson heard Zellhoefer walk around. Drawers clattered open. One of these days, the man might learn to mute his end of the connection. "I found a couple guns," he said a moment later.

"Not surprising considering the tenant."

"Nothing else to report."

"I know the evidence is a little thin," Johnson said, "but I think we need to treat Tyler as missing, too."

"Any idea where they might be headed."

Johnson sighed. "No clue."

TYLER HOPPED down out of the Yukon.

Trees behind him offered a decent bit of cover, and traffic on the state road was light. Tyler opened the driver's door and dragged the man out. He groaned when Tyler tossed him to the grass. Still alive, though three rounds into the torso would be fatal soon. "Where were we headed?" Tyler asked the dying man. No response came. "What am I going to be up against there?" Silence. "Are they going to kill Hope?" Nothing.

Tyler grabbed the guy's left arm and dragged him farther into the forest. Trunks and branches blocked any view of the road. "Being a true believer isn't helping you right now."

"I'm dead anyway," the fellow croaked as blood bubbled around his mouth. "Go to hell."

"Fine." Tyler put him out of his misery with a shot to the head.

Connor and the third guy were already dead. Tyler found the handcuff key in the pocket of the dead man who shared the rear seat with him. Once free of his restraints, he dragged the other two corpses near the former driver's. Someone would find them before long—probably today—but Tyler would be gone by then. Tyler wiped off the handle of the Glock, tossed the gun down, took his own Sig back from Connor, and collected a pair of topped-off spare magazines, making sure of their Swiss logos and model stamps. He flexed his wrists and hands a few times before continuing.

All three deceased men carried cell phones. Chains or whoever was in charge could reach out to any of them, so Tyler pocketed all three along with their cash. He walked around to the back of the Yukon and popped the hatch. A twelve-gauge Remington pump-action shotgun, plenty of cartridges, and a collection of lock-blade knives lay under a blanket and cargo net. "One-stop shopping," Tyler muttered to the trees. A scoped semiautomatic rifle and bullet-resistant vest would have been nice, but these men clearly didn't expect to encounter enough resistance to pack them. Tyler took the knife with the longest blade, the shotgun, and enough ammo to assault a compound—which he figured he would need to do. He set them on the backseat and draped the blanket across everything.

The Yukon was new enough to be keyless. Tyler found the fob in the dead driver's pocket and put it in his own. Once he climbed behind the wheel, he set the trio of phones on the passenger's seat. The engine still hummed, and the navigation system displayed the destination. It was a touch screen, and Tyler moved the map a little to see the surrounding area. Wherever they went was a good location to execute a couple people you didn't want to keep around. Even if Tyler had a rifle, he expected a dearth of places to set up and use it.

One of the rounds he put into Connor must have gone clean through and embedded itself in a door panel. Tyler figured he would need to keep driving the SUV, so he'd avoided messy headshots. Some blood splatter inevitably marred the interior, but he could clean it up. In the meantime, the tinted windows would prevent nosy people from seeing it.

Tyler put the GMC in reverse. It took a few instances of crawling back and forth, but he got the big SUV turned around without tumbling down the incline. Traffic remained light on Route 51. Tyler guided the Yukon down the rise, over the grass, and back onto the blacktop.

Now, he needed Hope to still be alive.

47

Hope remained in shock.

She leaned against a counter as things happened around her. People walked by in what seemed like slow motion. Voices sounded distorted as if originating underwater. How was her father still alive? Years ago, he left, never to be seen again. Her mother told Hope he died and even had him declared legally dead. Yet here Barrett Raines stood, looking like Hope would expect him to with an extra eighteen years on the odometer. The muscles she remembered being impressed by as a young girl faded some with time, but her dad still struck her as a tough man who had survived a hard life.

"Hope," he said, and his hands on her shoulders shook her out of her reverie. "It's good to see you. I know you must have plenty of questions, and I promise we can talk later. Right now, I need to prepare."

"For what?" she asked in a small voice.

"Three men are bringing this . . . Tyler fellow. I hear he might be dangerous. We need to take precautions." Her dad left to issue orders. "Rock, Chains, you stay in here." He pointed at a cluster of large men Hope didn't recognize. "You three, outside. Set up a perimeter. Regular patrols. If Tyler arrives cuffed in the back of a Yukon, great. Beat his ass a little and bring him in. Otherwise, kill him."

The trio grunted, nodded, and headed through the door. Chains approached. "A word, Barbell?"

"Go ahead."

"In private," Chains added.

"You can say whatever in front of Hope."

"She's kind of what I wanted to talk about."

"I'm sure you have questions," her father said. "The answer I'll give you is yes."

"What?"

"You were going to ask if I knew she was a fed when you showed me her picture and brought her in. The answer is yes."

Chains blinked a few times. He looked as confused as Hope felt. "You *knew*?"

"Of course. Hair and eye color fakery aside, I recognized my own flesh and blood."

"And you still let her in?"

Hope's dad patted Chains on the shoulder. The other man's expression remained sour. "She's my daughter. I knew I could really bring her in when it mattered. She loves me, and she won't act against me."

"You'd better be right," Chains said, and he stalked away.

"I am." He turned to Hope. His smile showed more lines on his face now, but it still reminded her of hundreds he'd flashed in her youth. It was hard not to reciprocate the gesture, but Hope managed to keep her face impassive. "I know you have a career, Hope, but we're family. I'm close to shutting this down. I had goals when we started these operations, and we're nearly there."

"This is why you've been ramping up?"

"You mean hitting places more frequently?" he asked, and she nodded. "Yes. I want to retire while I'm still young enough to enjoy it. I don't need millions of dollars and some Swiss chalet. I'm fine with a few hundred thousand and a nice place in Cabo."

"No extradition treaty," Hope said.

Her father smiled. "There are other perks, yes."

"People died, Dad. This wasn't just about stealing shit and funding your retirement."

"It was at the start." He sighed. "Things . . . got a little out of control. We probably should have dealt with Pop sooner. Trigger-happy son of a bitch was a liability. I was hoping Chains would show initiative and get rid of him, but I needed to give the order for it to happen." Hope wondered if Chains would survive into retirement. Eliminating members of the group theoretically increased the take for everyone else. Would Connor and Rock meet a similar fate?

Hope took a deep breath. If she made it out of here, she would definitely need some time with a Bureau shrink. Until then, however, she had to rely on her skills and wits to survive. Her father probably wouldn't order her killed, but he also seemed hellbent on his retirement in Cabo. Hope resolved to act before her status got reduced to that of obstacle.

THE LACK of traffic allowed Tyler to make good time.

The Yukon's willing V8 put down plenty of power. He leaned into the all-wheel drive system for traction rather than slowing much on curves. Hunger gnawed at him, however, and he also felt thirsty. Tyler wanted to skip drive-throughs to avoid giving someone at a window a good look inside the car. He passed a McDonald's with a crowded lot and pulled into a High's convenience store about a mile farther along.

Tyler left the GMC at the far end of the lot away from other cars. He went inside, grabbed the first two cold premade subs he saw and added a very large bottle of water. When he paid, Tyler grabbed enough napkins for a family of eight. He ignored the cashier's quizzical look and headed back to the Yukon. After wetting some of the napkins and wiping down the interior to remove blood splatter, Tyler got back on the road, eating as he drove.

The sandwiches—one roast beef and the other turkey—were mediocre, but he didn't want to be weakened and distracted by hunger. Tyler presumed Hope could take care of herself, but the group's boss would have brought in reinforcements. Connor and his two idiot friends wouldn't be the only muscle. If he thought the operation to be compromised, a responsible leader would circle the wagons and have men waiting to interrogate a potential rogue agent in Floyd Tyler Rayford.

As Tyler drew within ten minutes of his destination, he thought about the gang's mysterious leader. Memories of Hope played in his mind, too. During his therapeutic painting program, Tyler learned not to edit his thoughts. The subconscious discerned and processed things, and letting them bubble up sometimes made a difference. It helped Tyler get many things out of his head over the years—missions he undertook as a Green Beret, memories he thought he'd forgotten.

He wondered if his subconscious tried to tell him something now.

Hope never talked much about her father. Tyler knew the man bailed for good when Hope was a teenager, but before leaving, he'd instilled a love of cars and fast driving in his daughter. She presumed him dead, but this always seemed like something of a rationalization to Tyler. Getting a person declared deceased didn't require an actual body and was mostly a paperwork exercise.

Chains said she was off-limits. Couldn't even have any fun with her. Boss's orders. He wanted her alive and mostly unharmed.

One of Connor's goonish friends said this. Hope was a pretty woman, and both Chains and Connor were men used to having their way with people. Connor's intentions were base and obvious—and explicitly disallowed. Tyler witnessed women being mistreated in many ways during his times in Afghanistan. Sometimes, the barbarism of powerful men served as the most likely reason. Other times, those men had specific goals in mind, and they saw the violation of a woman as a means to an end. It sickened Tyler even as he recalled it years later.

I guess he has his reasons, Connor said in response to the leader quashing his friend's desire to do awful things to Hope.

"Shit," he muttered to the empty cabin. An obvious reason presented itself, and Tyler gave the Yukon more gas. He drove up State Street and stopped the large SUV about a quarter-mile from the destination. Barrett's Bike Shop stood by itself at least a thousand feet from the nearest building. State Street continued rolling past to the front and kept going across a nearby set of train tracks. Grass and trees lay behind the building. Those were the only places to get cover.

One of the dead men's phones buzzed. Tyler picked up the one humming on the seat. It was Connor's. The message came from a contact called Big Boss. *Where are you? Figured you'd be here by now.*

After scanning past texts to learn how the dead man communucated, Tyler tapped out a reply.

> Got hungry. We stopped for food. Should be there in 15-20.

> What about your guest?

> Fed the bastard a knuckle sandwich, lol.

Good. Hurry up.

The leader bought it. Tyler wrote the messages to fit Connor's overgrown frat boy style, and it worked. Small successes at the beginning of an op could lead to bigger ones by its conclusion. Tyler replaced the phone and approached the general store where he'd parked. A sign in the window said the place was closed on Sundays, and a large cross on the paper conveyed the reason. This whole area was still, quiet, and uncrowded. Tyler moved to the back of the building. He used the rusted ladder to climb to the roof. There, he remained low, padded to the edge, and lay flat.

Three men patrolled on foot outside the bike shop. Their routes and overlap were good but not great. At least one figure appeared at a window on the exterior. Tyler didn't see any sign of Hope, but she must have been here. He again wished for a working rifle with a good scope. In two seconds, he could drop as many sentries. Instead, he would need to take a slower and stealthier approach.

Tyler climbed down, retrieved the shotgun from the GMC, and headed toward the tree line.

48

"Why?"

It was a simple word, but it hung in the stale air between Hope and her father. He stared at her, unblinking and not answering.

"Why?" she repeated.

"Why what?"

"You know what!" Hope pounded the countertop. "You know damn well."

"I want you to say it," he told her in a tone much like the one she'd last heard almost two decades before.

"Why did you leave?"

Her dad—she needed to think of him as Barrett and stop personalizing the man based on childhood memories—leaned on the counter. "I needed to," he said as if those three words offered any real explanation.

"What do you mean?"

"I was no good, Hope. Your mother papered over a lot of my faults. We didn't want you to see the struggle. I couldn't maintain a job, and I'd started doing some . . . other work to keep the lights on. Your mom didn't want me to. Told me it was too dangerous. I'd get arrested one of these times." He let out a single, dry snort. "She ended up right. I got popped. I knew I'd be facing jail, so I left."

"You could have stayed," Hope said.

Barrett shook his head. "No. This was the best thing for you and your mother. I was an anchor dragging the two of you down."

"You didn't need to be. Mom really struggled for a while. We both did. You were there one day and gone the next. What kind of a man does that to a family he supposedly loves?"

"The kind who knows he's no good for them." He reached toward Hope, but she scowled and jerked her arm back. Barrett put both his hands up and continued. "It might seem hard to believe, but I did love you both. I still do. The best way to keep the family going was to remove the dead weight. You say your mom struggled for a while. She figured it out, though, right? She got a much better job and moved you both to a nicer place. Eventually, you went to college and joined the FBI."

"You know all this?" Hope asked.

"I kept tabs on you. Even when I was inside, I made sure to have someone get word to me."

"Running a gang even in prison?"

Barrett flashed a humorless smile. "I guess you could say I did. Like I told you, I knew jail was coming for me. Rather than have a few assholes try to dominate me, I took the fight to them. Even killed one in the exercise yard, so everyone called me Barbell afterwards."

"How are you not still in jail?"

"I didn't start the fight," he said. "Besides, he was a serial killer, and I made sure to learn things about people. You never know who wants good intel."

Hope snorted. "So you were a snitch."

"I did what I needed to do to get out. Since then, I've set things up so it would be hard to send me back. It's why Pop needed to go. He was ruining everything for the rest of us. No one was supposed to die on the jobs."

Hope leaned against the counter and took it all in. Over the years, she'd assembled a list of the things she would say to her father if she ever met him again. Now, none of them came to mind. A guy walking the perimeter outside passed in front of the window. Just after he did, Hope thought she spotted someone slipping down from the roof of a building farther along the street. It was the right size and shape to be Tyler. Connor and his crew should have been here with their captive by now.

If Tyler got rid of them and made it here on his own, he would be able to pick off the guys outside. He wouldn't rush things, however. Hope needed to keep her father talking and not thinking about late arrivals. "You said you knew I went into the FBI?"

"Yes."

"So you knew who I was when I became the driver."

"I did," he said. "Such a basic disguise could never fool me. I'm your father, Hope."

"You knew I'd be working against you," Hope said. "Even though I needed to make things look good and not draw suspicion, you must have known my ultimate goal was bringing everyone down."

"Sure."

"Were you just going to kill me if I got too close?"

"Of course not." Barrett recoiled as if she'd tried to strike him. "If the shit hit the fan, I would bring you into the group in full."

"Just like that?"

"You'd pick your father over the FBI."

"In the early days of my career. . . maybe I would have. I made peace with everything after that. I figured you were dead. Most criminals don't live long enough to play shuffle-board at the old folks' home." She shook her head. "Seeing you today doesn't change anything. If you want to leave here alive, you're going to need to come with me."

"Hope, there's no need for the situation to deteriorate." Barrett snapped his fingers, and Rock approached. "You have a choice. You can continue to be a fed, or you can be one of us. We'll go somewhere else, do our last few jobs, and we're done. You can get your own place in Cabo if you want." He extended his hand toward her. "Come on, Hopesy. What do you say?"

Hope stared at the hand and then at her father. "My name is Special Agent Hope Raines with the Federal Bureau of Investigation. You're coming with me."

"Have it your way." Barrett gestured, and Rock stepped forward. "If you get past him, we can talk again."

ONCE THE TREES and tall grasses hid him, Tyler took out his phone and dialed Roland Johnson. "I'm going to send you a pin."

"Good thing I have kids," Johnson said. "I didn't know 'dropping a pin' had anything to do with maps until a couple years ago."

"Same."

"This gonna be your current location?"

"More or less," Tyler said. "It's where the gang is holding Hope."

"You've seen her?"

"Not directly, but they have a bunch of guys guarding the place, and three men were bringing me here."

"I'm going to guess you didn't slip away peacefully and without incident while they all went to take a leak," Johnson said.

"Definitely not."

"I'm going to further guess I can't convince you to stand down and wait for me to get a team there."

"Same answer," Tyler said.

Johnson said. "Fine. Send me the location."

"Tell your team to hurry or they won't have much to do except clean up the mess." Tyler ended the call, opened texts, and dropped a pin icon with the address of the motorcycle shop. He slipped his phone away and moved closer to the destination. In the open spaces, shooting represented a bad option. The men inside might have a hard time pinpointing the exact location, but they would know someone was coming for them. Tyler wanted to retain the element of surprise as long as he could.

One sentry walked a patrol behind the building. He came close to the wooded area—probably within fifteen feet—but never walked into it. Tyler crouched in the shade of a tree and waited for him to turn around. When he did, Tyler stayed low and kept moving. He needed the man to complete another circuit to get into the position he wanted.

Tyler had worked his way just past the far edge of the building. No windows looked out at him here, and he crouched in a good hiding place from the guy on patrol. Tyler drew the lock-blade knife. When the guard turned and headed away, Tyler stood. He placed his feet carefully as he moved out of cover. Then, he mirrored his quarry's steps, adding a little pace each time. In about thirty feet, Tyler drew up right behind him.

A final surge got him into position. Despite being much bulkier, the guard was only about one inch taller than Tyler. His left hand clamped over the man's mouth, and in the next instant, the edge of the blade raked across his throat. The sentry stiffened in surprise initially, but his body grew slack as blood spurted and poured from the mortal wound. Once it was clear the man wouldn't make a sound, Tyler eased the corpse to the ground. He checked to verify no one watched and then dragged the lifeless man into the tree cover.

Away from prying eyes, Tyler checked the guard's weapons. Another knife and a pistol. He'd hoped for something to upgrade what he currently carried, but no such luck. Even though it didn't fit his Sig, another magazine of 9mms in reserve couldn't hurt in the case of a firefight, so Tyler took it. He noted the lack of walkie-talkies and an earpiece. Phones made great comms devices, but whoever set them up needed to do so intelligently. No one did here. Two guys remained on the perimeter—one covering the front and left, and the other on the right. So far, neither gave any sign they'd noticed what happened.

Tyler approached the window-free rear wall of the building. He was closer to the right side, so he put his back against the stone and shuffled to the corner. Tyler leaned out as little as possible while looking toward the front. The fellow on patrol watched the road running past and started to turn. Tyler ducked back into cover. He shuffled along and did the same at the left side. The guard stood in place just past the front corner of the shop. He gave no indication he planned on moving.

The guy on the right had worked his way about halfway down the building when Tyler checked again. The man slowed, peeked in a window, and shuffled his feet as if he were going to head back. Tyler scratched the hilt of the knife along the stone, and the sentry stopped. He turned, and Tyler shifted behind the building. "Walt?" the man said. "You need a break?"

Tyler said nothing. Footsteps moved closer. "Walt? Izzat you?" When the guard's body cleared the building, Tyler struck. He thrust the knife into the unsuspecting man's gut just below the breastbone. With his left hand, Tyler grabbed the larger guy's collar, spun him around, and slammed him into the wall. His hand covered a goateed mouth as he pulled the blade out and rammed it home repeatedly. Blood gushed from a bunch of wounds as the dying man sagged to the ground.

Two down. Tyler wiped crimson off the blade and his hand. He took the dead goon's phone in case someone tried to reach him. One sentry remained outside, and then Tyler and Hope needed to deal with an unknown number inside. Normally, he would fear for Hope's survival. He doubted the group's leader would kill her unless he missed his guess as to the man's identity. Still, with the FBI rolling a team to their location, Tyler wanted to have the situation well in hand before the feds swarmed the place.

49

"I ain't gonna hold back," Rock said.

"Me neither," Hope replied as they circled one another. The space where they jockeyed for position—some kind of storeroom—was long but not very wide. Shelves lined the lengthier walls, and many of them sat empty. Hope wondered if her dad's bike shop was legit or a mere front for what the group really did. Anyone could buy a few old cruisers for cheap and make a repair place look legit.

"You coulda been one of us for real." Rock glared at Hope. "I shoulda known 'Felicity Snow' was too good to be true. Pretty girls don't work on cars, drive fast, and end up with guys like us."

"Maybe the problem is guys like you. If you'd spent more time focused on the work and less time staring at my chest and ass, you might've figured it out sooner."

Rock charged and threw a wild punch. He put power behind it but not a great deal of thought. Hope deflected it aside. She'd always graded out well in the Bureau's hand-to-hand training, and she would need to be on her game today. Rock was taller, broader, and stronger. He followed with another cross, a jab, and an uppercut. Hope blocked the first two and avoided the slower third one. She tagged Rock on the jaw with a jab of her own. It wouldn't put him down or even hurt much, but it would show him she could land some blows of her own.

Mostly, it made him angry. Rock came at her again, this time seizing her shoulders and throwing her backward. Hope slammed into a shelf. Even though it was empty, it was still sturdy metal and affixed to either the wall or floor because it didn't give when she hit it. A narrow bar caught her right in the back. She bounced off, falling forward and catching herself on her elbows. Rock was right there and kicked her in the gut hard enough to bend her in half.

He grabbed her hair, punched her in the face, and then wrapped his hands around her throat. Hope tried to knock them away, but he was too strong. Instead, she got her arm behind his, nudged it forward enough, and bit as hard as she could on his forearm. Rock howled in pain as Hope clamped down. He screamed and pulled back as she tore some flesh away. While Rock stared at his bleeding wound, Hope regained her feet. His voice filled the room when he shrieked, "You bitch!"

"Takes one to know one," Hope said. "You're the one crying over a little bite." She smirked. "No way you could have handled me in bed, chump."

"I'm gonna kill you," Rock growled as he came toward her again.

～

TYLER USED the dead guard's phone to text the other.

The man shouted for Walt, so Tyler hoped he'd grabbed the correct cell. He sent a short message. *Come around to the right. I think I hear something.* Then, he waited.

Nothing. No movement and no response. Tyler waited a minute and tried again. *Dude, where are you?*

Soon, a reply came. *I'm not leaving my post. Check it out on your own. Get Norm if you're going to be whiny about it.*

Tyler muttered a curse and tossed the phone down. Just his luck to draw the one guy who didn't want to freelance. This required a change in tactics. Tyler moved to the rear of the building again. He kept his back against it and reached the left-hand corner. A quick peek showed him the remaining sentry stayed at his post, watching the street out front despite an obvious lack of activity. This place stood at the very end of the road immediately before a set of train tracks. There would never be much traffic or a slew of pedestrians. Keeping more than an occasional eye on the street was a waste of time.

Normally, Tyler would be fine with this, but time was the scarce resource at the moment. He didn't know when the feds would roll up and change the math for everyone, and he had no idea how long the leader would want to keep Hope alive. At some point, his relation to her wouldn't matter. She represented a threat to his freedom and the narcissistic life he'd built.

Tyler could probably sneak up on the guy, but he would also be moving past windows along the side. Even if the guard never spotted him, someone inside might. He wanted to keep the element of surprise as long as possible—both for himself and Hope. Tyler peeked around the side of the building again.

His run of bad luck continued. The guard happened to be looking in his direction, spotted him, and fired.

"Shit." Tyler ducked back into cover as the bullet whizzed past. So much for the element of surprise. With it gone, Tyler sank to his knees, leaned out under the sentry's follow-up shot, and dropped him with two rounds to the chest. Once the man fell, Tyler put a third into his head in case he wore a vest. No one else popped out from around the shop.

Tyler moved to the other side and checked there. Still quiet. As he advanced along the side, he heard a voice shout, "Hold your positions! Make the son of a bitch come to us." Must have been the leader.

If he wanted Tyler to come to him, it would be rude not to oblige.

50

Rock went back on the offensive.

Hope turned his punches aside. He tried to back up and kick her, but she raised her leg and pushed his wide. While he was off-balance, she elbowed him in the gut and bashed him in the face. Her hand stung, but Rock went down to the concrete. He'd pounced and tried to strangle her under the same circumstances a moment ago, so she wasn't about to give him a break.

Hope raised her foot to stomp on his balls. Rock shifted, and her shoe glanced off his hip as he scurried out of the way. She wobbled, and Rock—still prone—booted her in the hip and knocked her down. They got back to vertical at the same time and raised their fists. "You want to come quietly?" Hope asked.

"Screw you."

"You wish."

Rock's left hand came forward. When Hope moved to block it, he pulled it back and clocked her in the face with a hard right cross. She stumbled into the shelves again but managed to stay on her feet. A wolfish smile came over his face as he rushed forward to kick her. Hope scrambled to the side. Rock's foot hit the wall, and his leg ended up on the shelf with his back to Hope.

She punted his exposed gluteus hard.

He grunted, and his leg slid from the shelf. The process unbalanced Rock, and he crashed to the concrete. Hope scampered around him, kicking him hard in the ribs. When he rolled onto his back, she got her stomp in. Though his hand covered the family jewels, she used maximum force, and his multitude of curses toward her got lost in a series of grunts and groans.

From the corner of her eye, Hope saw Rock's right leg move. It found the pit of her knee an instant later, and she toppled backwards over it. While she managed to hold her head up and keep it from smacking into the unforgiving floor, the fall knocked the wind out of her. Hope sputtered and coughed as her lungs burned and struggled to take in air. Rock rose to unsteady feet, scowled, and raised his foot. She wanted to move, but her body wouldn't cooperate, and Rock's boot slammed into her stomach. What little air she had got blasted away again.

Rock's black boot went up and came down again, then again, and finally a third time. Hope wheezed as he crouched and got close to her face. "Still think you can take me on? You're a girl. You can't hang with me. Piss off." He drew his fist back and punched her hard in the face. She tasted blood. Desperation raged in Hope. She could barely breathe, and now, Rock might stand over her and beat her to death.

When his fist started coming forward again, Hope got her elbow up and nudged his wrist. It sent his fist out wide, missing her head by less than an inch. Rock howled in pain as his knuckles slammed into the concrete. He pulled his fist back and spun away. Hope sucked in a lungful of air and sat up. Her head swam, but she pushed past it, first getting to one knee before making it back to vertical.

Rock turned to face her, cradling his right mitt in his left. "You broke my hand, you bitch."

Hope spat a blood-covered tooth at his feet. "Boo-hoo. You gonna man up, or am I arresting you now?"

"God, I hate you." Rock's face—never very handsome—twisted in rage and pain. He came at her with his left fist now clenched. It would reduce his offensive potential, though he'd also tried some kicks before. Still, he was a strong guy riding the adrenaline wave of anger, so she would need to be careful and look for an opening. When he punched, Rock kept his injured right tucked against his midsection.

Hope moved inside a hook, raised her arm to blunt it, and drove her knee directly onto his wounded appendage. Rock screamed and retreated a step. He bumped into the shelving. Hope pressed the advantage. He managed to stop her punches, but she landed a kick to his upper left leg. Hope then did the same to the right. Rock grimaced as she scored another hit. He would need to lower his guard or find his movement compromised.

He lowered his guard. Rock caught Hope's next kick, pinning her calf against his outer thigh. He bent his right arm and raised it. From here, he could snap her knee with a hard elbow strike. Hope leaned forward and punched him in the solar plexus. Rock gasped and released her leg. She elbowed him in the side of the head, grabbed his face, and rammed his head into one of the shelving support posts. Rock blinked a few times but stayed on his feet. Hope stepped back and planted her right foot under his chin, dropping Rock to the floor.

When he tried to sit up, she moved behind him and got him in a headlock. "You're under arrest for a shitload of crimes . . . including armed robbery, grand larceny, murder, and assaulting a federal officer." With his right hand injured, Rock could only reach back with his left, and Hope avoided his attempted grabs. She made sure the crook of her elbow remained under his chin. "You have the right to remain silent."

"Go to hell," Rock croaked. He reached toward his lower left leg. Hope looked around his shoulders and spotted the small sheath and knife hidden there.

"Don't do it, Rock," she ordered. Somewhere outside, gunshots pierced the quiet. Her father barked an order a couple seconds later. Did one of the guards spot Tyler?

"Go to hell," he said again as his fingers brushed the hilt.

"Goddamn you." Hope slid her arm down, cupping Rock's chin in one hand and his forehead in the other. "Don't make me do it." He kept reaching, so she twisted, and the sound of his neck snapping reverberated as loud as one of the earlier reports. Hope let the corpse go and stood. "You son of a bitch," she said, kicking Rock's lifeless body.

From the doorway, someone clapped. Hope looked up. Her father smiled and spread his hands. "Good job, Hope. You passed the test. Now . . . are you ready to join me . . . or do you want to meet the same fate as your boyfriend?"

Hope raised her fists and spat blood onto her father's black leather boots. "Piss off, Dad."

51

Tyler imagined the layout of the place.

If it really were a motorcycle repair facility, the setup would need to be similar to his own shop. A front door for the public which led to some kind of waiting area and counter. Desks and maybe an office behind it. A stock room for parts. At least one service bay, though motorcycles could abide narrower and shorter spaces than muscle cars. He ducked past two windows on the right before coming to the front edge of the structure.

Tyler peeked around the corner. No one was there, but he confirmed two doors: one standard for customers to use and another garage-style to bring bikes in for service and roll them out again. The latter yawned open. Tyler could never get past such a gap unseen. To go around the other side, he would need to walk the perimeter again and hope no one spotted him at a window despite his efforts to duck.

The element of surprise was already gone. Might as well take the direct approach.

Tyler stuffed the pistol in the back of his waistband and brought the Remington to bear. It wasn't the trusty Mossberg model he was used to, but the twelve-gauge dwarfed the

9MM in stopping power. Whispered voices came from the interior. At least two men. Motorbikes needed fewer and smaller parts than cars, so the odds of finding a stack of tires to hide behind were small. Tyler would need to make his shots count.

When he heard someone moving, he leaned into the opening.

A large man scurried across the service bay. He glanced over, and his eyes widened. Tyler pulled the trigger, and the buckshot did its job. He spun back into cover as bullets whistled past him, a few deflecting off the stone and scattering gray dust. The rate of fire suggested semiautomatic pistols. There were no doors on the right-hand wall, but an enterprising soul could try climbing out a window to get into flanking position. Tyler kept an eye on them and didn't see anything unusual.

When the barrage stopped, he leaned to his left again. Quiet greeted him. No obvious cover suggested itself, though he could crouch behind a chopper. Tyler leveled the shotgun at the open space and padded toward the big bike. When he saw motion, he fired again and chased another man back into hiding. A closed door at the back of the shop led somewhere else. Maybe the storeroom. Tyler didn't see Hope anywhere.

Tyler took his position behind the chopper and pumped the Remington. Its distinctive *chick-chack* broke the silence in the stale area. His back remained about two feet from the wall, and he situated himself to where no one could try to sneak up on him from around the building. The two idiots in here would need to try and take him out the old-fashioned way.

If they worked together, they could make things difficult for a lone man assaulting the place. Tyler figured this gave them too much credit. Unless they used sign language, he didn't pick up on any communications between them—a major oversight with the combat math now significantly altered by the dead man. Quiet activity sounded from some-where at the other end. Tyler hunkered down and waited. One of the things he always preached to young soldiers was the value of patience. Waiting for the other guy to give himself away or make a mistake could save your life if you simply let the situation develop.

Behind the husk of another bike, someone moved. He stayed low, but he would run out of cover soon, and advancing didn't gain him any advantage. He kept going, however. Tyler went down to his left knee, scooted toward the defender, and pulled the trigger. A bloody spray preceded a brief scream as the second man fell dead. Tyler moved back into cover just in time for a barrage of bullets to scream over his head. In the gap between the seat and the engine, he saw the third guy stand up and step into the open. His weapon clicked empty a second later.

Tyler stood and fired again. The third and final man slumped to the concrete a few feet from the second. Tyler crouched behind the chopper again, set the Remington down, and took the pistol back out. He listened but didn't hear anyone else moving around. Three outside. The same number inside. Connor and his two friends on the ride most of the way here. Chains and company dug deep to find more goons, but they couldn't have many left.

With the area remaining quiet, Tyler stood and started toward the door at the rear.

～

"Report of shots fired," an agent in the SUV said.

"Where?" Roland Johnson asked.

"At the bike shop, sir. I'm patched into the locals. They've gotten two calls, and they're going to respond."

Johnson sighed. He remained at least twenty minutes away. They came south from the greater Pittsburgh area.

Bravo team—which started closer to the destination—should arrive several minutes before him. He dialed a familiar number. "How far away are you?"

"Seven or eight minutes, sir," Watson said.

"Two things, then," Johnson told him. "One, drive faster. Two . . . locals are getting reports of gunfire at our target location. They're going to investigate. It seems no one waited for us before they started shooting."

"Roger that."

"You have photos of Hope Raines and John Tyler. Make sure they're all right. Treat anyone else who's not a cop as a hostile."

"Understood."

Johnson hung up and put his phone away. "Sir?" the young agent asked. She looked like she'd finished the FBI's training program the previous morning. The woman rode in the passenger's seat, a computer on her lap and an earpiece in her right ear.

"Can you contact the locals?" Johnson asked.

"Yes, sir."

"Good. Tell them we have two personnel inside. A female FBI agent and a male informant."

"We're calling Tyler an informant?"

"We are today," Johnson said. "Hope is probably the only woman on site, so she'll be easy to identify. Tyler might still have his hair dyed blond. Tell them he's a middle-aged retired soldier who will look unhappy to be there." It seemed the perfect description. Every time Johnson met Tyler, he looked sour, and the impression extended to their phone conversations. Johnson wondered if Tyler was ever happy to be anywhere. When the woman didn't respond, Johnson pressed her. "Something I say confuse you, Agent Lilly?"

"No, sir."

"Make it happen, then." Lilly reached out to the Clairton police and advised them of what went on. She repeated herself on the description of John Tyler. When she ended the call, Johnson leaned forward and tapped the side of the driver's seat a few times. "Let's hurry. The locals might beat both our teams there, but I don't trust them to handle the scene properly."

52

———

Hope stared at her father as he closed the door.

"Just you and me in here, Hopester."

"Don't call me that," she barked.

He put up his hands. "All right, all right."

Hope glowered at him. For years, she'd imagined what she might do if she ever saw her father again—if he somehow turned out to be alive. In some of her thoughts, they had a happy reunion. In others, she wept with disappointment and refused to let him console her. In still others, anger overtook her, and she shook with rage before resorting to violence.

Today, she simply stood still and seethed.

"What do you want, Hope?"

"I want to take you in," she said.

Barrett wagged his head. "No. You're talking about your duty as an agent. I mean you. Hope Nicole Raines. What do *you* want in this situation?"

"Why? So you can tell me riding away with you to keep the gang going is the answer?"

He shrugged. "The roster's gotten smaller today. You'd get a bigger cut of any take."

"You're delusional," Hope said. "I'll never go along with you."

"Because I'm a criminal?"

She snorted and couldn't help a short laugh. "It's so much deeper than that."

"Tell me." Gunshots rang out in the shop. Hope dropped to a crouch. Barrett—she'd stopped thinking of the man as her father for now—smiled. "Don't worry. The walls are solid stone, and the door won't let regular bullets in. I've taken precautions."

"Of course you have," Hope muttered as she got back to vertical.

"It's my shop. I built it knowing I might get involved in . . . other activities."

"Did you expect your daughter to turn up at some point?"

"No," he admitted. "It was a complete surprise. I'd been following your life, of course. Social media makes things easy." He chuckled. "Your generation sure seems to like it. I knew you went to college and joined the FBI. When Chains told me he had a new driver, and she was a woman, a fleeting thought crossed my mind it might be you. You were always great behind the wheel."

"Why not just stop?" Hope said. "Pack up and move across the country? You had to know I would press on."

More gunfire sounded from behind them, including the distinctive boom of a shotgun. The first reports came a minute or two ago. Way too early for the locals to arrive. Tyler might have tipped off the feds. Still, law enforcement would announce themselves. Hope wondered if Tyler took on what remained of her father's gang. She needed to get out of this room and help him.

"I hadn't seen you in eighteen years," Barrett said. "Was it so wrong to want a father-daughter reunion?"

"Yes. You don't deserve one."

"You don't need to be—"

"No," Hope broke in. "Don't you tell me what I need. Don't try and mansplain my feelings to me. You walked out on us. Mom and I were gutted." Hope heard her voice crack but kept going, relying on years of residual anger to get her through the next few minutes. Her hands clenched into fists as she talked. "I was Daddy's girl, and then my daddy was gone." Barrett's face betrayed no reaction. "Mom did the best she could, but you ruined us. No matter what bullshit you might say about us being better off without you, you destroyed our family. I'll never forgive you for it."

"Hope, I—"

"Shut up, Dad. Barrett. I'm going to arrest you, and you're going to come with me. I'll attend your trial, and this time I'll actually know what happens to you."

"I'm not going with you," he said.

Hope raised her fists. "Let's do this, then."

"I'm not going to fight you, Hope."

"Have it your way." Hope whacked her father in the face with a right jab and a left cross. The harder punch turned his head, and he took a few steps to the side. Hope mirrored his movements. She now stood with her back to the door, and her father's boots rested a couple feet from Rock's body. "Give up yet?"

"I'm still not going to fight you. You should let me leave. If you don't want to have anything to do with me after today, fine. I'm your father."

"Biologically, yes," Hope said. "I'll never be rid of your DNA." She brought her hands up again. "Barrett Raines, you're under arrest."

"No." He tried to get past her, but Hope shoved her father backward. It took a lot of effort. Despite being nearly sixty years old, he remained taller, broader, and stronger than her. Considering his lifestyle, he couldn't let himself go, so the man remained in good shape. If he decided he wanted to fight back, this wouldn't be a cakewalk. "Let me pass, Hope."

"Like I told you, you're under arrest." Hope clocked her father with another hook and folded him in half with a hard kick to the midsection. Before he could straighten, she kneed him in the face. He rocked backward, and his heels caught on Rock's lifeless form, sending him sprawling to the concrete floor. Hope hurdled the body and pounced. She put her forearm across her father's throat. He grunted, and rage flashed in his eyes, but he offered no counterattack.

"I won't fight you," he said.

"I want you to, dammit!" She drew her fist back and walloped him in the face. Blood ran from his split lip. Hope hit him again, then a third time and a fourth. His nose cracked on the final one, and she stopped, fresh crimson dripping from her fingers onto his grease-stained shirt. "Barrett Raines, you're under arrest for robbery, grand larceny, conspiracy to commit murder, murder, and whatever other charges your sorry ass deserves." Hope stood and kicked her father in the side. When he rolled over, she knelt on his back, grabbed his arm, and wrenched it. He grunted, but she got both behind him and slapped on a zip tie.

From behind her, someone clapped again.

Hope spun to see Tyler standing in the doorway. The front of his shirt was bloody, but the way he held himself suggested it came from someone else. "Good job, Special Agent Raines."

"Thanks."

"I figured out your father was the leader on the drive up here. I wanted to tell you, but you were a little busy."

"Seems like you were, too," Hope said. "Not bad for a mediocre flyboy mechanic."

Sirens approached as Hope stood and wrangled her father to his feet.

53

____

TYLER RAISED HIS HANDS WHEN THE LOCAL COPS STORMED THE place.

"I'm FBI Special Agent Hope Raines," she said when staring down a couple of semiautomatics. "The man with me here is John Tyler, a consultant on this case."

"We heard he was an informant," the burly male officer said.

"Little bit of both," Hope said. "We're the good guys. The Bureau is going to want to haul away anyone else who's alive."

"I think we only have one survivor, ma'am," the cop said.

Hope and Tyler both shrugged and let the locals do their jobs. They stretched yellow tape around the perimeter. A van rolled up, and three men in white Tyvek suits climbed out. "Can't imagine a small place like this has such a large forensics team," Tyler said.

"They could be on loan," Hope said.

"They'll have plenty of bullets to pick up and blood samples to collect."

The two sat behind the counter and did their best to stay out of any traffic paths. A couple cops talked to Hope's father.

For her part, she never even looked in his direction. "Walk me through what happened," she said a moment later.

"Connor and two of his friends came for me," Tyler said. "They were smart about how they grabbed me, so I went along and looked for an opportunity. I got one on the drive here and took them all out."

"Connor's dead?"

"Three bullets in the left side, yes."

"I can't claim to be sorry."

"He made his choices," Tyler said. "They all did."

"How'd you know to come here?" Hope asked.

"GPS in their SUV. I just followed the directions. Once I was on this street and could see the place, I pulled over and assessed things. Three guys walked the perimeter. I got the first two quietly, but the third took a shot at me."

A tall, thin man in glasses and a blue FBI jacket entered the shop. He beelined for Hope and Tyler. "I'm Watson. SSA Johnson is on his way. Everything going all right?"

"We're okay," Hope said.

"You sure?" Watson frowned and pointed at Hope's face. Her lip was swollen and split, she'd probably have a black eye later, and her smile showed a missing tooth.

"I'll make a dentist appointment, but I'll live." She pointed into the storeroom where two Clairton PD cops still talked to her father. "There's the leader of the group. His name is Barrett Raines. He's—"

"Wait," Watson broke in, "Raines?"

"Yes."

"Is he . . . ?"

"He's my father," Hope confirmed. "I had no idea he was involved when I started this case. My mother told me he was dead. I guess now he'll get to die in prison."

Johnson arrived with several agents in tow a short while later. He pulled Hope away for a sidebar. Tyler watched the various agencies work and interact. Despite movies and TV shows often depicting the FBI muscling locals out of their own investigations, he didn't see any evidence of this behavior. Regardless of affiliation, everyone roamed the scene, looked at evidence, talked to one another, and collected statements from the survivors—Hope, Tyler, and Barrett.

Johnson looked a little silly with his tie under the Bureau windbreaker. "Thanks for your help with this one," he said as he and Hope rejoined Tyler. "I know you stuck your neck out a little."

Tyler shrugged. "I wanted to see them caught."

"Caught or killed?"

"They made their choices."

Johnson nodded. "So they did. I think you two are done here. We have a scene to keep processing. I'll have Watson drive you back to Hagerstown if it's all right."

"Sure," Hope said, and Tyler agreed. They headed outside to an unmarked Dodge Charger. Red and blue lights mounted into the grill flashed, joining the other vehicles in bathing the area. Chains sat inside an identical car. He must have taken off at some point. Tyler opened the passenger's door for Hope, who slid inside with a quick smile. He sat behind her, and Watson got the address for Hope's apartment.

Other than a short conversation at the outset, they made the drive in silence.

~

"I NEED A SHOWER AND FOOD," Hope said when she walked into her apartment.

Tyler followed her in, and Hope made sure the coast was clear before locking up. "Me, too," Tyler said.

"You probably ate more recently than I did."

"I stopped for lunch on the way to your father's bike shop."

Hope chuckled. "In a bloody SUV?"

"I avoided head shots, so it wasn't too bad." Tyler shrugged. "If you park far enough from the door, people don't notice."

"I guess." She pulled her shirt off and winced. Tyler pointed at her waist. Her tank top—which rose up when she doffed her shirt—sat above several fresh bruises. She poked them with her finger and grimaced.

"Seems like the guys treated you as bad as me," Tyler said. "I wish I could've gotten to you sooner."

"It wasn't your job to rescue me, Tyler."

"I know. Not sure you needed me to, anyway. You seemed to do well on your own."

Hope flexed her right bicep and patted it with her left hand. She knew she wouldn't win many posing contests, but she also knew women who spent more time in the gym and had less to show for it. "I guess I did all right. I'm getting a shower. Think about what you might want to eat." Tyler nodded, and Hope headed to the bathroom. A minute later, she stood under the hot water. It felt good on her sore muscles. Once she finished drying off, Hope changed into sweatpants and a plain black T-shirt. "You come up with anything?"

"I'm fine with pizza," Tyler said. "I pretty much always am."

"I knew I liked you for a reason." Hope took out her phone and opened the website for a good local place. She chose two pies, paid, and slipped her mobile away again. "You want to shower now?"

"Sure." Tyler headed down the hall. Hope turned the TV on, but the choices in the middle of a Sunday afternoon were uninspiring. She didn't care about sports and instead watched the national news for a few minutes before turning it off in disgust. A few minutes later, Tyler reappeared wearing a towel around his waist and an amused look on his face. He carried his clothes. "I don't have anything clean to put on."

"Pretty sure my stuff won't fit you," Hope said. She got up. "Here." Tyler handed her the clothes, and she combined them with hers in the washing machine. "This place actually has good appliances, so it shouldn't take too long."

"I'm waiting for food," Tyler said, "so I'm something of a captive audience."

Hope sized him up standing in her hallway. He looked a little ridiculous wearing just a blue bath towel. The blond dye wore off, and Tyler's hair was now some weird shade of brown with a little gray peeking through. "This is my ticket out of the doghouse," she said.

"I know. You should be back in the Bureau's good graces now."

"I certainly hope so."

"Any idea where you'll end up?"

"No." She moved closer to Tyler. The smell of her shampoo in his hair filled her nostrils. "I hope I have my pick of assignments." Her hand landed on his chest. A few bruises peeked out above the line of the towel. Hope's fingers ran over a tattoo on Tyler's right pectoral. "This might well be the last time we see each other."

"You might end up across the country," he breathed.

"I might."

"Sounds like we need a proper goodbye."

"Sounds like it." Hope wrapped her arms around Tyler's neck and kissed him.

"What about the pizza?" he asked as she steered him toward the open bedroom door.

"I chose a ninety-minute delivery time."

Tyler grinned. "You're a clever one, Hope Raines."

"Shut up," she said, "and get that damn towel off."

54

When Tyler got home Sunday evening, he texted Lexi to tell her he was all right. After expressing her initial relief and happiness, her next message made him chuckle. *What about your hair?*

Without thinking, he ran a hand through it. Even though the dye job mostly covered the expanding gray in Tyler's black hair, he was ready to return to his natural look. *Fading. I'm going to wash it out for good tomorrow morning.*

Oh well. We'll always have your blond period to look back on, Dad.

He smiled. While he would look back on this period, it would be for meeting Hope and taking down Barrett's robbery ring. Tyler needed a trip to the grocery store before cooking anything. Afterwards, he went to bed early. The next morning, he got up in time to wash his hair several times if necessary. It took five extra turns under the hot water, but the last vestiges of the blond color finally swirled down the drain.

Tyler stopped for bagels before heading to the shop. He'd been gone before doing extracurricular work, but this time saw him spend quite a bit of extra time away from the shop. Smitty and Ortiz deserved more than a doughy treat, of course. Tyler would give them a bonus in their next checks. It was only fair. He rolled up to Special Operations Classic Car Repair to find his two employees drinking coffee and chatting in one of the service bays.

"Morning, boss," Ortiz said.

"What's in the bag?" Smitty wanted to know.

Tyler patted the bottom of the stuffed paper sack. "Bagels for everyone. Let's have some breakfast before we get busy."

"Maybe it'll be a nice Monday after all," Ortiz said. They all walked inside. Tyler poured himself some coffee while Ortiz and Smitty chose a plain and a cinnamon raisin, respectively.

"I know I was away for a while this time," Tyler said. "Bringing a bag of carbs for breakfast doesn't make up for it. You two covered for me without complaint." He looked at Smitty and smirked. "Mostly." The older man grinned. "I'll take care of you in your next checks." Like many small business owners, Tyler outsourced payroll. The low employee count meant it didn't cost much, but he would have paid a little more to avoid the hassle.

Smitty waved a hand. "You don't need to give us extra money."

"I do. This was a heavier load than you signed up for."

"I agree with Smitty," Ortiz said, "but I also won't complain."

"There's the spirit," Tyler said. He toasted a sesame bagel when the other two were finished. The shop's refrigerator held only the basics, so there was no cream cheese, but everyone made do with butter.

"What are you going to do now, boss?" Ortiz asked when they all threw their paper plates away.

"Get back to work," Tyler said. "I could use some normal weeks. Regular and quiet would be nice."

"You think you'll get them?"

Tyler chuckled. "I guess we'll see, won't we?"

～

WHEN TYLER GOT HOME, Lexi's Accord coupe sat in the driveway.

He looked at his watch and muttered, "Shit" before getting out of the 442. With everything happening in Hagerstown and Clairton, he'd forgotten about his father's birthday celebration. The old man was turning 78, and he'd arranged a small gathering at his apartment.

"You forgot, didn't you?" Lexi said as Tyler locked the front door. She wore dark blue jeans and a red sweater and would probably be the best-dressed person there. Tyler wondered if he would need to punch some old man for ogling her.

"I remembered."

"When?"

"When I saw your car in the driveway," Tyler admitted.

"Daaaaaaaad!"

"It's fine." Tyler waved a hand. "Let me get a quick shower, and I'll be back down." He headed upstairs, took a fast turn under the hot water, and put on a black quarter-zip sweater, his nicest pair of medium blue jeans, and a well-worn pair of brown Clarks. Total time—nine minutes and fifty seconds. Not bad.

"Did you get Grandpa anything?" Lexi asked once Tyler returned to the main floor.

"I've been a little busy," he said. "Besides, I can't think of any non-morbid presents." Lexi pointed to a green and white gift bag on the table. White tissue paper stuck out of the top. "I knew I could count on you, kiddo. What did we get him?"

"*We* found a nice cardigan." Lexi crossed her arms, but the corners of her mouth turning up betrayed her amusement at the scenario.

"Can I sign the card?"

"It's behind the bag." Tyler read the sentiment enough to

know it would be good coming from the two of them, scribbled his name on it, and sealed the envelope. They both left the house and climbed into the white Tesla Model X SUV. It originally belonged to one of the men in Tyler's old Special Operations unit. Almost three years ago, a faction of them supported their former colonel in starting a company. Tyler did not. When they went after Lexi, he took the group out and kept the electric vehicle as spoils of war. He didn't drive it often, but he appreciated its instant torque, carrying capacity, and near-silent operation.

The drive to Evergreen Acres in Bel Air took nearly an hour. After getting through the gate, Tyler drove to his father's building. They passed a set of pickleball courts along the way as well as another group doing yoga in a field. One guest spot remained open, and Tyler snagged it. He and Lexi walked inside and rode the elevator up to his father's floor.

Zeke opened the door and smiled at them. "Glad you could make it," he said as he let them in. The old man leaned closer to Lexi. "Did he remember on his own?"

"Yes," she said, covering for Tyler's forgetfulness.

"Yes," Tyler repeated. Lexi carried the gift bag and card to a small table. Tyler's dad always kept the place neat and spartan, and even today, hosting a gathering, this remained true. He'd added a leaf to the dining room table, and someone probably hung the streamers for him, but the condo didn't really look festive. This fit its occupant, however.

A few other people milled about the place. They were all Zeke's age and probably fellow residents of Evergreen Acres. Considering his father's outgoing nature, Tyler expected to see more people here. The only person he recognized smiled and shook his hand. Geoffrey let Tyler borrow his Lincoln Continental the previous year when Tyler needed it. The older man still looked gaunt but happy. They chatted for a few minutes. A knock at the door brought a staff member carrying a cake. Two large 7 and 8 candles pushed into the icing later, the group sang an off-key—and blessedly quiet—rendition of "Happy Birthday."

Tyler—who drove here without eating dinner—circled the table and grabbed a few finger food items placed at the opposite end from the cake. He snagged a chicken tender, a few pigs in blankets, and three deviled eggs. It would do. The items in the veggie tray looked uninspiring and a day past their useful life. Once he'd munched the fare on his plate, he sliced off a piece of cake and sat next to Lexi.

Zeke opened his gifts, sharing a story either about the item or the person who gave it to him each time. Tyler smiled. His father could command a room. It was more than just being a master chief in the Navy. Zeke genuinely liked interacting with people, and he'd always been good at building and fostering relationships. Tyler was his father's opposite in many ways, but being an introvert and getting seasick on any boat tied for the biggest gap between them.

When he got to the green and white gift bag, Zeke pulled out the cardigan and grinned. "Thanks, you two," he said to Tyler and Lexi. "You know, the first gift my granddaughter here ever got me was a hideous sweater." Lexi blushed, and everyone laughed. "She was five or six, so I don't think she picked it out. I doubt her dad did, either." He didn't—Tyler remembered his ex-wife Rachel selecting the dreadful thing. Zeke never liked her, so maybe she tried to get a little bit of sartorial revenge. "Of course, I said I loved it, and I even wore it once." He held up the new item. "This is a hell of a lot better."

After another round of cake and coffee, the other guests filed out. It was just after eight, and Tyler realized his thought was uncharitable, but he figured most of them wanted to go to bed soon. "Thanks for coming by, you two," Zeke said.

"Of course, Grandpa."

Tyler browsed the cards. There were far more of them than people who attended tonight. One caught his eye. A beautiful blonde woman smiled on the front flap. "Dad, I wasn't aware you knew Anna Kournikova's mother."

The old man chuckled. "I think the picture is a few years old. She's nearly my age, now."

"Who is it?" Tyler asked.

"Irina," Zeke said. "She was a Soviet officer when I did some intelligence work. Making friends across the aisle, if you will, was pretty uncommon then. It was the 'eighties, and I think we were both smart enough to see how things would turn out."

"You've made some interesting friends." Tyler set the card down again.

His father chuckled. "By the time you're seventy-eight, you will have, too."

55

———

THE NEXT AFTERNOON, TYLER FINISHED THE BRAKE JOB ON A classic Camaro when Lexi's Accord pulled into the lot.

She joined him in the service bay. "Where's everyone else?"

"Ortiz had the day off," he said. "Smitty went home. I wanted to wrap this up before I took off."

"When can you put my car on the lift?" Lexi asked.

"In another ten years or so."

She waited a few minutes for Tyler to finish. He washed his hands, and they headed to the office. "I'm always happy to see you," he said, "but we just went to your grandfather's place yesterday. What's up?"

"We're due to get a pizza."

Tyler bobbed his head. "A few good options not far from here." He watched her tug on her ponytail. "What's the real reason you're here?"

She grinned. "I picked a major."

"Really? What'd you decide?"

"Criminal justice."

"Good." Tyler smiled. "I'm proud of you."

"Thanks, Dad."

"What are you going to do with it?" he asked.

"I don't know yet," Lexi said. "I don't want to be a lawyer." She grimaced, and Tyler was glad. He didn't want her to be a lawyer, either. There were way too many attorneys plying their trades in America already. "I think I'd like to be an investigator and work for an attorney . . . on the defense side."

"Good call. I can see you doing great work there." He looked at his watch. "Why don't you get a couple of pizzas delivered?" Tyler opened his wallet and tossed his credit card onto the desk. "I think there's still some beer in the fridge. You're not too far from twenty-one."

Lexi picked up her phone and started tapping away. "True. Grandpa's birthday starts the chain for the three of us. You're not gonna narc on me?"

"I'd really be narcing on myself for giving you alcohol," Tyler pointed out, "so no."

A moment later, Lexi picked up Tyler's credit card, tapped on her phone some more, and then set both down. "Done. Thanks for buying dinner."

"One of these years, maybe you can return the favor."

"I'll have to earn my way from intern to merely underpaid."

"You have anything lined up there?"

"Working on it," Lexi said. "I may not get into a law firm this time. People who have been criminal justice majors since they started have gobbled up the spots. Well . . . them and nepo babies."

Tyler spread his hands. "One day, this will all be yours."

Lexi wrinkled her nose. "Gee, thanks."

"Just don't change the name to Nepo Baby Classic Car Repair," Tyler said. "I might even make it a requirement in my will."

"No worries there," Lexi said.

"On the more immediate front, you still have two years of

college. I'm sure you'll find your way to a firm. They'd be fools not to take a chance on you."

"When they do, maybe we could even represent you." Lexi grinned. "On your knight-errant activities, of course."

"This time, I had the backing of the FBI," Tyler said, "but I like the sound of your deal."

"How is your fed girlfriend?"

"Punching her ticket to a better career. She made a big bust, and she'll get to go to a different field office and do more meaningful work."

"So she *is* your girlfriend."

Tyler chuckled. "No . . . and even if she were, I wouldn't presume to stand in the way of her career advancement."

"Why do old people have complicated relationships?"

"Probably so we can confuse the younger generations." Tyler grabbed his card and slipped it back into his wallet. "Enough about the FBI and Hope. Let's talk about you being an intern. You think I could get a break on the retainer if I needed to hire your firm?"

"I'd put in a good word for you," Lexi said.

Tyler moved to the fridge, grabbed two longnecks, and set one in front of his daughter. "Let's hope it's enough."

END of Novel #8

Tyler's next adventure is a personal one. When his father disappears, rumors swirl about the old man's real loyalties during his Navy years. Tyler has to find his father and sort out the mess in Collision Course, coming March 2025.

THE END

AFTERWORD

Thanks for checking out this novel! I hope you enjoyed reading the book as much as I enjoyed writing it.

I write mysteries and thrillers with action, snark, and flawed heroes. If this sounds like something you like, you can check out my catalog below.

The John Tyler Action Thrillers

1. The Mechanic
2. White Lines
3. Lost Highway
4. Four on the Floor
5. Forced Induction
6. The Low Road
7. Backfire
8. Redline
9. Collision Course (Spring 2025)

The C.T. Ferguson Crime Novels:

1. The Reluctant Detective
2. The Unknown Devil
3. The Workers of Iniquity
4. Already Guilty
5. Daughters and Sons
6. A March from Innocence
7. Inside Cut
8. The Next Girl
9. In the Blood
10. Right as Rain
11. Dead Cat Bounce
12. Don't Say Her Name
13. Night Comes Down
14. Concrete Angels
15. Conduct Unbecoming
16. Bleeding into Winter
17. Unreasonable Doubt (December 2024)

I generally release 3-4 new titles per year. For the most current list of books, please visit:

- https://tomfowlerbooks.com (direct sales)
- https://tomfowlerwrites.com
- https://books2read.com/tomfowler

(Notes: C.T. Ferguson appears in *White Lines*. John Tyler appears in *Don't Say Her Name*.)

While these are the suggested reading sequences, each novel is a standalone mystery or thriller, and the books can be enjoyed in whatever order you happen upon them.

Connect with me:
For the many ways of finding and reaching me online,

please visit https://tomfowlerwrites.com/contact. I'm always happy to talk to readers.

This is a work of fiction. Characters and places are either fictitious or used in a fictitious manner.

"Self-publishing" is something of a misnomer. This book would not have been possible without the contributions of many people.

- Stuart Bache for the cover design.
- My editor extraordinaire, Chase Nottingham.
- My wonderful advance reader team, the Fell Street Irregulars.